JIM COOPER

TWISTED TIES

A CHYNNA LENNOX MYSTERY

Face Plant

FacePlant Books
New Jersey

Cooper, Jim, 1956-

Twisted Ties / Jim Cooper-Print 1st edition

ISBN 978-0-9888213-0-9

Book cover design by Audra Dean DeFalco

FacePlant logo by Steve Cooper

Cover photographs: istockphoto.com/DNY59 (MB Photo, Inc.), istockphoto.com/ okapistudio (okapistudio.com), istockphoto.com/nullplus (software.photonullplus. de), shutterstock.com/Alersandr Hunta

The Twisted Ties All-Star Jug Band

My wife and kids - Sally, Stephen & Beth - who were always there to piece me together when I became unglued, which is more often than I care to admit. Thanks for not allowing me to give up.

My readers who suffered through an early draft and told me to keep going – Michelene Krawchuk, Andrea Stark, Stephen Cooper, Sally Cooper, my sister Joanne Adams and Sara Moritz, who went the extra mile on more than one occasion. Thanx.

Lt. Christopher Howard (Ret), Wildwood, NJ Police for keeping me somewhat real in police matters. Any mistakes or fantasies in this area are mine.

The Philadelphia Caron Alumni group who told me to stop whining and write the damn book already.

Anne Dubuisson Anderson – wordsmith extraordinaire – who asked the right questions and was always willing to answer mine. (http://anne-consults.com)

Stephanie Rubin – punctuation and grammar guru. Thank you for making me appear as if I know what I'm doing.

Rachel Simon – for the nurturing and positive way you forced me to believe in myself, and for telling me I was better than I thought I was. It's been a long journey from the TCS Writer's Conference – thank you for letting me ride the bus with you. (http://www.rachelsimon.com)

Dedication

This book is dedicated to the memory of Barbara Cooper and Sally Howard, two more avid readers I have never known. They showed me, in their respective ways, the irreplaceable value of the printed word. Hopefully this book is on their to-read piles as they sit on the beach sipping iced coffee and diet Pepsi.

One

A zippered black bag, its contours revealing a human form within, rolled out from the second floor apartment. My skin twitched violently as the wheels ricocheted off the saddle in the doorway and then slammed, like a gunshot, to the wooden porch floor. Someone that used to be alive and breathing, that smiled and was warm, someone I held in my arms was now lifeless pieces inside that reusable garbage bag.

"DaKota. I need to see her," I said jumping off the stairs towards the body bag, not sure if I could make it without collapsing and face-planting the porch floor.

A cop jumped on the steps, grabbed my arms and stopped me. "The best thing you can do is go upstairs. Please, Ma'am. Someone will be up in a few minutes. Please get back to your apartment and wait there."

I watched them load DaKota in the ambulance, slam the doors shut, reverse down the driveway then take off down the street.

Like jolting awake from a sweat-soaked dream my mind scrambled, running a frenzied reality check. Everything's okay, isn't it? What I just saw didn't really happen and I don't need to hold on to this clawing emptiness...

But she was gone. Just like that. Gone.

Sirens in the distance were a part of life, just another piece of street noise taken for granted. Now the wailing pierced through me like a chainsaw appendectomy.

"Please, Ma'am." The officer turned me around and guided me up the stairs.

Not knowing what to do, I sat on the sofa in my living room staring into the void, unable to process anything through the cold slog in my head. I grabbed a cushion and wrapped my arms around it, willing it to hug me back.

I was the one who found her, all because Zenobia wouldn't stop howling at three in the morning. A bad-ass Persian cat, Zenobia was prowling and screeching outside of DaKota's door, which was strange because she's deathly afraid of nature and would rather get hosed down in a crate full of slobbering collies than go outside. I got the key from my apartment and went downstairs to let her in. The cat shot through the crack in the door before I could get it halfway open. Then it hit me. The smell. A funky, metallic odor.

Behind me something stirred, a scurrying in the bushes next to the garage; rabbits, raccoons, or just my paranoia. I waited and listened. Nothing, save the cricket and cicada jam session in full swing.

Inside, the apartment was thick with quiet, only the faint hum of the fans in the bedroom down the hall kept me from believing I'd been struck stone deaf. I padded towards the hallway but suddenly rocketed out of my skin as the refrigerator picked that moment to let loose with a demonic bellow as the motor kicked on.

"Asshat," I said once I caught my breath. I felt my jean-shorts to make sure I hadn't pissed myself blue. Not exactly the message one wants to give off when confronting an ex-lover.

As I crept down the hall, a faint voice whispered inside me, "This is so wrong."

Thanks for sharing, now shut up.

Chynna Lenox's the name, schizophrenia's the game.

Slashes of hazy purple streetlight floated through the bedroom blinds, bisecting the full sized angel's wings tattooed on DaKota's sleek back, the damp bed sheet stopped at the curve on her hip, a sight that still makes my chest tighten. She was alone, laying on her right side facing the wall. Blonde strands of her hair danced like frenzied marionettes as two oscillating fans churned the dense humidity.

I took a deep breath of thick, rank air. "Hey," I said. No reaction. I knelt on the empty side of the bed. "Wake up, dammit. Talk to..." I stopped halfway as I put my hand on her arm. It was ice cold.

I pulled her shoulder toward me but the rest of her body came with it, as if heaving a statue.

"DaKota?" I leapt over her body to the far side. Her eyes were wide open and fixed, her lips purple and parted with a dark line drawn down across her cheek from the corner of her mouth.

Then I saw the blood, lots of it, dripping off the hem of the saturated sheet and pooling on the floor.

"Oh, shit," I grabbed her head in my hands and shook her.   "DaKota! Wake up! DaKota!"

Nothing. She was looking at me, but not seeing.

"Oh my god." I slammed back against the wall when I saw there was something sticking out of her chest. I turned on her bedside lamp.

The stream of shiny dark blood from her mouth staining the sheets sent bile into my throat. Her tongue, sliced from its roots, was impaled against her chest by a deeply embedded pair of shears.

"No. No," I moaned, climbing into bed and cradling her in my arms. I tried. I really tried not to think of all the things that tongue had done to and with me, but my brain was not cooperating as I just sat and held her, shaking. That's the way I stayed, rocking her lifeless body gently back and forth until the gray light of dawn filled the room.

I wanted the feeling of her weight pressed against me, blond hair tumbled over me and her body slowly rising and falling with each breath. I wanted it right now. Looking at my hands I willed that feeling from deep in my brain to come and comfort me. It conjured itself for a brief second and then faded, replaced by...

Singing. Singing from the kitchen...

"*We're knights of the round table...*". The Camelot song from *The Holy Grail*. To each her own ringtone. I forced myself to get up and answer it.

"You'll think me daft, but I had to ring you up. You showed up in my dream last night. I was dashing through a hospital and you were in a room somewhere but I couldn't find you and everybody kept telling me to bugger off. I woke up in a panic. All right, then?"

"Andi..." Words hung in my throat. I knew what I wanted to say. I didn't want to say it. Then I'd have to face it. Deal with it.

"Chynna? What's going on?"

"DaKota's dead." It came out in a big rushing sigh. A current flowed from the back of my head down my spine, eventually enveloping my body.

"Hang on. Be there in twenty," she said and disconnected.

It's not an unusual occurrence in my life for the people I love to make unscheduled exits, re-enforcing my belief that I wear bad karma like stink on a meth junkie. In any case I was getting mega-tired of it. Not that people were dropping like flies at every turn but it was time for death to visit someone else for a change.

First there was Taj–my older male cousin and my earliest mad crush. On February 28, 1991, six hours after the Desert Storm cease fire, Taj's squad was returning from patrol when their truck hit a land mine. The vehicle flew in the air, hit the ground and rolled, the edge of the truck bed sliced him in half.

Then there was Jannali–my eighth grade best friend. While on vacation in Aruba, she was struck and killed by a drunken frat boy from Wisconsin on spring break. He got to go home and graduate. She was shipped home in a casket on a cargo plane.

Dad–I'll get to him later.

Now DaKota. Who was that King whose touch turned everything to gold? Midas? Meet Queen Chynna, everything she touches turns to shit.

I thought about asking my mother if there were any unusual circumstances surrounding my birth that concocted a death curse inside me forever, but dismissed that idea as it meant contacting her, which is something I've thoroughly avoided whenever possible. Besides, I knew full well the bizarre environment in which I was born.

A collective of hippies, who did not know the original Woodstock was approaching its twentieth anniversary, remained squatting on five acres of farmland in North Carolina. I'm told there were thirteen untrained, self-proclaimed midwives on hand supplying my Mom with natural peyote buttons allow her to "turn on" to the birth experience. My father was in a teepee on the far end of the commune teaching a fifteen year old runaway the mystical wonders of the Kama Sutra.

Because all the cool baby names were spoken for, my Mom struggled with just the right combination of positive vibrations. At the insistence of her hippie-wives, she dropped acid while smoking her placenta until she finally settled on Karma Flower Cassidy.

We stayed on that hot and dirty cow pasture for ten years with only brief and welcome respites to Nana Lennox's house on Wrightsville Beach. For two weeks every July, Mom piled me in the dilapidated wreck of a car and drove two hours east to deposit me at her mother's cottage overlooking the ocean where I could breathe and feel somewhat normal. Nana's house was built on the edge of the dunes at the end of a sandy lane surrounded by scrub pine that provided patches of cool shade. After dinner, she and I would get lost on a pillow covered sofa bed on the front porch, bathed in warm orange light, while she read stories from a crumbling ancient collection of Hans Christian Andersen fairy tales that smelled of camphor and baked chicken. Listening to the wave's crash on shore in the darkness that surrounded the room, I was certain this was the safest place on earth.

After Mom left the commune (with the local Democratic election campaign chairman on his way to Washington to get Mr. Clinton to the White House), I decided that going through life as Karma Flower Cassidy, complete with a monogram advertising a fast-food chain, was not acceptable. After one hasty application to the courts, I became Chynna Lennox, taking Nana's married last name and my first name from a kick-ass Manga illustrator, Chynna Clugston.

Andi buzzed through my back door without knocking and silently sat on the sofa engulfing me in her arms, even though I had not relinquished my grip on the cell phone and cushion. Neither of us spoke. I was too numb to cry, but I felt a little bit safer with my head on her shoulder and her arms wrapped around me.

Andi and I are mismatched misfits; I'm Betty to her Wilhelmina, Anneke van Giersbergen to her Jesse James (the singer, not the asshole). I'm five foot two, she's six foot even. I have stumpy legs, she has gams up to her neck. My chin length red hair with creative green stripes on one side is the antithesis of her long latte and gold-streaked mane. She is a *most-women-want-to-rub-mud-in-her-face* beauty with an aquiline nose and full pale lips. My mug sports freckles whose number, size and shape depend on sun exposure. In the summer people often mistake me for having some fatal skin disease until they are close enough to realize it is just the marks on my face congealing. My nose is more of a ridged ski jump and I've always felt my mouth was too big for my face. Not Fantasia necessarily, but close.

"I'm sorry," Andi whispered. "Any notion what happened?"

Before I could answer, a pounding at the back door made us jump. A walking fire plug with gelled dirt colored spikes of hair crowning a mushy face burst through the door. His eyes were almost Asian, narrow but set far apart. His thin lips barely moved when he spoke giving off an air of boredom and swagger. At one time he may have been a hard-body, but a well fed gut strained against pants with shiny knees and a waistband permanently folded over from the pressure. The alcohol damaged capillaries in his jowls looked like little red lightning bolts streaking across his cheeks.

"You Lennox?" he said. I was about to answer when the cloud of Old Spice and cigarettes hit me.

"Who wants to know?" I said, coughing out the question.

"Gralewski. Detective Sergeant."

"How about some ID?"

Half snickering, he produced an ID in a wallet, holding it out just long enough for me to see his first name was Albert and read "New Jersey" and "Mercer County". Seeing as that's the state and county where I lived I let it slide.

"Who're you?" he snarled at Andi.

"Candice Bertenshaw. I'm Chynna's friend," she said, emphasizing my name.

"Where were you last night?" Gralewski asked me, ignoring Andi.

The hair on the back of my neck started rising, a good sign that someone, or something, was starting to piss me off. "Why?"

"Look," he said pacing through the living room, like he was furniture shopping. "I'm investigating Jessica Gibson's death. You, having found the body, are on the hook for cooperating with me here or down at the station. The choice is yours."

"I was here, asleep."

"That a fact? Any witnesses see you here last night? Your pal here spend the night?"

Andi's muscles stiffened but I answered before she said something regretful. "Oh, dozens. It was my usual Friday orgy."

"Wouldn't surprise me." He pulled out a pair of drumsticks from a stick bag I had hanging off the end of a bookshelf.

"Any chance you have a warrant?" I asked.

He said, "You really play drums?" He made a clicking sound with his teeth and shook his head tossing the sticks back in the bag. One missed and hit the floor. He stared at it for a second then left it there. "Real rock star wanna-be, huh? Guess that includes all the usual activities that go along with that life."

"You're the Shakespeare of vague euphemisms aren't you?"

"I don't know what that means but if you don't know what I mean then you must not be a very good drummer, if you catch my drift."

My witty repartee limit was being reached. I said, "I'm sure there was an English sentence somewhere in what you just said and maybe I'll try to find it one of these days but in the meantime you can just get the hell out of here. Now." Every muscle in my back was knotted. Maybe because he was marinated in cologne, maybe it was his overwhelming self-importance. Maybe I just didn't like the bastard within the first five-seconds and giving him as much crap as possible felt like the right thing to do.

"I have a better idea. Why don't I arrest you right here on the spot for withholding evidence and obstruction of justice? According to your downstairs neighbor, one Susan Roche…"

"She's not an insect. It's Ro-shay," I said, gladly correcting him.

He shrugged, "Whatever. You and the deceased were close pals, so to speak. So when I ask you a question you damn well better answer it without any wise-ass comments as I'd like nothing more than to wrap this up quick. And if that means all the hard core dykes at the Clinton Correctional Facility get a new punk slit to tickle, that's fine with me."

"Hang on, clever dick," Andi said standing. "So when, exactly, did you stop beating your wife?" Now I remembered why Andi and I were friends.

"Funny. Are you aching to be an accessory because I'd be happy to accommodate you."

"You loathsome git. Who do you think…"

"Sit down and shut up," he snapped. Andi grudgingly sat but the daggers were flying. Gralewski turned his attention back to me. "So what really happened?" He pulled a pack of Marlboros out of his coat pocket and shook one into his mouth. His fingers were fat and stubby; half his nails had caked bloodlines across the top probably from gnawing them down too low. It wasn't possible for him to be any skeevier.

"Don't even think about lighting that up in here," I said.

Pulling out a yellow disposable lighter, he chuckled, fired up his cancer stick and took a deep drag blowing a plume of blue smoke into the air. Scummy red eyes bore down on me, scanning my body as if he was inspecting a wrecked car.

"What's that 'M' mean?" he said pointing with his chin to the red and gold Scorpio symbol tattooed on my bicep.

"I belong to the Moose Lodge. What do you care?"

"Not hardly. Tattoos on skirts are skanky, and all the damn piercings. How many holes you got on you? There's at least half a dozen I can see but for my money there's got to be a few special ones, right?"

"None of your fucking business. Dick." For the record, I have four in each ear and a barbell in my eyebrow. I gave up the tongue piercing after three months because, contrary to several goth blog pages, it interfered with, rather than enhanced, certain DaKota-based activities and was a hassle to maintain. Thus far I'd taken a pass on some of the more sensitive areas.

"At least your pal downstairs didn't look like a pincushion, except for the scissors jammed in her chest. Now she has a real set of wings to go with the cartoons on her back, huh?"

Shaking, I stood. Intimidation was not my goal, being five feet two did not allow me the opportunity to tower over anyone.

"Get out. Now. You want to talk to me? Call my attorney."

"And that would be?"

"I'll let you know," I said.

He smirked, blew another cloud of smoke into the room and said, "Don't plan on going anywhere for a while," then headed for the door.

I didn't know what I should do next. What I wanted to do was repeatedly stab this bastard with rusty, white hot meat skewers, but I restrained myself.

"Wanker," Andi said.

"You're being too kind."

There was another knock at the door. This time, a mild face smiling behind rimless glasses peered through the glass panes. "Ms. Lennox, I'm Detective Sergeant Kal Douglas. Do you mind if I ask you some questions?"

"I thought that other creep was the detective."

"Detective Gralewski?" he said quietly, "We're partners on this investigation. May I come in?"

Standing behind me, Andi said, "You don't have to do this now."

"It's okay," I conceded.

Once we were seated in the living room, Detective Douglas asked, "How long have you known the deceased?"

Deceased. The word caught me off guard; it had such an onerous ring to it. No life or breath to it at all. "Two years. No, three. Three years."

Douglas started making notes in a small pocket notebook. "What was your relationship with her?"

I half smiled. "Complicated." I looked at Douglas as if I expected him to read my mind.

"Can you be a little more specific?" he asked.

"I'm sorry. We met at an audition. Neither of us got the gig so we decided to start our own band. We've been friends and band mates ever since."

He hesitated and then said, "Nothing more?" Unlike his partner there was no trace of smarmy innuendo.

"What do you mean?" I said.

"Standard question, Ms. Lennox. Your neighbor downstairs suggested that you and Ms. Gibson were a bit closer than 'just friends.'"

"Stop with the Ms. Lennox already. It makes me sound old. It's Chynna."

"Okay," he had a gentle grin. "I have to explore all possibilities. I am not making any judgments."

"Fine. Go on."

"Well?"

"What?" I asked a bit too innocently.

"Was that the extent of your relationship?"

"Yes it was." It really wasn't a lie. For the past two weeks we hardly spoke to each other.

After jotting a few notes in his pad he said, "Did she seem upset lately?"

"No." Just with me, I thought, but that shouldn't make any difference.

"Was she spending time with anyone new?"

Good question. I had to stop and think about that for a second. "Not that I know of," I answered but that had not occurred to me and right now, it added another knot in my stomach.

"When did you see her last?"

"Last Saturday night. A week ago. We had a gig."

More notes. He glanced out the window as if considering his next words carefully. "Was she upset? Did she mention anything about being in trouble or any new personal problems?"

"No. Everything was cool. The set went fine. We all hung out for a bit then went home."

"And you hadn't seen her since?"

"No," I said.

"I know this is not easy but tell me exactly how you found the body."

Douglas had me walk through each detail step by step. My story was essentially how it really happened, minus the time lag, I fibbed about coming down to talk to her before work and left the cat out of the picture completely; that and spending a few hours with a dead body before dialing 911. Minor details.

Douglas turned his attention to Andi. "Ms. Bertenshaw, were you here when the body was discovered?"

"God no! I rang up Chynna this morning and she told me what had happened so I came over straight away."

"Do you always call her early in the morning?"

"Not often, no. I had a dream about her and wanted to make sure she was all right so I called," Andi said.

"Why? Did you think she was in danger?"

Andi blushed but told Douglas about the dream.

He continued. "So you did not know anything about what had happened until Ms. Lennox called you?"

"No, I called her."

"Oh, that is correct. Yes."

I could see in Andi's eyes that she knew Douglas was playing with her, trying to lead her into making a mistake.

The Detective closed his notepad. "OK. That's all I can think of for now. Just so you can gear yourself up, here's what is going to happen over the next couple of days. Because this appears to be an assisted death, the county prosecutor's office is now involved. You will more than likely have to tell your story to Detective Gralewski again, probably within the next few hours, as that is the most critical time in any homicide investigation. They should have autopsy results back in a couple days, which will determine cause of death."

"The..." I swallowed hard. "The scissors in her chest weren't a big enough clue?" I said.

"We have to rule out anything else. For instance, if there were any other substances involved..."

"Substances?"

"Drugs, alcohol and the like," Douglas said, "They will not know for a few weeks until the toxicology report comes back. In the meantime, Detective Gralewski and I will talk to neighbors, your band, people you work with and anyone else they think is relevant."

"Great. Can't you do a solo? Gralewski will just piss off everyone and they'll blame me for his charming personality."

He smiled. "For the time being, please stay close. There is an investigative team downstairs going through the apartment for clues, fingerprints and anything else that might help so you will hear some moving around there for a while, but please stay out of their way."

Douglas walked over and put a hand on my shoulder, "I am very sorry Ms. Lennox. Here is my card. Please call me if you think of anything else that might help."

"Like impaling your pal on a rusty spear?" I said.

Douglas smiled and left. When the door closed I looked up at Andi, feigning a grin.

The Knights of the Round Table chimed in again. I didn't recognize the incoming phone number, but the area code matched mine so I answered it.

"Is this Chynna Lennox?"

"Yes," I said hesitantly.

"Jessica Martin-Slade from the Trenton Times. I need to ask you a few questions about the body that was found this morning. You are the upstairs neighbor, correct?"

"How did you get this number?"

She ignored me. "Did you hear or see anything? Who could have wanted Ms. Gibson dead? Do you think it was random or possibly drug related?"

Andi grabbed the phone out of my hand. "This is Ms. Lennox's solicitor. Under advice of counsel she has no comment at this time." Then she hung up.

"Not bad," I said. We both had crooked smiles on our faces, trying to hold on to a light note and keep reality at a safe distance. The phone started buzzing again. Another unknown number, this time a 215 Pennsylvania area code.

"Word is spreading," Andi said, pointing out of the window. "Take a gander."

From the front porch door the local press corps were visible; a half dozen or so TMZ wanna-bes. "You'll want a tale to tell them, if you want to chat them up at all."

"This really sucks," I sighed.

"Better think fast. It's Friday and we have an appointment to keep. My car is out on the street so we'll have to wade through the lot of them."

"Considering the morning's events don't I get special dispensation?"

"What do you think?"

Sponsors are a pain in the ass.

Two

"I really wanted to use. My mother ate all my cupcakes. I was really angry." George B.

"He just dumped me on the side of the road. It was my birthday and he just left me there just because I was talking to another guy at the bar. But he apologized when I got home." Stephanie F.

"He was watching lesbian porn. What am I supposed to do with that? I went absolutely crazy looking for some birdie powder. I was ready to blow it all. Ended up calling my sponsor instead who talked me off the ledge." Miranda H., transsexual.

"I smoked pot three days ago and I still feel like shit. Makes me want to smoke more." Greg N.

A random sampling from my group of twelve step-taking misfits of which I am a charter member. Our Friday noon Narcotics Anonymous, or NA, meeting is colloquially named "The Weekend Reminders" and gathers in the finished basement of a post Civil War, white clapboard church in a perpetual state of disrepair. The basement, however, was sort of clean and dry, and furnished for kindergarten through sixth grade Sunday school with low-riding plastic chairs. You know, the kind that drives your knees into your chin.

On any given Friday there are ten to fifteen druggies congregated to share our past and current addiction experiences. More people congregate in church cellars on any given day than on a year of Sundays in the main building, and the spirituality downstairs is a hundred fold. One of these days a few religious leaders might get a clue, but I'm not holding my breath.

Life has to be a royal mess to wind up attending these meetings. Why the hell else would anyone show up? I know mine was. I was never a drug addict, or so I told myself. Drug addicts spend all their time wandering around slums in inner cities mugging people and robbing convenience stores for coin. I certainly wasn't that kind of loser. Even after getting served with an eviction notice from my apartment and pawning the gold ring left to me by Nana Lennox for a score. Just bad luck, that's all. No way was I one of those city addicts trading hand jobs for drug cash. No, instead I was arrested for bringing new meaning to the term 'blow job' by going down on my dealer behind a Seven-Eleven dumpster in exchange for more nose candy. I woke up in a jail cell listening to a skeletal meth junkie puke her remaining teeth into the sink. That was my bottom–that's the term used by addicts to describe the realization that life is unlivable, no big burning bush; just a quiet knowing that I was a writhing bottom feeder and needed help.

My group is a place of safety, a place I can let go without judgment and re-connect with my higher power that I refer to as "Mom". Don't ask me about all the psychological implications of that. For me, psycho-babble is as pointless as pantyhose and women's clothing in any shade of pink.

It's also where I first met Andi. I asked her to be my sponsor based on the color and length of her hair. So much for motives.

The speaker that morning talked about her inability to turn her life over to her higher power, how she faked sobriety for ten years, taking occasional hits of Vicodin to maintain control and avoid the pain all while working the steps and sponsoring dozens of people. She finally realized her disease was not drugging but her own self-centered behavior.

When she finished, I dutifully listened to the group's reactions but had decided I was not ready to talk to anybody about anything. I needed to sort it all out for myself first, wearing a blank mask to avoid the inquisitions of others in the group. After several people shared I glanced at Andi whose gaze was boring into my skull. She didn't have to say anything, I knew what that look meant.

Fine. I raised my hand.

After acknowledging the speaker I said, "It's been a strange morning. I've been up since dawn dealing with the police and reporters skulking around my place so needless to say I'm tired and hungry. Right now I'm too numb to be angry and lonely but I'm sure they are waiting in the wings, ready to strike."

I was referring to the HALT acronym–Hungry, Angry, Lonely, Tired-used in twelve step programs as conditions ripe for acting out in ones addiction of choice.

"My former partner was murdered last night." A murmur of gasps and sympathetic moans coursed through the group. "I'm not feeling much of anything at the moment and really did not want to share but my sponsor thought it might be best if I did. So I'm just putting it out on the table."

After the meeting I received lots of hugs and offers of "Anything I can do to help". Most of the offers are genuine and spring out of a loss of something meaningful to say. But I know one or two are really saying, "If you want to spill the sordid details I'll be more than happy to listen."

Andi hugged me and I whispered "Thanks" into her shoulder. She hugged me a bit harder and made me promise to meet her for lunch around two. I walked home as I needed to make a vain attempt at figuring out what happened and time to let my attorney know he just elected to take me on as a client.

Three

The Slipped Disc was a building with a pituitary problem, a standard suburban two car garage in width but deep enough to fit two super-stretch limos end to end. It was my home-away-from-home as I spent most of my time managing the place.

Saturday was always our big day. Aside from the 'no-life-regulars', as the staff dubbed them, all the college and high school kids descended to go through shelves of used albums, CDs and DVDs hoping to find an overlooked used Metallica CD for $1.99, but instead taking home five CDs for the same price by Joe Unknown and the NeverWillburys because the cover art or song titles were blasphemous enough to make them feel rebellious. On the floor from front to back were, at last estimate, about fifty-thousand albums of all genres from Beethoven to Black Sabbath and all priced between ninety-nine cents and four bucks. The drawback was traffic issues. Walking through the place without stepping on the knuckles of album-sifting floor dwellers was a challenge. Most Saturdays there were enough squatting customers to whip any construction site in a butt-crack challenge. The store, nestled on Spring Street in Princeton, is a warehouse of minor audio memorabilia for which people are thankfully willing to shell out ten to fifteen thousand bucks a month, even with the explosion of digital downloads and iPods.

Years ago, I started as a part-time clerk while trying to scrape a band together. Jason Wibblesman was the store manager, a Birkenstock intellectual who coaxed me to his apartment under the pretense of discussing the similarities between afro-Cuban rhythms and haiku pentameter when all he really wanted was to hump my brains out, which he accomplished quite nicely. Our mutual lusts cooled after Jason morphed into a respected business person, investing in a dozen commercial businesses in town and living off the income. This left me to step into senior management at The Slipped Disc, as it were. Jason also had many different side jobs, depending on his whirling dervish moods. Few people were as smart as he was; a lawyer in four different states who held a PhD in

Behavioral Science and Computational Physics. Even so, he kept his office in a hallowed out enclave in the rear corner of the store.

The contents of his inner sanctum exploded in every direction and was lit by twin barred windows at the rear, one wide open to let in the summertime heat and humidity, while the other window sprouted a government surplus air conditioner going full blast while precariously balanced on a pile of warped album covers.

Jason's desktop clutter consisted of coffee stained file folders, crumpled sandwich wrappers, half-empty Styrofoam cups growing new life forms, and a half eaten bagel, the odors from which congealed into a supermarket dumpster aroma.

Behind the desk sat an overgrown prairie dog whose thinning wheat-stalk hair stood at attention as if he had stuck his tongue in a light socket. Today Jason was dressed to impress in knee-torn jeans and a button down shirt that had never seen an iron and had once been white. Lost among the desk rubble was a speaker phone, over which his scarecrow frame hunched.

"Mrs. Bradbury, your husband has skipped out, departed, vamoosed, flew the coop, went over the wall. He boarded a plane for London yesterday. From there he could be ensconced in a Libyan bunker for all I know."

"Was he alone?" asked Mrs. Bradbury.

Jason rolled his eyes; 'Who' was always more important than 'where'.

"No, Mrs. Bradbury. He wasn't. He was accompanied by..."

"That's OK, Mr. Wibblesman. I know who it was. You've been very helpful. Thank you." Then the phone went dead.

"Hopefully your gratitude extends into a timely bill payment," he said staring at his desk.

I slammed the open window shut. "Jesus, Jason, make up your mind with the damn windows. Are you looking for pneumonia?"

All he could manage was a half-hearted "Eh" as he leaned back in his squeaky wooden Captain's chair and lit a cigarette, taking a drag that burned down half the stick, then blowing out enough smoke to qualify as a human forest fire.

"When are you going to quit those things?"

"I was graced with one mother. I'm not in the market for a replacement. If you don't like it, go stand outside. This is my building and smoke free it isn't."

"Jesus. Chill."

"That's a very hip thing to say now isn't it? 'Chill'. If only people had the balls to say what they mean, because your hackneyed colloquialism translates into 'Hey, I'm sorry I'm such a flaming asshole to suggest something that's none of my business but really pisses you off so please don't yell at me anymore.'"

"When was the last time you got laid? Never mind, I don't want to know but it certainly wasn't recent enough."

He stared at me as if I had just spoken in a long-forgotten, ancient tongue. "Now that we've established my sexual frequency, what is today's crisis?"

"When are you going to hire a cleaning service? This place reeks from all the crap on your desk," I said. "What is all this shit anyway?"

"An intensely intricate filing system. Do you want me to alter it to meet your specifications or are you just tormenting me for your own amusement?"

"A little of both. I need a good lawyer and as I can scarcely afford one on the crappy salary you pay me, I'll settle for your services." Before he could object I explained the day's events.

When I was done the silence curled inside the hovering cigarette smoke. He took a last drag and threw the butt in a Styrofoam cup, the ashes sizzling in whatever liquid festered inside. "And?" he said.

"That's not enough?"

"Let me guess. The first detective is a bloated Winnie-The-Pooh with military hair and the manners of a trough swilling hog?"

"Could not have put it better."

Bucking his chair forward, he said, "I wish you luck on your quest for legal representation."

"Bite me."

Four

Antonella's was packed wall-to-wall with screaming, polo shirt clad Princeton yuppies loudly swapping humorous anecdotes about their latest vacations and live-in nannies. Andi and I opted to dine alfresco and sweat out the humid July afternoon.

"What's going to happen with the band?" Andi asked.

"Good question. We have a gig tomorrow night. I'm hoping Spag can step into DaKota's spot."

DaKota wasn't her real name of course. Her Connecticut socialite parents played it safe in the eighties and went with Jessica Holt Gibson. By age fourteen, however, Jessica decided her name would only get her into the country music hall of fame and that's not where she was headed. She fully intended to sit next to fellow guitar legends Jimi Hendrix and Jimmy Page in the Rock and Roll Hall of Fame in Cleveland.

Andi dug into a healthy grilled chicken salad with fresh looking greens, tomatoes, cucumbers and light balsamic dressing on the side. I opted for primo comfort food; a cheese-steak slathered in sautéed mushrooms with grease dripping from the sandwich into congealing white slush-puddles on my plate. And onion rings. With only a modicum of guilt and ignoring the arterial hardening evidence before me, I wolfed it down. With tomorrow's gig I'd work it off. Being a drummer helps keep food guilt at bay.

"We're a bloody hooverette today, aren't we?" Andi said.

"And proud of it," I said, leaning back and noisily slurping the remnants of my soda.

She asked, "Why are we friends, again?"

"Because without me you'd become like them," I nodded toward the restaurant, "just another over-privileged asshat with more emotional attachment to your car than the people who care for you."

"And here I thought it was because I could kick your arse any time I felt like it."

"Dreamer."

When the check came Andi glanced at it for two-seconds and said, "The tip is four eighty so the total is twenty-eight-sixty, call it twenty nine and you put down the extra forty cents for your choice of nibbles. All right, then?"

"Where were you when I was tanking algebra?"

We paid the bill, walked a bit through town and then settled on one of the tree-shaded park benches on campus. From nowhere a wave of sadness washed over me. "I keep imagining what she went through, you know?" I said eventually. "Was she conscious at the end? Was she raped? Did she know her killer? God, I hate thinking about it."

"What happened..."

"I told you..."

"That's not what I mean."

I folded my arms across my chest, tucking each hand under the opposite armpit, and drew my legs under me.

"You know, we broke up."

"That was convincing. Want to give it another go?" Andi said, with that look sponsors get that says, "It's your choice but if you don't fess up it'll haunt you until you do and then I can say I told you so".

"Not really. No."

"Out with it. You're going to have to get the story straight anyway so you might as well start practicing."

My hands settled into my lap as I took a deep breath. "She didn't want the relationship anymore. I didn't know why and still don't. God, I didn't even see it coming. We had a big fight at Antonella's a couple weeks ago."

"Just how big?"

"Big enough to get kicked out. I kept asking her what was wrong, what had I done. She'd been acting like an asshat lately and maybe if she told me what was going on, I could help. All she kept saying was that there was nothing going on. It was just over. She'd had enough."

Andi let that settle for a moment and then said,   "Did you ever find out why?"

"She never said. She basically told me to mind my own fucking business." I looked up at Andi, my eyes becoming glassy.

"What?"

After a pause I said, "I didn't call 911 immediately."

"Come again?"

I told her exactly what happened earlier today and she went all wide-eyed on me.

"So instead of being embarrassed you'd rather get nicked for lying. Where's the logic in that? On top of not coming clean about your relationship."

"Thanks to Susan they already know about the relationship. Anyway no one saw me when I let the cat in."

"You're certain?"

"All was quiet."

"Let's hope it stays that way," she said, reaching out for me. It felt good in her arms even though my brain had me in DaKota's, which fueled a spark of desire deep inside me. I came to and with a slight touch of embarrassment disentangled myself her and said good-bye.

Five

Weariness took its toll on me as I walked home; what was a few blocks felt like miles. All I wanted to do was flop into bed and pull the covers over my head to make it all go away. I didn't want to think anymore so I just concentrated on my shoeless feet hitting the sidewalk. From Memorial Day to Labor Day, my feet remain unshod as much as possible. Maybe it's a throwback to my early commune days. All I know is that I'm more comfortable with bare feet, garbage strewn pathways notwithstanding.

The blueprints for the chopped up Victorian I called 'home' must be stamped "Design by Lego". My Vandeventer Avenue estate consisted of three apartments piled on top of each other, three floors of duplicated interior floor plans wrapped in worn out beige stucco with white trim and hunter green shutters. Each floor has a white porch railing on the front facing the street; however the sole entrance is through an external staircase at the rear with a small landing on each floor. I live in the penthouse. As I came up the walk only a couple of scavenging press dogs remained camped out front. A simple flip of the finger was my response to all their barking.

All was quiet as I ascended the stairs. The curtains were drawn across Susan's first-floor window and door, but that's not unusual. Outside of a few passing 'hellos' I didn't know all that much about her other than she looked like an anorexic Prince Valiant and dressed in clothing designed to hide as much skin as humanly possible, no matter the temperature.

Pausing on the second floor, now wrapped neatly in screaming yellow police tape, images of the day's activity flashed in my head.

A surprise package awaited me once I reached the third floor in the form of Zenobia, sitting quietly but with regal impatience.

"Yes? Something I can do for you?"

Her tail twitched but the gaze didn't falter as if my obvious stupidity was annoying her. She gave off an air to say that there will be no conversation on the matter; my apartment was her new home and I better damn well open the door soon.

"Why me?" I said with a sigh. Her countenance didn't change and when I cracked the door she paraded inside ahead of me and began the inspection.

The back door to my digs opened into the kitchen, a room I seldom used with the exception of the old folding leg card table functioning as a storage area for six months worth of junk mail. I reminded myself, yet again, that I really needed to go through it. Maybe that million dollar check was somewhere in that pile. The kitchen was separated from the living room by a half wall trimmed in some sort of faux wood that was in vogue during the nineteen sixties. The hallway to the bathroom and bedrooms lay off to the right. Small, yes, but how much more did I need?

I opened the fridge and was greeted by a bright white light, and not much else.

"Shopping," I said under my breath, "Must go shopping."

Grabbing a lonely carton of orange juice I opened it, took a swig and immediately sprayed rancid OJ as close to the sink as possible.

"Jesus", I said, sucking water straight from the sink faucet to rinse the moldy scum out of my mouth. I didn't have the courage to look in the carton itself, especially when the whole mess was trash-bound. After scrubbing my teeth in the bathroom, twice, I peeled off my clothes leaving a trail down the hall to my unmade bed. Living on the third floor was great in the winter when all the heat rose to warm my bod. In the summer, though, it was a killer. The tightwad owners did not supply air conditioning. I switched all three oscillating fans on high and melted on the bed for thirty minutes of gymnastics, trying to find, without success, a comfortable position to get some sleep. Frustration finally yanked me out of the twisted sheets. I kept thinking how good a shower would feel but since I don't have a shower, a swim in the ancient claw-foot tub would have to do.

I turned on the spigots and, after picking up the clothes I abandoned on the floor to toss them in the giant garbage bag I use as a laundry hamper, I was drawn into the second bedroom. Everything was where it was supposed to be; drum kit, scattered piles of videos and DVDs, and the cockeyed bulletin board that sported pictures, messages, random liberal bumper stickers, and hand-drawn doodles.

A picture of DaKota and me lodged in the frame of the board caught my eye. It was taken backstage after a gig, both of us sweaty and smiling. Our second Cadillac Grille show in Philadelphia, a Friday night two years ago. Constant thunderstorms kept the crowd to a minimum but we cooked on stage nonetheless. We have one song called "Scatterbrain" that is arranged to allow overlapping solos. We sort of 'borrowed' the structure from an old Phish jam where each band member takes four bars to solo on top of a driving drum rhythm. The space to solo shrinks every four bars until guitars and violin end up jamming together. It sounds like a handful of quarters in a food processor if it doesn't work right but that night it flowed like melted chocolate. In the middle of the piece DaKota turned to me, sweat running down her face and neck, guitar slung low across her hips. I thought she was going to drop to her knees and hump her blonde wood Fender at any moment. I saw smoke in her eyes. The electricity was thick and overwhelming.

After the show, we speed-loaded her van, dodging the ongoing downpour. DaKota and I finally jumped in the front, soaked to the skin, the rain cascading in sheets down the windshield. The wipers were on the fritz so we sat and relived high points of the gig and watched all the windows steam up.

"Someone is going to think something lascivious is going on in here," I said. "Should we rock the van back and forth to fuel their imaginations?" We started rocking side to side on the bench seat, hands pressed against the damp windows, barely moving the chassis but laughing hysterically.

She reached over and grabbed my arm. Her eyes were deep and dark. She lifted a hand to touch my face. For a moment I wasn't sure what she was doing. Then, suddenly, I got it. I tried not to tense up but this was blindsiding me. The thought had never entered my mind. I realized another woman was about to kiss me. DaKota put her face right in front of me and softly touched her lips to mine.

Sirens, flashing lights and whistles were exploding in my head. Yeah, that felt like any other kiss, I thought, making an outside attempt at rationalization.

"Are you uncomfortable?" DaKota whispered.

"No," I practically screamed, trying to breathe. "No, it's just something I've never done before."

"What, kissing?"

"No, no. You know..."

Our mouths met again softly at first, and then with increasing hunger as she pushed me down on the bench seat, her lips and tongue exploring my mouth, stopping from time to time just to stare into my eyes. Pulling my hand to her mouth she kissed and licked my fingers, all the while her eyes not leaving mine. A burning desire flushed my body. I kissed her back with a deep need. She peeled off my wet clothes, then hers; our hands exploring smooth curves and soft heat. The rain beat harder on the van's metal roof. I tasted the mixture of salt-sweat and musk on her skin, fueling a desire I never knew was there. The sensation of her tongue trailing down between my breasts was delicious; her hair softly tickled my sides, my stomach and eventually my thighs. Thick and wet like never before, I quickly gave into DaKota's soft slithering tongue, crying out and not caring who heard, feeling only muscle-wracking sensations rip through me.

"Oh God," I breathed as the waves ebbed into a glowing pulse.

She crawled under me and we lay in each other's arms, with my head on her shoulder. My finger traced the brown skin around her navel, teasing the silver belly-button ring. Her breathing was soft as I watched her breasts rise and fall. She gasped and purred when I touched the tip of her erect nipple.

"Time for me to return the favor," I said.

"Only if you want to."

Sliding across her damp skin, sensing her need and inhaling her musk, I said, "Bet your sweet ass I do."

Another first. And then a second. And a third.

Steam drops wriggled down the inside of the windshield as the rain pounded on the outside. DaKota's musk filled the air. My fingers gently trailed through the sheen on her stomach.

"You're insatiable," DaKota murmured.

"I was enjoying myself."

"Obviously."

"You weren't?"

A Scarlett O'Hara sigh escaped from her lips, "Not at all. Faked the whole thing."

"Bitch," I said, playfully biting her thigh.

I crawled on top of her and we lay entwined, sweat soaked skin melded together.

"Have women always been your thing?" I asked.

"No. I just go with what attracts me. Gender just doesn't enter the picture. I've been with two different guys in the past."

"How many women?"

"Just one."

I closed my eyes, feeling safe and contented as her hand combed through my hair, my head rising and falling nestled between her breasts. "Anyone I know?"

"Doubtful. She was older, much older. She started getting all clingy and possessive, calling me every half hour to see what I was doing. I never found out for sure but I think she had someone following me. Way too bizarre so I ended it."

"And I'm the rebound?"

She pulled my head up to scowl at me nose to nose. "No, you're the fucking idiot for asking such a dumb fucking question." Her hand pulled my chin up to her face to kiss me softly and deeply.

Outside, the rain on the van continued its metallic drumming. Then slowly it started changing. Changing to…to…a…splash. A splash on… tile.

"Dammit." I came to and ran into the bathroom; water was flowing out of the tub onto the floor.

In the steam filled room, I mopped up the floor with whatever I could grab; towels, T-shirts and underwear from the bag/hamper, and threw the sopping pile in the sink. Once the water drained a bit I slowly climbed in letting the heat engulf me.

The hollow sound of one last drop falling from the spigot into the tub echoed in the empty bathroom. My head fell back with a dull thump against the condensation covered tile, eyelids fluttering closed. Flashes of DaKota tightened my chest, all the looks she had, all the smiles, the laughter. I tried to slow it all down to grasp something, anything, out of those visions that would give her back to me. Everything was moving too fast and exhaustion kept me from keeping pace. My mind wouldn't stop, seeing her playing on stage, the last phone call and our last meal at Antonella's where everything fell apart. Searching through the words looking for a clue, looking for a reason where there was none. I wanted to wake up and see her sitting in the living room, playing her acoustic Taylor guitar and see her smile at me as I walked in the door.

The images accelerated, twisting everything that kept me sane, sending blasts of heat and light to my brain and quaking shudders through my body. I let it come. Tears burst out and streamed down my face. My hand, dripping with hot water, lifted to my mouth trying to stem the wail of sobs.

After a second wave, the tears gradually subsided. The taste of salt covered my lips. Little by little normal breathing returned. I cupped handfuls of now lukewarm water and splashed my face, feeling like I was washing inches of grime and crust away. My pruned toes pushed the hot spigot to reintroduce steaming water into the tub. Tendrils of warmth sculpted around my body, wrapping me in a false sense of security. I felt sad, but protected. All I wanted now was to sleep.

Six

The roar of the ocean filled my living room, compliments of the ocean waves loaded in my iPod, which was now plugged into the stereo; surf rolled out of the studio monitors, substituting my brain clutter with images of those days curled up next to Nana Lennox in Wrightsville, the closest I came to absolute peace and serenity.

I threw on shorts that were once black sweat pants but now had the legs torn off, and my black tank top that read, 'Guitarists have good licks but you can always count on a drummer for a great banging'. I curled up in the corner of the sofa; a glass of Coke with ice was perspiring onto the Wal-Mart pressboard table, my sole new piece of furniture when I moved in. I switched on my lamp filled with frosted sea glass I scavenged off the beach, filling the corner with soft light.

The ocean continued to fill the apartment. Waves rolled along the sand in a rush. First one wave hit, receded, then another crashed in, followed by…

"Dinner!" Andi entered carrying a paper sack in each arm containing take out packages.

"I figured you would not eat unless supervised." She had procured one large roast beef and Swiss hoagie, a bag of sour cream and onion chips, a can of Coke for me along with a salad, and a bottle of water and the local paper for her. The last thing I felt like doing was eating but I went along not wanting Andi to feel bad for her effort.

We sat in silence, eating to the rhythm of the waves. Andi pulled out the section of the newspaper with the Sudoku puzzle and filled in all the blank spaces in about thirty seconds.

"I can't stand those things," I said.

"Keeps the mind sharp now doesn't it? Besides it's not math, it's just logic."

"Whatever."

Without warning, Andi screamed and jumped out of the chair, which was closely followed by a fierce pounding on the back door which made us both jump.

"Bloody hell…" she said looking at the floor.

"Ah. Say hello to DaKota's former roommate," I said picking up Zenobia, who had apparently rubbed against Andi's leg unannounced. "She seems to have picked me as her new keeper. You want her?"

"Hell no. The last thing I need is a ninja cat."

Another pounding at the door. Through the glass I could see what looked like a Hispanic woman in a gray suit and white blouse. Moving behind her was somebody with a camera, and it wasn't the disposable kind but a shoulder mounted broadcast rig.

"So much for a quiet dinner," I said. "These creeps have no shame whatsoever."

"Allow me."

I grabbed Andi's arm. "Just remember anything you say or do will most likely be seen by everyone on the eleven o'clock news."

"Possibly."

Andi grabbed the unopened can of Coke and shook it vigorously.

"Yes?" she said opening the door.

"Chynna Lennox?" the woman asked, whipping a microphone under Andi's chin.

"No. Now bugger off." From the kitchen I heard *snap*, *fizz*, shrieking, dripping soda and the slam of the door as Andi walked back in the kitchen triumphantly to wash her soda soaked hands.

"THAT was fucking awesome." I stuck my fist in the air and got pumped back.

"Ta. Bunch of twits."

It felt good to laugh.

"OK. Now, you need to get some kip. Come on." Holding onto my hand she yanked me back to my bedroom.

"Get in," she said pointing to the bed. She turned two of the fans on as I climbed on the bed.

"Move over," she ordered

"Excuse me?"

"Shut up and move over. No snogging involved. Promise." Andi propped all the pillows against the headboard and sat with her back against them. I looked at her cautiously.

"Here," she said quietly, pulling my arm, and then positioning me next to her with my head on her shoulder, her arm around me, holding me close. She pulled my leg up so it crossed over her thighs.

"Go to sleep." One hand was gently rubbing my back. I felt her steady breathing underneath my head.

"Mmmmm. That feels good. Thanks."

"Shut up."

I did.

Seven

A dynamite blast of thunder rattled the windows, and my insides, hard enough to jolt me upright in my bed, still clutching a pillow to my body with both arms. Teeming rain sizzled on the street. A blinking red light next to the bed caught my eye…4:37…4:37…4:37…The power must have died and come back on. Shaking the cobwebs from my head, the dull light outside started to register.

"Holy shit," I whispered through the gravel in my throat. The fans were going full blast, shoving the sultry air around the room. One of these days I would get myself a window air conditioner, I promised myself for the twentieth time.

Then I remembered going to sleep. Andi was gone.

To my surprise, I was naked. How the hell did that happen? My head was too foggy to recall getting up in the middle of the night to disrobe. My brain shifted as the Knights started singing.

"Just wanted to make sure you were OK."

Dammit, not today. "Snevley, what the hell do you want?"

"Hey, just wanted to offer my condolences, you being the bereaved widow and all. How about I come over and you give me an in depth interview?"

"The days of you and I doing anything 'in depth' are long past. Besides the only person you go in depth with is you. You come near me and I'll gouge out your eyes with a broken drumstick."

"Hey, is that any way to treat a close intimate friend?"

"In this case, yes."

Christian Snevley is a reporter for *The Trenton Chronicle*; a local train wreck of a scandal sheet that is not sleazy enough to be sold at supermarket checkout stands with all the other tabloids yet still manages to mask gossip and innuendo as real news. Snevley stood six feet tall, three inches of which was spiked blond hair atop a well sculpted, muscular physique that he worshipped in his spare time when he wasn't making up the news. His apartment had more mirrors than a disco ball, which should have been a big clue when I moved in with him-one of those great mysteries I chalk up to a gigantic character flaw. It's a toss-up whether his narcissism or workaholism destroyed our short-lived relationship. I eventually realized that competing with either was as hopeless as finding water in the Sahara and I left him but carrying a bag full of anger as I went.

"Come on. I'll make it worth your while," he said in what he thought was a seductive voice but sounded closer to oozing snot.

"You are repugnant and there isn't anything you have I could possibly want."

"Oh really?"

By his tone I knew he had something to dangle in front of me and was playing it to the hilt. Once a fifteen year old, always a fifteen year old.

"I'm not in the mood for games, asshat, so just spill it."

"What am I, a moron?"

"Yes."

"No way. You talk first, on the record, and then we'll see."

"On the record, go to hell," I said and hung up. What did I ever see in that pusillanimous pipsqueak? Okay, so he has a hot bod and is a master at the gift of gab. I must have been stoned to the gills the night we met.

The phone sung again and I snatched it up without looking at the caller ID.

"I said 'go to hell' asshat!"

There was a moment of silence on the other end followed by, "Swell. I always get the frigging lunatics. You treat everybody like that?"

Great. Just great. Gralewski. "I'm sorry. The, um, press has been hounding me." That wasn't totally outside the realm of truth.

"I'll be at your apartment in five minutes. Don't leave," he said then hung up.

Gralewski paying me a visit reeked of bad news coming my way. I punched in Jason's number.

"Yeah?"

"I see I've reached the home of the Seven Dwarves and you must be Grumpy because you sure aren't Happy or Bashful."

"Did you call just to abuse me? Why aren't you here? What do you want and my guess is that it's something I'll regret."

"Charmer. I'm about to be visited, for the second time, by your favorite storm-trooper and something tells me I need a trusty lawyer by my side, but I'll settle for your company."

"Pro Bono naturally."

"Bring Bruce Springsteen if you want to."

"Juvenile." A deep sigh emanated from the earpiece. "Fear not Isolde, Sir Tristan approaches."

"What? Who?" I said but the line went dead.

Suddenly, the back door flew open and I assumed it was Detective Dumbass. Forgoing underwear, I grabbed the first T-shirt and pair of shorts I could scrounge off the floor.

"I've got some more questions," Gralewski grunted as I entered the kitchen. He made no pretense of letting his eyes lasciviously ride the elevator over my barely clothed body. I made no pretense of crossing my arms over my chest.

"Oh do come in. I see you're not wearing your swastika armband. They run out down at the station? Keeping the extra-portly size in stock must be a bitch."

He was wearing a pale yellow short sleeved shirt and a brown paisley tie that hung four inches above his bulging waistline. He tossed his suit jacket in a heap on my mail-strewn table.

"On the night of the murder, where were you?"

"I already told you I was here sleeping."

He snickered, "Yeah I know, but what were you doing before you were allegedly here sleeping that conveniently no one can corroborate."

I sighed and said, "I was at the store until 10pm. Stopped to get something to eat..."

"Where?"

"Hot Wings on Tulane Street."

"Which you better believe I will ask them to verify," he said pointing a stubby finger in my face.

"Be my guest and please get your scummy hand out of my face," I said and moved toward the table to create some distance when he snatched my arm and pulled me back, his pocked and beat up nose an inch from mine.

"And if I don't? What are you going to do about it?" he breathed.

Struggling from his grip wasn't an option; something told me it would just make things worse.

"Let me go," I said softly and slowly.

"You should play nice with me," he said, "It wouldn't take much to make you look like the psycho-dyke who attacked me when I arrived, leaving me no choice but to defend myself." Our eyes locked and I was not going to give him the satisfaction of breaking the stare.

"Poof. Gone," he said flinging open his free hand to emulate a puff of smoke. I felt his grip loosen just enough that I jerked my arm free.

He continued, "You didn't happen to pay a visit to your pal downstairs when you got back last night. You know, trying to reconcile things? Patch up hurt feelings? Celebrate with some blow and a rough fuck?"

Hitting him with a stick sporting a dozen nails driven into it seemed a proper course of action at this point. I put that wish on hold and said, "You get all your social skills by watching porn on the net, don't you?"

"Okay let's try a different topic, like you and the deceased having a knock down drag-out at a downtown restaurant, from which you were asked to leave. Funny how you forgot to mention that to Detective Douglas or me. Apparently you and your carpet-munching friend were a hot item until said brawl, leaving one jilted and angry drummer dyke."

"You can't be serious."

"As a heart attack."

"I should be so lucky." I grinned.

"I wonder what other details you didn't provide us? The coroner told me your pal had red and inflamed nasal and bronchial passages consistent with heavy coke use and or huffing. He won't know for sure until the tox reports come back. You being the junkie..."

"Ex-junkie," I cut in.

His mouth formed a tight grin. "Once a junkie, always a junkie."

Once I stopped being snarky his comment finally registered. "Coroner? The autopsy was done already? Awful damn quick isn't it?"

"This was given high priority."

"Why? They just took her away about twenty-four hours ago."

"Because it was. That's all you need to know. Now, if you don't mind, I'm just going to have a look around."

"Doubtful," a voice from the door said before I could.

"Oh great," said Gralewski, shaking his head. "Hey, I hear Greenpeace is out humping whales. Why don't you go rescue them and leave the real work to me?"

Jason threw his worn satchel on top of Gralewski's suit coat. "I assume that, one, you were not invited in and two, you do not have the required court authorized warrant so you've got about thirty-seconds to vacate the premises before I notify the local constabulary and have you booked for trespassing, and perhaps breaking and entering."

Local constabulary. Suddenly I felt like Mary Poppins walking the London streets, meeting Burt and jumping into chalk pavement pictures.

Gralewski stared Jason down then broke into a smile. "Okay, Mr. Attorney. Have it your way. Tell your client that I'll be back later, with a warrant, and not to pack too much. The correctional facility has a nice selection of orange jumpsuits she can pick from."

"Eat shi…," I started but Jason grabbed my arm and pulled me back, his way of telling me to shut the hell up.

"This search warrant will be based on what evidence?"

"That's not really your concern now, is it?" Gralewski croaked, swaggering up within a couple inches of Jason's face.

"It's very much my business as you well know." Jason pushed his glasses up the bridge of his nose. "Some advice, Detective? You really need to invest in a toothbrush. Your breath may be misconstrued as a concealed and highly offensive weapon."

Every muscle in the detective's jaw tightened, his fingers clenched into fists. I was doing my best not to burst out laughing.

Throbbing veins coursed through the Detective's thick neck. "This isn't over, and she's going down." Flinging his jacket off the table and sending Jason's satchel to the floor, Gralewski burst out the door.

"Thanks," I said after a deep breath.

"A complete throwback to the nineteen forties. Most unorthodox."

"Something's strange, though," I said, "the autopsy is already done. That's a bit quick isn't it?"

"Thoroughly due to your friend's well-heeled and politically-connected Connecticut parents who pulled a few strings at the Coroner's office. On my way over I called the assistant M.E. to find out when the autopsy was going to take place. Apparently DaKota's father and the Governor of New Jersey matriculated at Harvard together and have maintained a long-term acquaintance. You can speculate what transpired from there. The autopsy was completed and the body is already on its merry and legal way back to Connecticut. Officially, the funeral is scheduled for the day after tomorrow."

"What? How the hell did that happen?"

"'All things are subject to interpretation, whichever interpretation prevails at a given time is a function of power and not truth.'"

"Who said that?"

"Nietzsche."

"And your point?"

"It means God resides in Connecticut while you and I slum in a leper colony. Get acquainted with the idea."

Eight

After checking in at the store, I headed for the University gym for a swim. A ritual between work and gigs, it helped wash off the crust of the day and get me energized to play at night. Being the good person she is, I was able to twist Andi's arm into finagling a pool membership for me.

The water was cold and gave me something to fight against as I swam laps. I kicked hard but forced myself to breathe steadily as I made my way from one end of the pool to the other. After three laps my body kicked into automatic pilot, which let my brain focus on the band.

Brain Sponge had been described in the blogosphere as 1) kick-ass bitches, 2) the most amazing rock goddesses since Heart, and 3) complete crap. Okay, so we can't please everyone. My goal is to have fun, play all out, and make money. Maybe we'll be discovered someday. I keep praying to Mom to send a good label executive to one of our shows but so far, she hasn't come through. I'm still working on the recovery concept of things happening in Mom's time, not mine.

On bass guitar, Geoff Kurtzman, my ADHD computer wizard. On electric violin, Katrina Gorski, zaftig Harley-rider–think Christina Hendricks body with Fiona Apple's looks. Yes, our audiences are male dominated. Then there is Spag. Standing six foot twenty with a straight, brown waist-length pony tail and ZZ Top goatee, our rhythm guitarist invariably sports three silver chains clipped to his jeans that trail across his hips and end in a back pocket. Both arms are tattooed in multi-colored sleeves of dragons, guitars and naked nymphs. Spag and DaKota traded guitar licks with DaKota taking most of the leads. Whether Spag could fill the new void in our sound remained to be seen.

I stayed in the water until few people remained and then made a hasty exit to the locker room. It's an old reaction that makes no sense, at least that's what my head thinks. My guts sometimes tell a different story, and it's all Kyle Borkferder's fault. In high school, I had this mad crush on the sniveling little git, until one day at the end of a field hockey session during gym class I gave Kyle the flirtiest 'hi' I could muster as

I passed the boys picking up the equipment. Seconds later all I heard was a whispered 'thunder thighs' that was distinctly Kyle's voice, the scar from which lingers to this day no matter how much logic I apply or how much I try to turn it over to Mom. My legs are thick and muscular from the drumming and swimming, and every so often I look at them in the mirror and think they belong on Dumbo. It's one of those things I have mostly surrendered; a resentment that has grayed with time, but pops up every now and again, especially when I'm feeling vulnerable. I often daydream of meeting Kyle one day on the street and using my thunder thighs to lodge his nuts in his throat.

On the way home, I stopped for a roast beef and Swiss on rye with lettuce, tomato, cucumbers, spinach and roasted peppers, a bag of chips and a coke. A typical pre-gig protein/carb extravaganza. Once engorged, I packed up the car and headed for the club.

We're regular jukebox heroes at Gofer Phang, a 1960's era dive on the southern edge of town off Route 206. The outside still looked like a log cabin tucked in the woods. Inside, the black walled hall had a three tiered floor leading from the stage, each tier devoid of tables and chairs but containing its own bar. Faded posters of local bands long forgotten remained stapled to the walls. It was an originals club, in other words, no cover bands. Everyone who played here wrote their own material.

The band prepped backstage in Phang's so-called green room, a black walled enclosure that smelled sickly sweet, like a bad diner's ladies room, and was about as big. Furnishings were neo-modern 60's era dumpster, with two olive green dinette chairs and a faded Three Musketeers bar colored sofa in need of recovering. And re-springing. And decontamination.

Gig prep took its usual course. Katrina focused on tuning her electric violin. Tonight she was dressed in a cutoff white tank-top and black leather pants tight enough to look like body paint, her thick chestnut mane tied back in a simple pony-tail that hung to her waist. Spag, in his usual T-shirt, jeans and chains, warmed up with flaming thirty-second note riffs, his spider fingers blurred as they scrambled up and down the guitar neck. Geoff sat in the corner playing with his new iPad while white ear buds hung from his head that were connected to his iPod. Pad, pod, pud…whatever. He was the keeper of the Kool-Aid in the cult of Apple. Dressed in a Philadelphia Eagles football uniform, complete with pads and black greasepaint under his eyes, Geoff had a helmet with a New York Giants logo sitting next to him on the sofa. I stopped questioning Geoff's on stage wardrobe the night he showed up wearing a tuxedo jacket, ruffled shirt and bow tie over a pink ballerina tutu.

My routine consisted of opening a black flip-top cylinder that contained a bright pink mass resembling Silly Putty, called a Putty Pad. I squeezed the black container, pulling the gunk out and pressing it flat on the counter top; instant practice pad. I grabbed a pair of sticks and limbered my fingers and wrists by banging away on the pink splotch.

"You okay jumping in on DaKota's leads?" I said to Spag.

"Shouldn't be a problem, as long as you're not expecting a note-for-note imitation. Some of the stuff she does…ah, did…I'm sorry."

"Don't be. This is new for all of us and it will take getting used to. I'm not expecting anything."

"I am," said Geoff donning his helmet with a smile.

"The only thing you should be expecting is a visit from the dudes in the rubber truck," Katrina said. "You are just too strange. Do you purposely shop for your clothes at garage sales?"

Geoff shot back, "Hey, I don't have double D boobs to flash all over the stage to attract drooling horndogs. I mean, why don't you just play topless and get it over with? Between you, Chynna and DaK…well between you and Chynna I have to find some way to get some attention."

"Oh yeah," I said with a sigh. "This is going to be a rip and a half."

The set was passable. We felt the lack of coordination with DaKota not there, but Spag pulled through like a trooper. Even the audience felt restless and disjointed. During "Gunn This", an extended variation on the "Theme from Peter Gunn" played double speed with fluctuating time signatures and wild strings of thirty-second notes, my energy took a nose dive. It happens every now and again, especially when I'm distracted with the rest of my life and right now, DaKota had me off balance big time. Energy sags sometimes trick me into pushing harder and improvising fancy fills I normally wouldn't dare to attempt that naturally end up sounding like crap. I had to focus on straight ahead basics.

Around one in the morning I slumped on the couch backstage, chugging a bottle of fruit punch PowerAde and munching half-frozen orange wedges straight from the freezer. Trust me, there's nothing better.

Perspiration covered my body from head to toe, soaking my gray tank top, black running shorts and Daffy Duck sweat socks. Anyone who doesn't like the feeling of a drenched T-shirt sticking to their body, or streams of water running down legs and arms best consider picking up a flute. I felt energized and sexy, but smelled like an end-of-term boy's gym locker.

All this felt a bit more than strange. DaKota supplied a unifying energy to the band, even post-gig, running around high-fiving and fist-pumping everyone. Somehow, through all her maniacal gyrations on stage, she managed to pick up on little fills or riffs we all did and would say how great they were or how the song really came alive with some new piece. Spag often called it 'Team Gibson'. Now the thread that connected us all was gone. Surrounded by band mates, I felt oddly alone.

"Hey, you ok?" Katrina grabbed both my hands with hers and squatted down in front of me with a crunching, squeaking sound produced by her one-piece leather chaps, of which the jacket was unzipped low enough to display a ridiculous amount of cleavage. She was dressed to jump on her Harley and head home. Sparkling emerald eyes searched my face.

"Yeah," I said. "I just miss her, you know? She's here but she's not. Strange…"

After a solid hug and a promise to call, Katrina strutted out the door under the drooling eyes of every male backstage.

"Good thing all your heads are connected," I shouted. They all looked like kids who got caught with their hand in the cookie jar.

Nine

"I'm scared, Angel. My ribs are sore and my jaw aches..."

There was no one better than Humphrey Bogart, especially in all the Bacall films. I spent Sunday morning with my butt planted on the couch, alternately watching old movies and eating what little remained in the apartment. *The Big Sleep* flickered on TV but my mind kept wandering, thinking that I really needed a Phillip Marlowe to figure out just what the hell was going on. Actually a savvy, tough Ms. Marlowe was more to my liking these days.

What would Marlowe do first? After he dumped that slut Carmen back at the Sternwood's he...

Went back to Geiger's place. The scene of the crime.

DaKota's apartment. Just maybe...

In my kitchen cupboard sits a Daffy Duck head coffee mug used primarily as a holder of some loose change, dust, a couple bent paper clips and a key to the second floor. A gnawing something in my gut tried to warn me about going through DaKota's apartment at all. Foolishly, I ignored it.

I carefully crawled through the police tape trying not to tear it off the porch or doorway, and inserted the key.

"What do you think you are doing?" I jumped at the voice behind me. Susan Roche stood on the steps, hands on hips.

She was dressed in a white starched blouse buttoned to the neck and pressed navy slacks. Susan was the type who applied her make-up with a trowel; somewhere an inch below the surface was skin of some sort that had never seen the light of day. She looked like a fugitive from a wax museum. There was minimal interaction between Susan, DaKota and I. She kept her distance; cordial enough but with obvious walls protecting her space, like the blinds on her windows that were never open.

"You take one more step and I'm calling the Police. I'm sure they'll be very interested to hear about this, among the many other things I'm sure you've neglected to tell them."

"Wait a minute," I said climbing back through the Police tape, wondering what had happened to the quiet, reserved Susan I thought lived downstairs. "What does that mean?"

"It's bad enough I have to put up with all the noise you two make," she said. "This was a quiet house and then all of a sudden we have guitars and drums with which to contend. And that's just the half of it." She dropped her voice to a whisper. "It's disgusting. You two deviants carrying on up there. Makes me sick just to think of it. How can you do that? It's revolting and not normal. Why don't you just move to New Hope? There are plenty of those types of people there."

"Susan, wait," I said as she started down the stairs. I walked over to her on the landing. She was two steps down which brought us eye to eye.

"I'm sorry. I didn't know you felt that way or that we were causing you any discomfort. Had I known that I would have done this long ago." I quickly grabbed her head, pulling her to me and smashed my lips against hers. I tried to wriggle my tongue in her mouth but her lips were sealed tight. All I could feel was waxy goo rubbing off on my mouth. She squealed and pushed away from me but I held firm. After about fifteen seconds I let her go.

"Oh," she stammered, "you…you…"

"Yes?" I asked in my best sweet and innocent voice.

"You'll regret that. Believe me." She stormed into her apartment, slamming the door behind her.

"Asshat," I murmured.

After washing Susan's grease off my face, I reassessed my approach, planning to return once the Roche dust settled and under the cover of darkness.

Ten

A distinct advantage of living where I do is having a place to mooch a meal every so often, thanks to the head chef at La Monde, the town's restaurant for rich, white snobs. The fact that the chef is also a sort-of step brother helps as well. Brendan Patrick McCullough is the oldest son of the wife of the man who last divorced my mother. Got that? Calling him a 'sort of step-brother' is a bit of a disservice. He kicked my ass when it needed it most and, against mother's objections, footed the bill for three months of rest and rehabilitation at Caron Treatment Center, the facility that ended his long standing love affair with Jack Daniels.

Sunday meant dinner service only at LeMonde, so late morning was a good time to just "unexpectedly" pop in. The restaurant itself took up almost an entire block on Witherspoon Street, but the kitchen could only fit seven people without creating a human bumper car atmosphere. I entered through the restaurant's back door and was surprised to not find the usual bustle and smells of the evening meal's prep; sautéed garlic, onion and the warm aroma of comforting spices. Today, Lysol and ammonia were more like it.

"Pat?" I stopped and listened. Not a sound. It was a little creepy. My nerves started to tingle a bit, which happens when things in my life are not in the order they should be, or at least in the order I think they should be. DaKota's deathbed flashed in my mind. If I found another dead body I was going to stick my head in the oven.

Pat's office was nestled down the back hallway. His laptop was there and the lamp was on, so he was around somewhere. I heard a faint scraping and a bump, like a wooden chair dragged across linoleum, coming from what sounded like the main dining room.

I crept back into the kitchen and gently pushed open the swinging door to the dining room just enough to see Pat and a blonde pony-tailed woman in yellow sport shirt and white shorts in more than a friendly embrace. Even from this distance I knew a good tonsil exploration when I saw one.

By the time I had orange juice poured in a coffee mug, Pat plowed through the kitchen doors, abruptly stopping when he realized I was there, shit-eating grin plastered to my face.

"Please. Don't stop on my account," I said.

"You know you're a real pain in the ass. And your timing sucks," Pat said.

"Sorry. My, we're a bit touchy this morning."

Without answering me, he started yanking things out of the fridge and banging skillets onto the stove. I think he was making me breakfast but I knew better than to interrupt. When Pat went quiet it was best to steer clear until the storm blew over. I went back to the dining room, now empty, to watch the early morning pedestrians. Through the mottled glass windows they looked as if they were walking underwater while busying their way down the sidewalk.

I pulled a chair from the table over to the window and noticed a scrap of paper on the floor. Just something the cleanup crew missed, I thought. There was a series of numbers handwritten in red ink, perhaps a note someone dropped. I looked around for a garbage can but saw none so I stuffed the paper in my pocket.

Pat came out a few minutes later carrying a bacon and mushroom omelet with home fries for me and a cup of coffee for him. He sat and sipped, staring out of the window while I devoured breakfast. A gold ring on his left hand reflected the sunlight, the initials 'BPM' gently etched on one flattened side, which he presently was twisting back and forth with the thumb of the same hand; his thinking tell.

My stepbrother had an easy face, fair skinned with traces of freckles. People commented on his chestnut hair flecked with blonde at his temples, saying that it gave him a dashing appearance. Pat's eyes always sparkled to let you know his smile was genuine, which is probably why he's done so well with the restaurant.

"Sorry for snapping," he said into his coffee, and then quickly put his mug down. "Hey, I'm sorry about DaKota. Why didn't you call me? I just heard about it this morning."

"Thanks. I haven't been thinking too clearly lately and Andi's been my faithful guardian, keeping me occupied so I don't have time to sit and stew about it." After another forkful of his wonderful omelet I said, "By the way where is everybody? Why isn't the crew prepping for tonight?"

"We're closed today. The annual full kitchen scouring is set to start within the hour. I'm here waiting for the crew to arrive."

"On a Sunday?"

He shook his head. "Traditionally Sunday is our slowest day of the week, which sounds odd, I know, but such is life."

We sat in silence. I was torn about how to bring up the blonde, not sure if I should gently steer the conversation around to what I saw, somehow, or bull my way straight through it at the risk of pissing him off. "So. Tell me about this one." So much for subtlety.

"What?" he said, then it dawned on him what I meant. "Oh," he said with a hard edge in his voice I was not used to hearing. Was he that upset about me seeing them? I had trouble believing that. This was something else.

"So I take it that was the 'I love you but we can't see each other anymore' scene?" I ventured a guess.

His jaw tightened and he said through clenched teeth, "Yet another on the long list, dammit. Being a chef and having a relationship are mutually exclusive."

"All of them want their shot, thinking they can change you, that it will be different with them. They will be able to make you realize being with them is more important than being a chef and that you'll delegate all your responsibilities to someone else and walk in the door every night at 5 p.m."

His lips tight, he continued to twirl his BPM ring with his thumb and stare out of the window.

"Why am I getting the feeling that this one was different?"

"You think?" he said avoiding my gaze.

"So why is this the first time I'm hearing about it? Who is she anyway?"

He sighed. "Carolyn. All together different. Wonderful woman. Kind, warm, funny."

"How long has this been going on?" I said, shoving another forkful of omelette in my face.

"About a month."

"A month and I don't know about it? Something's not right here. Why all the secrecy with you and Ms. Carolyn?"

"Mrs."

I dropped my fork on my plate. "Bingo."

Pat blushed a bit. "It just sort of happened. We knew what we were doing. She came in for lunch one day and I couldn't keep my eyes off her. It was slow so I just decided to introduce myself. We talked through most of the afternoon about…well…everything. It all just sort of clicked and we became comfortable very quickly."

"Secure in the knowledge that Mr. Carolyn would graciously not mind?"

A deep sadness crossed his face. "That's why she was here today; to stop things that neither of us wants to stop before the shit hits the fan."

"Are you nuts, Brendan?" When I was really serious I always reverted to his proper given name, kind of our little code to say, "I'm not playing." He sighed and gulped the rest of his coffee.

"Now you know why I've kept it on the Q.T."

"You're head over heels in love with her, aren't you?"

"Yes."

Pat always wore his emotions on his face. I said, "You're so obvious. Your eyes go all gooey and you get that crease at the top of your nose. You're a dead giveaway. You had the same expression when you were all googly-eyed at April Horseface."

"Houseman."

"Whatever."

He smiled sadly and gazed out the window.

"Drop this one, Brendan," I said quietly. "It's going to be nothing but trouble. Serious trouble."

"I know," he said.

"But you're not going to are you? I can feel it. Shit." I picked up my plate and utensils and headed back to the kitchen. This has to be my Mother's fault; she could open her own store named *Scars 'R' Us, Emotional Crippling Our Specialty*. Anyone in the path of her pompous brainwaves became infected. Dad was the first, although he didn't help much. I was the one who found his baked ass hanging in their bedroom closet in a psilocybin induced euphoria. His experiment with autoerotic asphyxiation failed. The faded Grateful Dead T-shirt he wore sported a psychedelic design that read, "Far out." Indeed he was, never to return.

I was on my way out the back door when Pat came into the kitchen and yelled, "Hey!"

"What?"

"You're welcome," he said, leaning on the doorframe, coffee cup still in hand.

I went back in and gave him a hug and kiss on the cheek. "Thanks. Just don't get in over your head, okay? Listen to me for once in your life. I mean where else am I going to get my one decent meal a week?"

"You might have to learn to cook" he said as I bounded out the door. "Or better still, pay for one like the rest of the world!"

I didn't know those were the last words I'd hear him speak for quite some time. If I did, I would have stayed for at least one more cup of coffee.

Eleven

All was quiet and dark on the first floor as I crept inside DaKota's apartment and gently closed the door, feeling as if I'd walked into an oven on Thanksgiving, the closed windows barricading any hope of circulation. Traces of rancid, death-smell lingered, I suppose once an odor like that gets into the curtains or the walls it never fully leaves. I reached to turn on the kitchen light but stopped short. Attracting attention would not be helpful right now. I remembered there being a flashlight in the kitchen drawer next to the sink. I rummaged through the clutter, hoping that any sharp knives were blade down.

The flashlight I found produced only a dim beam that showed little, so I smacked it against my palm, trying to coax some additional power from the batteries, but without success. Everything in the apartment looked the same, but the feeling was empty. All the energy DaKota generated into these rooms was gone leaving the space abandoned and lifeless.

I couldn't bring myself to go back to her bedroom just yet so I started with the second bedroom, the home of all her guitars, amps, desk, computer and the accompanying memorabilia.

I was looking at the pictures on the wall when the flashlight beam died. I shook the rattling batteries and a protesting dingy light flickered back on spotlighting Mouse Mouse, a computer mouse in the shape of a real mouse complete with pink nosed snout and whiskers, laying on its back on the floor. I hadn't touched anything else in the place, but some inner voice wanted me to right Mouse Mouse. Kneeling, setting the device on its rubber ball on its pad, the flashlight picked up a glint of neon pink plastic peeking out behind some books sitting on the bottom of the book shelf. I reached in and extracted a jump drive. It wasn't more than two inches long and had a pocket clip built into the case. There was a palpable energy whispering in my gut, something I've slowly come to recognize as Mom telling me to pay attention and take some action. I slipped the thing into my pocket for later inspection.

Without warning, the clicking of the apartment door opening echoed from the kitchen. I doused the flashlight and froze. Maybe I didn't close it all the way and the wind pushed it open. The kitchen floor creaked under the advancing footsteps as pulses from a flashlight blinked down the hall. Oh, shit. Where do I go now? The window? Yeah, right. Nice two story drop. As quietly as I could I forced myself to move into the walk-in closet, scrunching into a side space in a dark corner around some sort of column. I could hear footsteps but no voices. DaKota's scent still lingered in the closet, the smell from her hanging clothes rushed through me and tightened my chest.

I quietly grabbed an empty wire hanger from the rod and straightened the top hook. It wouldn't kill anyone but would leave some nasty scratches and punctures. I willed myself into invisibility, squeezing deep into the corner. Mom, please keep me safe, I prayed, and please help this person not to commit a crime or kill me, or worse.

Unnerving silence coupled with the oppressive closet heat created veins of sweat bleeding down my face and back. Staying in the closet shaking with fear had little appeal but what choice did I have? If he was silently waiting right outside the closet and I walked out, I'd be screwed. If he was already gone and I stayed in the closet I'd feel like a five year old hiding from the boogeyman. The hell with it.

I reached to push open the closet door when a massive crash shot me back into the corner. Another crash followed, then another. It sounded as if someone was thoroughly trashing DaKota's apartment. Glass shattered, loud thumps of objects being thrown vibrated through the floor.

For a brief moment, silence, then the destruction calamity resumed just outside the closet doors. Pounding thuds shook the floor, each hit making me jump and ringing as if someone hurled a fistful of rocks into a piano. DaKota's guitars. My stomach groaned at the thought of her instruments being trashed. The ringing stopped as more objects were thrown, a couple slamming directly into the closet door. I had to cover my mouth to keep from crying out the words shouting in my head, "Stop it! Mom, please make him stop!"

I could feel tears running over my hand. I was too frightened to realize that I was crying. Don't breathe, don't sniffle. Please don't come in the closet, I prayed. Mom, please keep me safe. Please keep this person from harming me and themselves. Footsteps crunched through junk on the floor. Getting closer, then stopping.

The bi-fold closet door slowly scraped open, my spine twisting with panic. Clutching my ready-made weapon, I coiled my muscles, ready to bolt through whoever stood in the doorway. It was my only chance. I took a deep breath, preparing to pounce...

Then, the closet door slowly rattled closed.

Shuffling footsteps moved out of the room. A wave of dizziness slithered through me. Breathe. My arms were shaking from fear and relief and my legs felt like jello. Staying upright was a tough enough task for the moment and I let my body lean into the corner, but the rest didn't last long.

I jumped and gasped audibly when the vicious pounding started, a hammering of metal against metal over and over again. Repeated blows growing more intense coupled with heavy grunts from the pounder. What the hell was going on? The wave of destruction continued. More glass exploding, more stuff hitting the floor. I realized there was no way Susan could not be hearing this from her place downstairs. Call the police, I thought in an attempt to send my will into the ether.

Who the hell was doing this and why? The person who killed her? Part of me wanted to disappear and another part wanted to walk out and see who was wreaking havoc. Of course, there was the possibility that seeing whoever it was would be the last thing I ever saw, which helped be stay glued to the closet floor.

A sudden quiet was quickly shattered by...a gut-wrenching screech. Rat-like and terrified at first then, an agonized wailing, struggling in tortured pain. My throat clenched. Shivering at the sweat running down my back, I prayed the shrieking would stop.

Finally, silence. I didn't know what to do, force myself to stop shaking or focus on not puking.

Please leave, please leave, please leave...

I saw the flickering flashlight beam return under the closet door, the shuffling footsteps working their way back through the debris in the second bedroom. I closed my eyes, trying to hold back the fear and concentrating all the strength I had left into an attack-ready force.

The next thing I heard, however, was the creaking of the kitchen floor. Could he be leaving? I held my breath until I heard the closing of the back door.

I waited, listening. What if it was a trick and the destroyer was still here, silently drawing me out. Braced against the walls, I didn't want to move for fear of collapsing all together but I was drenched in sweat and the air was stifling. I finally exited the closet somewhere between ten minutes and ten hours later.

What my dim flashlight revealed was nothing short of tornado wreckage. The faint beam spotlighted a large pile of splintered wood and fiberglass chunks held together by a tangled mass of nylon and steel spaghetti. DaKota's four guitars were obliterated into worthless rubble.

Everything was torn off the walls, amps kicked in and pushed over and music sheets with DaKota's scribbles shredded into obscurity. In the rubble, I saw half my face peering back at me. I pulled out a two by three inch pewter frame that held a picture of the two of us. I choked inside. She hadn't erased me completely. The picture was taken at a club in Philadelphia. We had gone to hear our musician friends, The Andy Browne Trio, and it turned out to be one of those spontaneous nights where many of our musician friends showed up, everyone had a good time and the band was on the money. Just looking at the picture now I could see the relaxation and happiness in both our faces. It made me wonder all the more what had happened. What had I done?

DaKota's bedroom looked just as bad, like a bargain table at The Gap exposed to eight hours of wild eyed mall Christmas shoppers. Everything was everywhere. Her favorite poster of Louise Post in her Veruca Salt days wearing a blue tank top and baseball cap, guitar hanging from her shoulder, was ripped off the wall and torn into pieces in the corner. I spotted the victim of the metallic hammering, a pilfered STOP sign that used to hang on the wall. It looked like it had a horrendous case of the mumps with dozens of rounded quarter sized dents pounded into it.

I felt dirty shuffling through her stuff, like being covered in dumpster garbage. The mattress where I had sat just yesterday was overturned and hacked up. Her jewelry box and perfume bottles from the top of the dresser were swept off into the nearest wall, a mixture of scents dripping in long thin fingers. Clothes covered every surface in the room. The dresser, all the drawers yanked out and tossed at random, except one. The one containing her underwear, or as DaKota called it, her animal sex gear. Then it hit me. The smell. Like wet, human shit. The stink grew heavier around the dresser.

The bile crept up my throat as I cautiously pulled open the drawer that I knew contained silk and lace panties of every color and style, but were now stained by the guts of a greasy, dead rat still vibrating with death spasms, slit from chin to ass, spewing its red gelatinous viscera over every piece of fabric.

I slammed the drawer shut and jumped into the hallway, damn near falling over all the junk on the floor. I let the wall prop me up as I gagged and hurled, my guts splashing on the floor.

I didn't remember dropping the flashlight but its dreary beam lay behind me in the hallway. The nauseous waves eventually subsided and I caught my breath as I crawled to grab the light and made my way to the living room.

The damage there was equally complete. Everything was overturned, shredded and smashed. The kitchen floor resembled a minefield of glass and ceramic shards; every glass, plate and cup from the cabinets lay in jagged pieces on the floor. In the living room, tables were upended and sofa cushions oozed their foam innards, mushrooming out of the slashed fabric.

A wave of heavy sadness crept over me. This is not how life was supposed to end. What the hell had she done? All the laughter, joy and love that existed was gone. I couldn't imagine what DaKota would have felt if she were here and seeing all this. In that sense, I was glad she was gone.

In the distance I heard a siren wail. Had Susan called the Police after all? Deciding I really didn't want to hang around to find out, I headed for the back door, stopped, went back to grab the framed picture of DaKota and I, then quietly made my way outside and upstairs.

Twelve

It had to be three in the morning, I thought, climbing the stairs to my apartment, physically exhausted and emotionally spent. Sleep. I know I needed a serious bath but didn't know if I could muster the energy to take one. Even the thought of getting undressed seemed to arduous a task. Still debating the issue, I opened my back door and released a force that knocked me flat on my ass. Pain shot through my leg as my foot slammed into the white porch railing. Unfortunately, my landing was cushioned by an empty clay flowerpot, pieces of which were now etched in my left ass-cheek. Something flew down the wooden staircase and dashed across the gravel driveway leading to the street

"Jesus!" I spat, "What next?" I said to no one. Without thinking I tore down the stairs and out of the driveway. Pissed off didn't begin to cover what I felt.

At the front of the house I quickly looked both ways on the road. Nothing. At this time of the morning it was possible to hear the flash of lightning bugs, but stillness blanketed the neighborhood. The sirens I heard had vanished.

"Shit." My curse echoed through the neighborhood with only the crickets answering me. I sighed and headed back to the house.

Blonde curls. That's about all I could conjure from whatever body-checked me. Male and blond curls. There was some vague image of a smooth face but my brain kept morphing the image, the eyes, nose and mouth growing and shrinking like a daffy duck cartoon.

Nothing looked disturbed in my place, although I half expected it to be trashed, assuming whoever was in my place was responsible for trashing DaKota's not fifteen minutes earlier.

I locked the back door and propped a chair under the doorknob like they do in the movies, not knowing what good it would do if someone was desperate enough. I climbed into bed and lay there wide-eyed, listening to every creak and sound, and seeing nothing but blond curls on a featureless face. What the hell was he doing in here anyway? Looking for something? If he found it I sure couldn't tell. It had to be fairly small since he didn't appear to be carrying anything as far as I could see while kissing the porch floor. I wanted to know who it was without meeting him if possible. Having witnessed the destruction downstairs, his loving treatment of rodents, and possibly humans, I was not in a great rush to bump into him in a dark alley or anywhere else for that matter.

Sleep? Forget it. It was five in the morning when, entangled in damp sheets, eyes wide open, I switched on the small tensor lamp on my bedside table (well, the legless floor tom-tom from an old drum set with a sheet over it that I use as a bedside table) and grabbed the pilfered picture from downstairs. I was having trouble comprehending that face being gone, that a photograph was all I had left of DaKota's smile. What had happened? Memories of the last couple weeks continued to haunt me, daring me to pinpoint exactly when it started, exactly when she first pulled away.

I pulled the picture over and sat it on my chest. I have decent boobs but my 36C's were not going to create any visibility issues while lying on my back. How could someone who looked so alive, so happy, not exist anymore? My mind has trouble wrapping itself around absolutes, particularly death. I just wanted one more chance to watch her sleep, her head settled deep into the pillow right next to me as it so often was. My hand moved reflexively to trace the contours of her face, but only rested on the empty pillowcase next to me that felt cool for a brief second before turning hot under my hand. I wanted her face there so badly, to watch her pink lips as she breathed in a deep sleep, to gently run my fingers over her smooth cheek, and brush back a wayward strand of hair that was tickling her nose.

I still don't consider myself a lesbian. It wasn't like I woke up one day and said, "OK, today I start fondling women." DaKota and I just fell together, and now that she's gone…I just don't know.

I looked up at the ceiling and said out loud, "I don't know what you've got in store for me, Mom, but it's getting really weird and it's starting to piss me off. I know I'm not supposed to ask 'why' because that's a management question and I'm not in management but I'm having trouble seeing the reason for all this." After saying the serenity prayer to myself, I looked back at the picture. It wasn't fair and even if I knew all the answers it still wouldn't be fair. This is my eternal struggle, Chynna's

Way or Mom's Way. The results of my best thinking had sent everything I owned up my nose so I knew I had no other option except turning everything over to Mom, even though it still drove me bonkers from time to time.

Had I known I was holding a key to the puzzle that was DaKota in my hands, maybe I could have avoided all the pain that was to come. Again, Mom played her mysterious game for some sordid reason and it's not up to me to question why. That's what I'm supposed to believe even when every bit of me wants to play it differently.

I put the picture gently back on the table.

Thirteen

"If one of those oil refinery tanks blew up, what would a fireball of that proportion look like from seat 8A in an incoming 737 at Newark? Or would the plane melt right out of the sky?" I asked.

"That's a cheery thought isn't it?" Andi replied without taking her eyes off the book in her lap. Morbidity hung in the air as we drove north on the New Jersey Turnpike heading for DaKota's funeral.

"What's so engrossing?" I asked.

"It's a book about numbers. All these bizarre factoids, similar to that list in Harper's magazine."

"And my subscription just ran out. What are you talking about?"

Andi's concentration broke as if coming out of coma. "Hmm? Oh, right. Listen to this. 'Number of people who could be provided with sources of clean drinking water per year for the cost of a submarine: 60 million. Number of miles driven by the average American car before it emits its own weight in carbon dioxide: 10,000.' This stuff is wild."

"Sorry I asked," I said, looking in the rearview mirror for some sanity and support, but Geoff's eyes were closed and the ever-present white ear buds remained fixed to his head, eliminating any hope of witty conversation. Spag and Katrina were meeting us there, driving in Spag's rolling tank of a Buick. Fitting five people in either of our cars was just not going to work so we decided to split up.

For the first time in more than twenty years The Slipped Disc was closed. After much cajoling, we convinced Jason that it would be better for all concerned if the store was not left solely in his hands. I always felt it better to avoid disaster than take it out for dinner and a movie.

From its hilltop perch, Mason's Funeral Home scowled over Stanford, Connecticut, its colonial facade broken by modern bay windows providing a view of the I-95 glass tower hotel-business complexes and the partially gentrified industrial shoreline of Long Island Sound.

My immediate instinct was to turn the car around, gun back down the hill and go home. Heaviness overwhelmed me, keeping me from doing either. Among the shiny Jaguars, Caddies and Beemers in the lot, my faded red bomb stood out like a chewed hangnail.

I killed the motor and glanced in the rearview mirror. "Hey. Are you getting out sometime this week?" I yelled at Geoff.

Geoff crawled out from his backseat cocoon and I yanked the white wires out of his ears. "Unplug for this one, G-man."

"I don't know," he said, "all this natural sound might just flip me out."

"These places creep me out," Andi said.

Geoff stretched and said, "I once dated a girl who lived on the second floor over a funeral home her uncle owned. One weekend she wanted me to do it with her in one of the display coffins. I was so freaked out I couldn't even get it up."

"And we need to know this because?" I asked.

"Oh that's tacky," Andi chimed in, but with the slightest smile.

A handful of people milled about in the DaKota Gibson room; excuse me, Jessica Holt-Gibson room. Five people lined up to the right of the casket, I assumed it was Mr. and Mrs. Gibson and various relatives.

A statuesque blonde woman stood in front of the open casket bathed in the sunlight from the bay windows. Her hand covered DaKota's folded hands as she whispered to the lifeless body. The woman's long blonde mane, with every strand in place, contrasted perfectly with the full length navy blue dress hugging her hourglass frame. Black wrap-around sunglasses sat on top of her head, pushed back to reveal a sad and intense gaze. Even from a distance, there was a familiarity about her. Something about her eyes that struck a chord inside me and trig-gered Mom into whispering unintelligible warnings. Whatever it was lay just outside of my mental reach.

Geoff broke my concentration whispering, "Oh, man I didn't know this was open casket. This is not cool. I'll freak if I go up there."

"Just stay with us. You'll be okay." I said.

From the back of the room we spotted Spag and Katrina already seated and headed in their direction.

"Been here long?" I whispered, sitting in the row behind them.

"Ten, fifteen minutes," said Spag.

"Speed demon."

Kissing the first two fingers of her right hand, the blonde woman placed them on DaKota's lips, and then pulled her hand back as if clutching something precious to her chest.

"What was that all about?" I whispered. She was more than a friend, that much was obvious. Maybe she was a relative, but if that was the case she'd be milling around with the reception crowd. A sad smile gently emerged on her face as she rested he hand back on DaKota's.

"Come on," I pulled Andi's arm and we walked up the center aisle as the woman turned to leave, walking away with her head up but no tears on her face. Her stride halted as she looked at me, a small spark of recognition flickering across her face. She acknowledged me with a slight nod as she strode from the room. How did she know me? What was it about her that felt familiar?

Andi took my hand as we approached the casket. I held on tightly.

DaKota's hair was spread out over the white pillow. Way too much make-up had been applied to her face, probably her mother's doing. DaKota was not into cosmetics and rarely needed them anyway. She was dressed in a simple black dress, a thin silver chain around her neck and a gray link bracelet with a single charm, that I think was supposed to be a bird, on her left wrist. I touched the bracelet enough to move it slightly up her arm, and then gasped. There were marks on her wrists, rough reddened lines like wearing a tight rubber band too long. Her other wrist sported another bracelet. With a sympathetic gesture I put my hand on top of DaKota's and casually moved the bracelet with my pinky. The same marks were visible. Pointing this out to everyone at that moment might come off as a tad ghoulish so I kept my observations to myself.

"She looks nice," Geoff was able to squeak out, if only to keep himself breathing. She looked like a mannequin, I thought, but added that to the list of unexpressed thoughts.

Through the window, a flash of color caught my eye. An ocean blue Jaguar convertible wound through the woods away from the funeral home. The brake lights flashed as it dipped down the hill and out of sight.

"Hey, check this out," Geoff said. To the right of the casket, an artist's easel held a collage of pictures intending to trace DaKota's life. One picture displayed a formally dressed older couple I assumed were her parents, cocktails in hand, staring back at the camera with less than a smile. DaKota rarely spoke about her parents other than to refer to them as George and Martha, not Washington, but rather the social misfits from *Who's Afraid of Virginia Woolf.* She had no pictures of them at her apartment and when I mentioned meeting them it remained only a matter of humorous discussion. The collage chronicled DaKota at various stages of her short life. A couple of the standard elementary school portraits complete with hair in different phases of length and disarray. One older picture showed a scowling girl barely hiding a mouth full of metal. I never knew she wore braces as a kid. I felt like I was learning more about her now that she was dead. Certainly my face wouldn't be among the snapshots, or any of the Princeton clan.

"Thanks," was all I could say as I rested my head on Andi's arm. She tucked me under her wing and squeezed my hand tightly. Spag and Katrina appeared and enveloped the three of us in a communal hug.

The crowd had doubled in size since our arrival. I scanned the faces and it hit me that, except for our little troupe, everyone was closer to the age of DaKota's parents. Were we her only friends?

An older version of the couple in the photo stood off to one side of the casket. Her Mom stood erect, an elegant black dress clinging to a well-toned body. Her watery gray eyes betrayed little while her straining face broadcast her devotion to the nip and tuck lifestyle. Apparently her surgeon held a grudge. Her smile reminded me of Jack Nicholson as The Joker. Next to her, in a hand tailored black suit, DaKota's Dad stared into space through black-rimmed soda bottle glasses. He passed bellying up to the Botox bar, a bad decision as he was creepier than a Chucky doll, and about as tall, with salt and pepper hair that hung in a Beatles bang just above his untrimmed Brillo pad eyebrows. He stared straight ahead, oblivious to the activity around him. Maybe he was still in shock, I thought.

"Mrs. Gibson?" I said.

"Holt-Gibson," she corrected.

"I'm Chynna Lennox. DaKota and I were in a band together. We..." I really didn't know what else to say without being obvious.

"Oh", she said. We shook hands but she offered nothing else.

I introduced the remainder of our party. "We just wanted to express our condolences to you and Mr. Gibson."

The stretched muscles in her face tightened, her capped teeth grinding hard enough to make her jaw bone bend outward. Any further facial tension would have split her skin like a broken condom.

I extended my hand to Mr. Gibson but quickly yanked it back when he started babbling, out loud, to no one.

"No, Dave, that's not what I told you to do. I don't want to put one nickel of my money into this project. I want one hundred percent financing in place within 30 days. Is Peter there? I want to talk to him." His eyes darted to me. He saw my hand and gave it a quick shake as if shooing a gnat. Confused, I wasn't sure how to react. Then I saw the Bluetooth device pasted to his ear.

I looked back at DaKota's Mom, an incredulous expression on my face. All she offered was a practiced grin.

"You're not serious," I said to her, as she turned her attention to the next person in line, purposefully ignoring me. Dad was still staring in to space listening to the chatter in his hairy ear.

"Hey!" I said to DaKota's Dad and got no reaction. "Hey!" This time giving the Chucky-clone a shove. He stumbled but maintained is footing, looking at me with a mixture of surprise and annoyance. He wasn't that much taller than me so I was able to go nose to nose with him. I wanted to use a claw hammer to scrape the smug arrogance right off his face. "This is your daughter's funeral, asshat!"

Dark eyes swam behind thick lenses, "Nicholas?" he called, his eyes never leaving mine.

"What? Who the hell is Nic..." but before I could finish protesting two giant hams clamped on to my arms and lifted me off the floor.

"Get off of me!" I screamed. Everyone in the funeral home craned their heads to get a glimpse of what was happening.

Andi, Geoff and company were also registering pleas to cease and desist. Once outside, I was released and King Kong silently walked back in the building.

Geoff said, "What the hell was that all about? God, you would have thought we were the anti-Christ."

"This is bullshit," I said, fuming, and heading back for the door.

"Hang on," Andi said pulling me back.

"Let me go."

"No. This is not the time or the place."

"I don't care."

Andi whirled me around to face her. "Lennox! No. I agree he's a complete nutter but not here, not now. Think of DaKota. Is this what she'd want you to do? I don't think so. This is more about you being cheesed off than honoring her memory."

I was torn between wanting to rip his goddamned head off and the images of DaKota now flashing through my brain. Looking at Andi, I knew she spoke the truth.

"Let's get the hell out of here," I said.

The silent tension was an inch thick while driving home on Interstate 95. Crossing over the George Washington Bridge and heading back down the Turnpike I thought that whoever killed DaKota was still out there and that her parents appeared to care less. Rushing the autopsy, rushing the funeral. The whole deal was a major thorn in their sides and all they wanted to do was get past it. My body tightened in anger. I was not about to let this go. Maybe I could get Snevley to write an expose on them. Public humiliation was too good for them. Bastards.

"Would you please slow down," Andi said breaking my fantasy. The speedometer read close to ninety-five.

I looked up as we came over a twisting hill and was confronted with a sea of red lights. Five lanes of traffic stopped dead ahead. I tromped on the brake and may as well have been stepping on air. The pedal went straight to the floor. I pumped it. Nothing happened.

"Shit!" I yelled.

"What?" said Andi.

A wash of red light was only a hundred feet away. I quickly down shifted to second. The engine bucked as if hitting a hurricane wind. I was still doing sixty-five.

"Brakes gone!" I replied in a panic.

The cars were now about seventy feet away. I slammed the car over to the concrete median, hoping to scrape the barrier to slow down.

"Turn the engine off!" Geoff hollered from the back seat.

Fifty feet. An SUV the size of Utah stood fast in the right lane. Was there enough space to squeeze between the SUV and the barrier? No more time to think. I hugged the barrier. I didn't want to destroy the side of my car but I didn't want to rear end the SUV either.

"Careful! Careful" Geoff screamed. Andi leaned into me and braced her arms on the dashboard. Twenty feet. I didn't have a choice. I eased to the right, scraping metal against stone, watching sparks shoot out and the side mirror tear away. Andi snapped her head around to face me. Her eyes were crystalline.

"Shit, hold on!" I said.

The car shuddered, and then I remember flying.

Fourteen

The grooved silver steps of the escalator popped up out of the ground not six inches from my bare toes, each step growing as it ascended. I had the vague sense of being in Macy's at the mall, but couldn't turn my head to look around. Funny, I had been standing on the beach at Surf City just seconds ago, watching the waves break on the shore and feeling the surf run around my ankles, but my left foot was sinking deeper in the sand than my right foot as the water flowed back to the sea. It sank deeper than it ever had before, almost halfway up my calf, while my right foot remained planted on top.

The rhythm of the waves had altered to the routine of the stairs, each appearing one right after the other, never missing a beat, unwavering in its regularity, each step identical to the preceding one. The hypnotic regularity created an odd peace; the moving staircase and the soft hum of its operation. Silence filled the remainder of the store. Not a single person walked past or tried to get on the escalator. A thousand perfumes congealed into one massive nasal assault.

The next step popped right out of the ground with a Honer b-flat blues harp along for the ride. I don't know how I knew it was a b-flat, the thought just lodged itself in my head.

The first bent notes from the harp whistled through the air, not coming from the instrument on the escalator but existing in the ether. At the top of the escalator sat an old black man in a dark yellow leisure suit and tan hat, wailing away his soul singing John Lee Hooker's "I Got My Eyes On You". How was he sitting on the gliding staircase without moving? The stairs just seemed to float underneath him as if he wasn't there.

"Do "Play That Funky Music"," I called and was immediately embarrassed at such a ludicrous request. Why the hell did I ask for that?

"He's too far away now. He can't hear you."

I snapped my head around to see DaKota standing a pace behind my right shoulder. She was wearing a full cowboy rig: black hat, tan leather chaps, broken in brown leather boots complete with spurs and a tan rawhide holster with a forged brass buckle and a pearl handled Colt .45 nestled on the side. Her face kept morphing into Sharon Stone's character from *The Quick and the Dead* and then back to her own. I wasn't sure who she was.

"Don't you even want to fight back?" DaKota/Sharon said.

"God, I'm sorry DaKota", I said. For some reason, tears started streaming down my face.

"Some people deserve to die." She was smiling at me when she reached out and gently shook my shoulder.

"Chynna, listen to me. Chynna...Chynna...Chynna…"

DaKota's image got fuzzy and finally shattered. Echoes of voices and sounds collided then faded but something was still shaking my shoulder.

"Chynna... Chynna... Chynna..."

The thick haze slowly dissipated. I became aware of cold air and a mechanical humming. Cracking my eyes open, I squinted to focus on the harsh white light. The blur focused into an unrecognizable white acoustic tile ceiling.

Okay, that is definitely not my ceiling. I think I'll take this slowly until I figure what the hell's going on.

Without moving a muscle, I checked things out by moving my eyes. To the left, a large white curtain hanging from a steel rod attached to the ceiling. Great, I've fallen asleep in someone's bathtub. At least they had the decency to cover me with a sheet, I thought as I strained to look down. This was like a bad airplane tour. "And, ladies and gentlemen, if you look to your right you'll see..." some guy in a long white coat with a stethoscope dangling from his neck and I have no idea who he is. Great. Just great. I turned my head toward the lab coat. Even though the motion was slow, I felt my brain playing catch up.

"Whoa, that was interesting," I croaked, my throat parched and scratchy.

"Don't fight it. You'll be groggy for some time yet. Here take a small sip." He offered me a baby sip cup with a straw sticking out of it. The water was ice cold and stung at first but gradually felt soothing. My nose itched like mad. Lifting my right arm I felt the twinge and looked to see an I.V. stuck under my skin. Scratching became problematic as my face was now equipped with an oxygen plug shoved up my nose.

"I guess I should call you 'Doctor' something."

His eyes twinkled as he smiled. "Dr. Anders would be good."

"That works," I said, my eyes still playing tricks as if I was trying to see underwater and then popping through the surface.

"Glad you like it. I've grown attached to it over the past ten or twelve years," he pulled up a metal swivel stool and sat. Even through the haze he appeared to be the casual type, white coat over a busy plaid button down shirt sans tie and a pair of khaki's. He had curly brown hair that was losing the battle for territory with his forehead, small close set eyes and a sharp nose. He put his clipboard on the side table next to my bed and turned to face me.

"Chynna, you're at Overlook Hospital in Summit. We performed emergency surgery on you last night."

"What…wait…are you kidding? When…how?…" I moved to sit up, but several red hot jolts of pain shot through my left shoulder and down my back. I felt Dr. Anders grab me and slowly ease me back into the bed.

"Slow down, and don't try moving all that quickly. I did some delicate work on you last night and it needs to set and heal for awhile."

"That really fucking hurt," I said through a staggered breath.

"All the more reason to be still and listen to your Doctor."

I grunted as pain subsided further. There was a blur at the end of the bed that wasn't there before. I think.

"Hi," said the blur.

Anders made the introductions. "Chynna, this is Doctor Eileen Kane."

"Ugh. I don't know. All these MD's. I feel so special."

Anders smiled. "Only one MD per customer."

I must have looked confused. Dr. Kane said, "Chynna, I'm not an MD. I'm a clinical psychiatrist."

The soothing female voice took me by surprise. Kane moved around the bed and slowly came into focus. She was both plain and beautiful, looking like anybody's Mom. Well, looking like anybody's Mom who kept fit and looked outstanding in jeans and a white blouse. She reached over the raised sidebars of the bed and grabbed my hand. I was immediately comforted by its firm dry warmth, the perfect grip to hold a child's hand, I thought, for a walk down a sandy road near the beach.

"Chynna," said Dr. Kane, bringing me back.

"Oh, hi," I smiled.

"How are you feeling?"

I did a mental check over my body and all systems appeared functional. "Fuzzy. A little nauseous. What happened anyway?"

"You were in a bad car accident. Do you remember anything about it?" Her eyes were more warm honey than brown. She wore only a trace of makeup and had a small scar just above her left eyebrow line, a small indentation an inch long sitting on top of thick but groomed brown hairs.

"Accident?" all I could see was a gray haze in my mind, clouds shifting and swirling around each other. "I can't remember."

"That's okay. You were knocked about pretty well so you may be groggy for a while." Her voice was deep and came from her chest in soothing tones. It was the way she said "about", coming out as "aboot" that tipped me off.

"You're from Canada."

Her laugh was natural and deep. "Very good, Chynna. At least we know your brain wasn't rattled too badly. Waterloo. I grew up there. I've had a private practice in New Jersey for ten years and work here at the hospital counseling those who need it."

That didn't sound good. "I need it?"

"I don't know if you do or not. That's up to you. You've been in a serious car accident."

"Yeah, you said that." In the haze, a flash of scraping metal echoed in my brain. The SUV. No brakes! The brakes…nothing but air. Geoff screaming "Be careful!" Oh Christ.

"Shit! Andi! Geoff! Are they ok? Are they alright?" I moved out of reflex and immediately regretted it.

Both Kane and Anders cradled me back on the bed. "Chynna. Listen to me," said Kane. "From what the Police say, you made the correct decision trying to stop the car the way you did. Any other way would have been much, much worse. You probably saved a few lives reacting the way you did."

My breathing slowly returned as the waves of pain receded. "You didn't answer my question," I eventually croaked.

Kane pushed down the railing and sat on the bed next to me.

"Doctor?" she said looking up at Anders.

"Geoff has a nasty concussion and a few stitches in his head but he should be ok. We released him last night. Candice, I guess you call her Andi, is still in intensive care. She has several fractures in both her arms and some serious head trauma, but Dr. Warmer, our Chief neurosurgeon, thinks she'll come through okay if she can stay out of trouble for the next twenty-four to forty-eight hours."

"What kind of trouble?"

"Infections, swelling. I could go into a lot of medical jargon but I think Dr. Kane said it best. They are both alive because of how you reacted. Plowing into the other cars would have been a disaster all around."

I turned to Kane a little too quickly. "Ugh."

"Take it slowly."

"I want to see Andi. Like, right now."

"You are not going anywhere just yet."

Dr. Anders moved to stand next to Dr. Kane. His eyes betrayed some sadness. I started sweating. "What's wrong?"

It was Anders who spoke. "Chynna, given the seriousness of the accident, you are lucky to be alive."

"Every time you say that it's followed by something I don't want to hear."

"You were brought in by a LifeFlight helicopter because no one thought you would make it. Your left side was badly crushed in the impact. We were able to repair the damage to your left arm and shoulder. Your lung collapsed and three ribs were broken. We had to repair a lot of tendon and muscle damage in your leg. Somehow you managed to escape the head injuries your passengers incurred. Unfortunately, we could not save everything. Your left foot…it was just too badly damaged."

My eyes slowly moved to the end of the bed. I hadn't noticed that my left leg was elevated enough to see where the sheet went straight out. There was no little tent where my toes should be.

"Oh, shit," I said staring at the ceiling. Why wasn't I hysterical? I wasn't anything. Images danced in my head, images so random that making sense of any of it was fruitless. The dance moved faster and faster; playing kickball as a kid, faces of school mates long forgotten, boyfriends, Christmases, Halloweens. All faster and faster until the film snapped and tore away leaving only whiteness, a blank screen.

"Call Pat, please?"

After stumbling through who Pat was, promises were made to notify him. I wasn't in control. Something forced my head to turn to Dr. Kane, "Don't leave me, okay?"

"Not a chance," she said, smiling and holding on.

Fifteen

Dreams haunted me throughout the night, strange and bizarre images of unknown people backstage at The Phang, reporters surrounded the band with micro-recorders in one hand and long-neck blue bottles emitting mad scientist smoke in the other, all chattering the same banalities at once. I felt an inward glow at the attention while outwardly remaining aloof.

Then the voices grew louder, and louder. The bodies of the reporter's grew larger, their faces sprouting bloated oozing abnormalities. My stomach tightened as the voices began shouting, and the bodies stretched with every new deformity. The monsters closed in, each disfigured as if seen through a fish-eye lens. Danger crept in, a cold sweat dripped down my spine. The vocal cacophony grew to a pitch that clawed at my brain, grabbing and twisting my insides. Oozing pustules burst on the faces of the ghouls as they advanced, clutching my body with sticky, viscous tentacles that pulled me in every direction, tearing me apart. At the instant my body split, the dream cloud burst.

I blinked. All I heard was the hum of the hospital room and my gasps. Sweat drenched me from head to toe.

"Good morning, Child." A squat dark-skinned woman complete with neat dreadlocks sporting rainbow colored beads on the end of each dread appeared next to me.

"Are you okay, Princess?" she said in a dancing West Indian accent, wide dark eyes set in an oval face, full lips and a wide nose. She was outfitted in nurse white pants and an aqua top decorated with small palm trees and pineapples. If she had told me she had just left the beach I would not have been at all surprised. She had a gold name badge pinned to her blouse that read "Armani".

"Mmm, Hmmm," she hummed, placing a sturdy hand on my forehead. After jabbing the thermometer in my ear she smiled at me. "Looks like you broke that fever you were working on yesterday. That's a good sign. We need to keep the infections away or Doctor will grow upset."

"DaKota," was all I could think to say.

"Who now?"

I was about to ask if anyone had contacted her, told her where I was, just so she wouldn't be worried. Then I remembered why I was in the hospital, where I had been and what had happened.

"Nothing." I said quietly.

"Something else?"

I shook my head but then changed my mind. "Thirsty."

After I slurped some water I said, "Let's go find a beach and sit in the sun."

She smiled. "Maybe tomorrow, Honey. Right now you need rest. If you get too excited Doctor will be unhappy with me."

"How's Andi?" I asked.

She thought for a second. "Oh the young lady with you in the accident. She fight the good fight. I can find out how she doing for you later on."

She turned to go. "I like your name," I said. She turned back to me.

"You are one of the few people who have been able to talk about my name without mentioning Giorgio. Thank you. It's an Afrikaan name meaning 'faith.' I knew I liked you when you came in. You mind if I look at your aura?"

I wasn't sure how to answer that. "Go for it."

Armani stared at me but was focused somewhere else as if she was looking through me to the bed. Placing her hands two or three inches from my body she moved them back and forth following the pseu-do-contour of my shape. Her hands sped up and slowed moving independently of each other, occasionally stopping in one place followed by Armani whispering "hm hum" and flicking one hand or the other away from me, as if tossing something away.

After several minutes of these gyrations, Armani grabbed my hand in both of hers and refocused on my face. "You certainly are one complicated young lady."

"And all this time I thought I was easy."

"Far from it. As expected, there is powerful healing going on inside you and I was able to pull out some of the negative energy. You have a strong yellow presence, that's joy and creative energy, but it's shadowed with orange."

"That's bad?"

"None of it is good or bad. It just is. It is who you are right now. You have some pain and grief to go through still but you're going to be just fine, child."

I was glad somebody thought so. I wasn't so sure.

Sixteen

Two days crept by and Pat was still MIA. I called LeMonde and was told he was off for a few days but no one knew where. I can't remember the last time Pat took a day off. Something wasn't right but I felt useless to do anything about it. The drains had finally been taken out and I was mobile enough to get my first really good look at 'it' while the bandages were changed. I don't know what I expected; maybe a hideous nightmare of a bloody stump with shredded skin and bone. Perhaps I've watched too many Steven Segal movies. It wasn't too awful. The skin at the end displayed all sorts of colors from bruising, deep purple and yellows with some green thrown in. At the end, the skin was sutured in a red, frown shape and looked a little swollen, and was crimped like handmade calzone. No bones, muscles or any other junk hanging out. I almost felt disappointed. Morbidity took over and I wondered what the missing foot looked like and where it was now. Was it all lonely in some fridge downstairs? Just what did they do with all those limbs anyway? I never even got a chance to say goodbye to it, which wasn't fair, considering it didn't do anything to anybody. It just sat there in the car while its sister pumped the useless brake pedal.

Speaking of which, I really wanted to know what the hell happened to my brakes, and, for that matter, my car. No one had said anything about it so far. I just had the oil changed and the damn thing inspected earlier in the summer. Can brakes just instantly stop working? I did not want to entertain the idea of intentional tampering but the recent events of my life certainly did not rule it out. But why?

Before Armani redressed it, I tried to hold my leg in both hands as if I was examining a newly caught flounder, but my left arm still didn't want to stretch that far without feeling like white hot rods were being jabbed into my shoulder. I looked at my right leg in comparison trying to gauge the exact location of the cutoff point. It looked to be about six inches above the ankle. I straightened out both legs, side by side to be sure. For some reason seeing only one foot struck me as kind of cool. Maybe it will be a new fashion thing. I tried wiggling the toes that weren't there but couldn't remember which muscles to use. I did it on my right foot, paying attention to the muscles and tendons that were flexing. I tried to duplicate it on the left side. The muscles flexed, with a couple painful tugs, but that was all. Without warning, a sharp electric current charged up my leg and exploded across my body.

"Shit," I grunted.

"What's the matter?" Armani asked.

"It hurts! Everywhere! Dammit."

Armani started massaging my leg and just as quickly the pain subsided.

I was breathing hard and everything looked blurry through my watery eyes.

"What the hell was that?"

"You just felt a phantom pain, child. Doctor can tell you more about it but all amputees deal with them. It's your brain trying to talk to your foot, but no one is there to answer."

My body seized as another bolt shot through me. This was worse than any muscle cramp I'd ever experienced, like sticking my finger in a light socket and not being able to pull away. When it subsided I said, "Is this normal? One right after the other."

"Mm-hum. They can come in groups."

"For how long?"

"Depends. Everyone's body react differently."

Over the next fifteen minutes, three more episodes wracked me into a sweaty exhaustion.

"This sucks," I said.

"You just lay back and try to get some rest. Talk to the Spirit. She is the true helper and healer."

Laying in wait for another jolt of pain was not fun and I made my displeasure known to Mom.

"You can knock this pain stuff off any time now. Tell you what, if you keep those jolts away, I'll, umm, I'll...oh I don't know. Go to church or something."

My prayers have never been that formal and certainly have never been unreasonable, at least to my way of thinking. Hey, whatever works as long as no one gets hurt. People could worship watermelons and that would be fine with me. One emphatic notion embraced by twelve step programs is that blaming God is a waste of time. It's all that child-hood-ego-psycho-babble stuff about being in control and behaving like a five year old when events don't go as planned. The key catch phrase is 'Turn it Over'. Right now, Mom's assistance was less than helpful and releasing all of it into her hands did not feel like the most expeditious route to solving any problems, which is all the more reason to let it go. See, this is not a good thing, being in my head. That's where all the bad shit lives. Three years ago I'd be hatching a plot with the nursing staff to give me any sort of heavy duty pain meds to avoid the frustration. Certainly that thought still occurs to me, but I don't want to go back to that lifeless life. So I call Andi. Only Andi was somewhere else in the building and not able to pick up the phone from what I was told. My cell phone had all my program numbers, which is sour grapes anyway because the last time I saw it was in the cup holder of my car, the same car that may now be compacted into a ton of twisted steel.

"Okay, Mom," I said out loud, "you are not making this easy and I'm really feeling angry about all the stuff that's going on. I guess now is when I'm supposed to turn it all over to you and just sit back, right?" The words 'there is a reason for this' floated through my head. "Yeah I'm having a little issue with that concept right now, thank you." I took a deep breath. "Okay. It's all yours. Show me what I have to do. I'll be patient and wait right here."

Armani explained each piece of material applied to my leg from plain cotton gauze to an off-white surgical sock, a "stump shrinker" she called it. Her bandage work was unquestionably professional, which made me feel better. If I had done it, the results would look like torn paper towels wrapped in drumstick tape. An aura of leg pain was stirring in the distance. My hand shook as I ran it down the dressings, barely touching the surface. As a teenager I wore an ACE bandage on my wrist for a week, the results of kissing the street after a failed bike jump off a poorly constructed launch ramp. The stump shrinker felt the same way. I rubbed it back and forth, applying a little more pressure with each movement.

That evening I finally got the damn catheter out, thank Mom, and Dr. Anders insisted I get up on my foot with a crutch so I was finally allowed to pee like a normal human being and wash my cruddy body. It was just a sponging but that alone made me feel a thousand percent better. I still couldn't get in the shower with the bandages on my left leg but just scraping off the stink was more than enough.

Later, as I was absently leafing through a "Modern Drummer" magazine that Katrina had dropped off, Satan dropped in for a chat.

"Knock, Knock."

"Oh, Christ. What do you want?"

"I heard you tried to drive on a three foot concrete median. I knew you were crazy but this I just had to hear in person."

Snevley stood at the door, dressed in a blue oxford button down, sleeves rolled up exposing thick forearms covered in barely visible dark blond hair. The hallway lights glistened off his faux gold Rolex. I don't ever remember seeing him wear jeans the whole time we were together but today he was poured into a pair of faded Levi's. If he wasn't a complete dick I'd have asked him to come in, close the door and crawl under the sheets. Maybe that's what got me in trouble the first time around. His smile revealed repulsively whitened teeth and his gray eyes still had that boy next door twinkle; a piranha in yuppie clothing.

"I thought I saw you hitching a ride on the highway and decided to mow you down. Must have been a trick of the light."

"Aww, Babycakes, I know you don't mean that. I have nothing but your well being in mind. I just had to make sure they were taking good care of you." He walked in and pulled a chair from the wall to the bed, turned it around and straddled the seat. He dropped a brown paper bag on my rolling table.

"Do come in. Have a seat. Can I make you a drink? And what the hell is that?" I said pointing to the brown paper bag.

"No thanks. I can get my own." He grabbed a plastic cup, poured some ice water from the pitcher, threw it back as if it were a shot of Jack Daniels and tossed the cup over his shoulder, banking it off the wall and into the trash can.

"Not bad, huh?" he said. I wanted to wipe that arrogant grin off his face.

"Snevley, I'm not impressed. Is there something you want because I'm really tired."

"OK. Fine. Here I spend my day off hauling my butt up here out of genuine concern and…"

"Genuine concern my ass."

"Which isn't half bad, I might add."

"Don't make me gag. You never paid this much attention to me when we were together. What the hell are you after?"

"Not a thing, Babe,"

He knew I hated being "Babed".

Getting up from the chair, without putting it back, he headed for the door.

"I guess you aren't interested in hearing about your brakes. Later."

Then he walked out.

I wasn't expecting that.

"Snevley get back here!" I yelled, hospital rules be dammed. I watched the door. Nothing.

"Dammit." Sliding off the bed onto my right foot I hopped toward the door using an idle I.V. stand as a medieval crutch. The sudden draft made me remember I was wearing nothing but a hospital gown. I didn't know if I could hop my way to the door, much less catch up to that little prick. It seemed like forever but I finally got into the hallway, looking to my left, towards the elevators. No Snevley. He had to walk by the nurse's station. Maybe he's just in the men's room or something, I thought. I took two clanking bounces down the hallway.

"I do repeat myself. Not half bad at all." The voice came from behind me. I looked back; he stood on the other side of my door, leaning up against the wall, his arms folded over his chest and his eyes glued to my half exposed ass.

"Good Lord! What are you doing in the hallway, young lady?" Armani surged toward me, nostrils flaring like a Pamplona bull and I was a red cape about to be gored. She whisked me back into bed. Snevley offered to help but I told him to back off.

"Don't you ever pull a stunt like that again, young lady. You hear me?"

I nodded through the steam escaping from my ears.

"Asshat," I said once Armani had departed. Snevley resumed his position in the chair.

"That's not a very polite thing to say, especially since I brought a peace offering," he said nodding to the brown paper bag. "Hospital food is edible only by genetic mutations. This is something you'll be able to keep down."

I gingerly looked inside the brown bag and saw a perspiring can of Coke, what looked like a sandwich from Grace at Alpha Bagel, the local Princeton deli I frequent, and a package of Hostess orange cupcakes. My mind jumped into handsprings but I wasn't about to give Snevley the satisfaction of scoring a hit.

"Looks okay," I said in an attempt at sullen indifference. Snevley closed the door so I could eat in peace. "Go ahead. You know you want to."

With a mouthful of roast beef and Swiss, lettuce, tomato, coleslaw and Russian dressing on rye, I mumbled. "How did you know what to get?"

"A good investigative journalist knows how to develop information."

"So how'd you find out?"

A genuine smile creased his face, a smile I returned. It felt like I hadn't smiled in years and it felt wonderful.

"This is perfect," I said, "but this doesn't change anything. You're still an asshat."

"At least my reputation's intact." Snevley sat on the window sill. The outside light reduced his body to little more than a silhouette.

"How much have they told you about your accident?"

"We've managed to fit most of the pieces together except for the actual impact and I can live without recalling that. Why?"

"It wasn't an accident."

I stopped in mid-chew. "How the hell do you know?"

Snevley didn't get a chance to answer as the door flew open.

"There you are. It took forever to find you and the dolts who work here are useless. I'm going to see you get transferred NYU Medical or Mount Sinai where they have a decent staff who speak English and don't need green cards."

"Mother," I said gagging down what was in my mouth to keep from spitting it out. Outfitted in a charcoal side stitched jacket over a matching sleeveless dress, Nina Ricci if I had to guess, she looked manufactured; her drawn and stretched face had not relaxed since the dawn of man.

"At least you could have called me. Imagine having to find out about your little mishap from Felicity Thorne-Michaels, and wasn't she so smugly happy to bring me the news. You realize, of course, that this is my busiest time of year what with Ross vying for a Senate seat against that hideous tramp. I can't even bring myself to say her name. There is no end to the lunches, parties, those dreadful speeches, but it's all for the best in the long run. I had to cut short a very important meeting with the New York GOP Leadership PAC organization to come here."

"I'm fine. Thanks."

From inside her black Prada bag came the shrill beeping of what turned out to be her iPhone.

"Oh, God," she sighed dramatically looking at the device. "I'm late for the god-awful Young Republican luncheon and a smarmier group of hard-ons I've never known. All twenty-something Gatsby wanna-bes who when they aren't trying to impress you with their credentials are grabbing your ass or your tits. This is going to cost Ross plenty. Ciao, darling," she said, absently patted my leg through the covers and marched out of the door, probably into a waiting limo.

After we each took a breath Snevley said, "You can still see me, right? I mean I didn't become invisible all of a sudden did I? What the hell was that?"

"Hurricane Lilith. Mother. You mean you couldn't feel the warm familial bonds flooding the room? I'm actually sort of surprised she took the time to venture out of the city all this way at all. I wonder what that's all about."

We sat in silence and I went back to devouring my sandwich.

Snevley said, "When I was twelve, I had an uncle that I didn't see all that often but there was something about him I connected with. He contracted emphysema and had to live with an oxygen tank by his side. One day, out of nowhere, the thought popped in my head that I needed to see him. Something inside was talking to me, placing my uncle's face in my mind as strongly as if he were standing in front of me. I talked to my Mom about it but she was too blitzed to give me anything but the usual I will-talk-to-your-father-and-we'll-see line. I knew what that meant but the feeling stuck with me for the rest of the day. Within twenty-four hours it was gone. A week later my Uncle died. I never got to see him again."

"Touching, but so what?"

"Since that incident I listen when that voice talks to me, no matter what's going on. Even if I think that voice is talking shit. I listen to it and follow it. I heard that voice again when I heard about your pile up. The voice said I needed to go see your car. By the way, what everyone is telling you is true, you're lucky to be alive. I have never seen anything that twisted that didn't involve mangled bodies. Here."

Snevley reached into his shirt pocket and handed me three pictures of my post accident mass of crunched steel. I couldn't see how they even got us out. It looked like it had already gone through a trash compactor. Grace's lunch started churning in my bloated gut.

"Yesterday I conned a mechanic into joining me at the junkyard, told him it was a vital murder investigation and his inspection was critical to the case. Your brakes failed right?"

"I almost put my foot through the floor," I said, as a shiver crawled up my spine.

"No surprise. Your brake line had been sliced just enough to let the fluid leak out slowly."

I could feel the blood drain from my face. "Shut up."

"No lie. I found out where you were parked at the funeral home from your bass player who, by the way, needs to unplug from cyberspace and join the real world for a while."

"You leave Geoff alone," I said. "Without his toys he's wound tighter than a virgin's daughter so just leave him be."

"I stopped at Mason's and found a stain on the drive that could be brake fluid but it has long since evaporated or washed away in the rain. In any case, your brake line was definitely cut."

This was impossible. What the hell did I ever do to anybody? "Sure it wasn't just worn out?"

"Not a chance. The cut was too clean. I saw it." Snevley normally gets his smug face on when he knows he's right about something but he looked at me in a quiet fashion, as if he was concerned about someone else besides himself.

"Son of a bitch," I murmured.

The other thought bugging me was why would anyone want to hurt me like that? What did I do to make someone wish me bodily harm and not care about any other consequences as well? I couldn't think of anyone I knew who hated me to that degree.

"Made any recent enemies?" Snevley asked.

"I was just thinking about that and came up blank except for that jerk-face detective...and you. This isn't some sick attempt to get back in my good graces is it?"

"Don't flatter yourself. I have another feeling."

"Do I want to hear it?"

"Probably not."

"You really know how to make a sale." I said, wincing.

He smiled, hung his head for a second then looked back at me. "I don't accept that all this is a coincidence."

"Coincidence with what?"

"DaKota."

"Oh, come on! You can't be serious. You really think there's a connection? That's a bit of a stretch."

He shrugged and said, "Possibly. Possibly. But, let me ask you, did you notice anything strange or see any suspicious people at the funeral?"

I brought the funeral parlor into focus in my mind; just flashes of images colliding together. "I don't remember anything unusual, but then again the whole day was unusual. DaKota's parents provided uncharted dimensions to the term 'douche bag'" I related the warm exchange I had with them.

"Nothing else?"

Sadness started creeping in with images of DaKota lying in the casket, standing there with everyone and not knowing that we'd almost be killed within the hour. The moment was frozen in my mind as one of the last times I'd be standing with both legs and feeling a bit guilty for not paying more attention to it, not having a clear picture of what it looked like in my mind. And now, along with DaKota, my leg was gone. Why did I take it for granted? I was too busy with everything going on around me, DaKota, the funeral parlor, the woman at the casket...

The woman at the casket.

"There was one person there that looked like she recognized me. A woman. Came in and stood by DaKota. She didn't talk to anyone. She kissed her."

Snevley looked puzzled. "Who?"

"DaKota."

"And nobody noticed?"

"I don't mean like that," I said. "She put her hand to her own lips then placed her hand on DaKota's lips. Then she turned and left. I think she recognized me." I saw her face in my mind, smiling in recognition. How did she know me? Maybe I just imagined the whole thing.

"She drove an ocean blue Jag convertible." I said.

"How do you know that?"

"I just realized it. We were standing at the casket and I saw a Jag roll down the driveway. It had to be her. No one else had left."

Snevley asked, "But you didn't actually see her in the car?"

"No, but who else could it be?"

"It would really help if you knew who she was."

"Well, duh, Dick Tracy. Even I could figure that out."

"Did you get a license plate number?" he asked hopefully.

"No. Light colored plates."

"That narrows it down to only forty-three of the fifty states."

"Bite me. She didn't look like the type to mess with my car. More like Connecticut or Princeton money. Classy looking, late forties or early fifties."

Snevley sighed, lost in his thoughts, "I noted a few names from the sign in book. Maybe one of them knows something and I'll get lucky." He suddenly smiled at his own comment. "Speaking of which," he said, standing next to the bed.

"Keep dreaming, paperboy. You had your turn."

He was just about at the door. "Hey, Snevley. Thanks for the food. That was cool. And let me know if you find out anything. Call me here as I assume my cell phone is embedded in the dashboard of my car."

"Whoa, almost forgot." He reached into his pocket and produced a shiny little flip-phone. "Here's another present." Before I could thank him he said, "This one isn't from me. I'm just the messenger. Power it up. It's a pre-paid phone with fifteen hundred minutes on it. Look at the contacts."

The phone came to life and I saw a list of a dozen first names already in the contact folder, first names I knew all too well. They were all from The Weekend Reminders, my Friday twelve-step cronies.

"One of them, David, tracked me down. Your group heard what happened and since you weren't answering their calls they figured your cell phone was probably a casualty. They wanted to make sure you stayed in touch with them."

"Wow," was about all I could say without losing it.

"Try not to annoy the staff too routinely, okay?"

"Sure," I said trying to smile away my tear filled eyes.

This totally blew me away. I looked up at the ceiling and said, "Thank you. I guess you are watching out for me, huh?"

By the time I fell asleep the phone was down a couple hundred minutes.

Seventeen

The next day the band appeared en masse.

"I brought you a few goodies to keep you occupied." Katrina said as she presented me a stack of papers, magazines and a Patricia Briggs paperback. Ms. Gorski is one of those vampire-werewolf people. She's patiently waiting for the right vampire to come along. Seriously. Katrina has the Pagan High Priestess triple moon symbol tattooed on her left thigh.

It was the first time I'd seen Geoff since the accident. He had a butter-fly bandage on his forehead and his left arm was in a cast upon which was drawn a purple amorphous blob with massive teeth and tentacles sprouting in all directions.

"Oh, that's cute."

"I know a guy who draws," he trailed off as if this was explanation enough.

"God, I'm sorry," I said looking at him.

"Eh," he said with a wave of his good hand as if shooing a fly. From Geoff that was high praise.

"Hey, has anyone seen Pat or gone to the restaurant to tell him what is going on?"

Katrina said, "I stopped by Le Snobbitorium yesterday but he wasn't there. Don't worry, Hon, he'll turn up."

Their visit was ruined by a short, perfectly toned man in black spandex bike gear parading into the room. Short salt and pepper dreads flopped on his head as he dashed toward me; his annoying smile was just too damn cheery. Stitched in yellow over the left breast of the T-shirt spray-painted on his body was 'Carmine'.

"Ready to stretch the leg out?"

"I'll give you a hundred dollars to disappear," I said.

"Now how could I face myself if I took you up on that? Besides, you don't have a hundred dollars anyway. I scoped out your stuff while you were asleep."

"Nice. Where's the wheelchair?"

"Uh-uh," he said, pointing to my crutch.

"Are you serious?"

"Come on champ. You hop to physical therapy."

"You're ancestors were part of the Spanish Inquisition weren't they?"

"*Nobody expects the...*"

"Don't. Just don't."

The band filed out and as we headed to the PT room, Carmine said, "Today is your lucky day. You get to meet your temporary new best friend."

When Dr. Anders first talked to me about getting fit for a prosthetic foot, I was imagining a Luke Skywalker contraption, complete with high-tech metallic construction and instant response to my every motion. So much for the movies.

The device, while still looking uniquely space-age was a conglomeration of titanium, wood and plastic that just seemed to hang on my knee.

"It's very simple," he said holding the contraption in front of me. "This is a supracondylar cuff. Your leg goes here and the straps go around like that, see? It holds on to your knee."

"It doesn't look like it will stay on."

"Of course it will. Here is the sock you have to put on to help stop chafing and blistering."

I sighed. "This is sounding better and better."

Carmine slipped one sock over my stump then slipped on the temporary prosthesis.

"Hmmm. Too much play," he said moving the cup from side to side around my stump.

"Is that bad?"

"Actually it's good. Over the next couple months you'll use more and more socks, 'plys' we call them. You want more because that means the swelling is going down. Once you reach about 16 ply, then you are probably ready to be measured for a permanent prosthesis."

He tried different plys and finally settled on four. "That's excellent. Usually this early it's a single ply, two at the most. You're way ahead of the game."

"If you say so. When do we road test it?"

"Right now." He undid everything and handed the apparatus to me. "Your turn."

Carmine knelt next to me and guided me through the installation process. I felt like the Terminator during that gross part when all his flesh is melted away.

"Let's go. Up," he commanded.

"Now? I was thinking maybe in a couple days after I've settled in and got used to it."

"That gets boring. This is much more fun."

I stood up. Slowly. "So far, so good," I said, more to convince myself than anyone else.

"Here," he offered his arm upon which I immediately clawed in a vice-like death grip. It was about five steps to what looked like a set of gymnastic parallel bars for little people. It might just as well have been five miles away.

The first step with "the foot" was more of a drag.

"Use your knee. It still works. You are used to not thinking about walking. It's been a natural movement since you were a baby. You will get there again, but now you have to think about it for a bit. It's kind of like learning to walk all over again. You're lucky because you have a BK and can still use your knee. Here we go."

"The only BK I know is Burger King."

He chuckled and said, "It means a 'below-the-knee' amputation."

I launched my body onto the parallel bars putting all my weight on my arms, and nearly collapsed on the floor when the pain shot through my still healing left side.

Carmine had me in his well-developed arms in an instant. "You can't put all your weight on your arms; even if they were both functioning properly you'd never make it. Use your hands to guide you along the bar, not support you."

"This is not going to work," I said.

He waved my comment away. "You're young, strong. I have a seventy year old woman with two prosthetics can walk miles without sweating."

"Yeah I know. Uphill. In the snow. Good for her."

Inching back and forth on the parallel bars was akin to ice skating for the first time. I spent most of my time making sure I didn't fall and look like an ass. I didn't fully trust that putting all my weight on this gizmo was going to work.

"You're doing fine," Carmine said, walking back and forth with me outside the bars. "Now let go and do it."

"Are you nuts?" I said panting. "I'll fall flat on my ass. Not that there's a lack of padding to save me."

"I'll catch you. And the padding on your ass is fine."

"Flattery will get you nowhere."

"Never mind. Walk."

I stood at one end of the bars and took a deep breath. "OK. I'm going to let go. Just let me stand here a minute. Shouldn't you be next to me in case I collapse or something?"

He sat at the opposite end and folded his arms over his chest. "Never happen."

Gingerly I shifted my weight. Slowly. My hands were still on the bars but just resting there. I pulled them an inch off the bar, ready to fling them back the instant something went wrong. But nothing did. I just stood there, weight on my feet, and slowly put my hands to my sides.

"Hey, how about that?" I said, beaming.

"See? You should always trust me. I know what I'm doing. Now, take a step."

"Do I have to?" I asked.

"No dessert tonight unless you do and they make a righteous German chocolate cake here."

"Sure. Hit me where it hurts." I figured it was safer to make the first step with the prosthetic foot, that way I could keep my weight on my good leg. I lifted it and clumped it forward about six inches.

"There. Does that count?"

He just stared at me.

What the hell, I thought; I'm going to have to do this at some point. What am I afraid of? So I fall down. So I fall down and smack my head on the parallel bars and knock myself into a coma and never regain consciousness. Who would get my drums? And the store? They'd have to get someone new in there quickly because none of the people there now would take over and where would that leave Jason? He's no good with disruptions like that and...

"Excellent!" said Carmine, breaking my train of thought.

"Huh?"

"You did it!"

"Did what?" I looked down and somehow my good foot was about ten inches in front of the prosthetic foot. "Well...of course I did it. I just needed time to get ready that's all." I hoped I could do it again since I didn't know what I did the first time.

Carmine made me walk at least another hundred miles that afternoon. He called it gait training. I made a crack about not being a racehorse and he just chuckled. Bastard.

After the stroll I was on the leg lift bench, a medieval device designed to strengthen leg muscles by lifting weights with the injured limb using a leather padded winter hand warmer on your leg. The weights were out of sight in order to make you feel worse when you think you've been lifting a hundred pounds when, in fact, you've been pumping only twenty. Add to that my private tormentor standing there eating some sort of power bar and telling me, "Aw come on, five more. You can do it."

"Are you sure this is good for me?" I said, drenched in sweat. My leg felt Freddie Krueger'd, coarsely flayed into raw meat. "And if you say 'no pain, no gain' I'm going to tattoo my name on your face with a broken Coke bottle."

"You'll have to catch me first. You're doing fine. Five sets of fifteen lifts at twenty pounds. In two days we'll have you up to five sets and fifty pounds."

"Why not make it easy and just take the rest of my leg off now so we can skip all this and go grab a beer. Can I go home now?"

Carmine grinned. "Not yet. We have to work your arm back into shape. Come over here." I'd like to work my arm back into shape by beating him with an I.V. stand. He brought me to a contraption that was essentially nothing more than an upside down bicycle balanced on its front tire, only without the tires and the pedals staring me in the face.

"Put your hands on the pedals and work it just like your feet riding a bike. We'll start easy on this one."

"Good."

"A thirty pound resistance and two hundred rotations."

I stared at him. "Easy? When was the last time you had a psychiatric evaluation?"

It wasn't as bad as I thought it would be but my left arm was throbbing and I was exhausted. Physical therapy is God's way of letting you know why it's not a good idea to injure yourself, because the pain of getting better is infinitely worse than the injury itself. "Just think," I said, "I can look forward to doing this again tomorrow. Joy." He smiled as we entered the elevator. "You'll be dancing the tango again in no time."

"And me a musician." The elevator stopped at the fifth floor. The doors opened but no one got on.

"Come on," Carmine waved, holding the door open.

"But I'm on seven."

"I know. We're taking the scenic route."

The elevator doors started closing so I gingerly hopped my way out into the hallway. I was beyond exhausted and, were it not for the crutch, I would be face-first on the hospital floor especially since the rubber pieces on top were blistering my pits.

"Come on. I'm wiped out. I can't take anymore." He just kept walking. "This better be good, and whatever it is it better include a seventy ounce Coke with a pound of ice." Every muscle and joint in my body was screaming for a rest. Carmine walked ahead of me and turned into a doorway.

"Is this another dammed test…" I stopped in the doorway and gasped. Andi lay in bed, eyes glassy but open, with a weak smile on her face. Carmine pulled a chair over next to the bed for me to sit. I took her hand. We both had tears running down our faces.

"God I'm so sorry. I'm so sorry," was all I could say.

"Shush," she said, her voice quiet and hoarse. There was little of her hair left to be seen under the bandage cap covering her head. Both eyes had purplish yellow bruises underneath. We just sat there quietly looking at each other and smiling, not needing to talk. After a bit she squeaked out, "How are you?"

"I'm fine. Really. I'm OK."

"You lie," she said.

"Yeah, and what are you going to do about it?"

She smiled and closed her eyes. Her breathing became deep and regular and I knew she was out. It didn't matter, I was grateful just to have her there…alive.

Eighteen

Hospital life was tedious when not in physical therapy. I was lying in bed, absently rereading a pamphlet on erectile dysfunction when a pair of large tortoise-shell sunglasses and a navy blue and white scarf covering the face of what appeared to be a woman, peeked around the door. From under the scarf I could see strands of blonde hair. She smiled meekly, slipped into the room and sat silently in a chair next to my bed.

"Um," I said, "I think the waiting room is down the hall."

She immediately started sobbing. From what I could see of her face, her skin looked puffy and now reddened from crying.

"I'm sorry," she said through the sobs. She undid the scarf. Her straight blonde mane fell halfway down her back. She slowly removed her glasses. Her right eye was horribly purple and swollen shut. Even through the damage she looked familiar but I couldn't place her. Something about her face wasn't right, apart from looking like someone tenderized it with a baseball bat.

She glanced quickly at me then away. "It's not as bad as it looks." She said, I guess in reaction to whatever expression was plastered on my face. "I'm glad to see you're still here," she said between sniffles.

I blurted out the questions in my head. "Who are you? What happened?"

She started sobbing again so I handed her the tissue box from the table next to my bed.

"Thanks," she said, blowing her nose. "Oh, just being clumsy. Fell down the stairs." She looked at me with her opened red-rimmed eye then looked away.

"You're here to see me? Really? I mean you are vaguely familiar but I just can't quite …" Then the tumblers in my brain fell into place. Blonde hair. DaKota's funeral. The restaurant. Pat. "You're Carolyn," I gasped.

She nodded.

"What are you doing here? Where's Pat? How do you know DaKota?"

She squeaked out, "I read about your accident in the paper. I was hoping he had been here. He hasn't, has he?" she asked, hopefully.

"No. No one has seen or heard from him. Have you talked to him at all?"

"I've called a dozen times and no answer. I'm scared."

A really crappy feeling gnawed at me. "Your husband found out, didn't he?" Her head snapped up at me. "Pat told me. I know about the two of you." My stomach clenched tighter. "You didn't fall down the stairs. Your husband did this didn't he?" She broke down sobbing, nodding her head.

I jumped up throwing off the covers. "You've got to get it together. Did your husband know who it was? Did he know it was Pat?"

Flames erupted inside me. I had to go do....something. I couldn't just lie here. How could I not do something? Damn it, damn it, damn it! Not knowing what else to do I pushed the nurse station button.

Armani's voice came through the intercom above the bed. "What do you need, Honey?"

"Carolyn! Did he know it was Pat?"

"Chynna?" said Armani.

"I need to speak to Dr. Anders. And Dr. Kane," I shouted back at the intercom speaker. I didn't know if that's where the microphone was, but it was the source of her voice and that would have to do for now.

"They won't be back until Monday. Is there something..."

"This is an emergency. I need both of them," I yelled.

Carolyn was shuddering as I grabbed her arms. "Did your husband know where Pat worked? How did he find out?"

"It was my fault. I usually erase all the text messages off my phone before I go into the house. Not that he looks at my phone every night, or even at all. But for some reason he did that night. Pat had been..." she blushed and looked at her lap. "He'd been particularly eloquent that day."

A friggin' poet. Great.

Carolyn turned her face away to hide her eye as Armani marched into the room. "What's the matter? You in pain?"

"No. My leg is fine. Please get Anders and Kane for me. I have to get out of here. Now. Today."

"But it's Satur…"

I cut her off. "I know what day it is, dammit. Just get them for me, and while you're at it, this woman needs medical attention."

"No. Please," Carolyn begged.

"She's been assaulted. Dr. Anders needs to check her out for other injuries."

"I can take her down to Emergency…" Armani offered.

"No, she's going to stay here with me until Dr. Anders arrives. Go get them now!"

"I cannot…"

I swung my legs around and grabbed my crutch. "Shit I'll call them myself if I have to."

"Get back in bed now…" Armani protested.

"Get out of my way!"

I pushed my way out the door and hobbled down to the nurses' station.

"Young Lady, you come back here."

There was an empty desk strewn with papers. I started rifling through them, randomly throwing pages left and right.

"Hey," said another nurse, reaching for me. "You can't do that!"

"Back off!" I shouted and took a swipe at her with my crutch.

Hopping to the desk with a computer, I leaned on the crutch and started punching keys looking for some sort of directory.

I called out, "Will someone help me here? I need Dr. Anders' phone…"

Before I could finish, I was airborne.

"Put me down, God dammit." I struggled but a muscular hulk had me from behind and was squeezing hard. Pain shot through my shoulder and arm.

"Shit. You're hurting me." I kicked my legs out, which turned out to be monumentally stupid. Searing pain blasted through me. The next thing I knew, I was on my back in bed.

Armani grabbed my arm and straightened it out and starting rubbing it with alcohol. It felt icy.

"No!" I screamed, fighting to pull my arm back. Two massive arms dropped across my chest and pinned me to the bed. Another bolt of pain through my left arm into my shoulder.

"What are you doing? Dammit, that hurts. Get off me! No! Don't do it! No!" I felt the prick in my arm and a flood of tingling warmth throughout my body. I struggled vainly but everything was starting to swirl and swim, the pressure was leaving my chest. My eyes fluttered. The last thing I remember was seeing an empty chair next to my bed. I thought maybe Dr. Anders came to get Carolyn. Good. Then blackness.

Nineteen

"Welcome back."

Doctors Anders and Kane were standing next to the bed smiling down at me.

"Hi," I yawned. The inside of each arm itched. I bent them to scratch but felt a jab and the pull of adhesive tape against my skin. An I.V. tube stuck out of each arm.

"What time is it? I really slept a long time. What's all this for?" I said, holding up my arms.

Dr. Kane grabbed my hand. I remembered what happened the last time she did that. "What, did I lose the other foot now?"

Her dazzling smile made me feel better instantly. "No, of course not, but I want you to tell me what you remember about the past couple days."

"I've been here, lying around doing nothing."

"Any visitors?"

"Well, Geoff, Katrina, Spag. Snevley was here."

"Who else?"

I tried to think. Something on the edges of my brain was sloshing around.

"How about a woman in sunglasses and a scarf?"

"Oh. Yeah. Carolyn. Is she okay? Did you fix her up?" I said looking at Anders. "Does she know where Pat is?"

"Slow down there," said Anders, now on the other side of the bed. Dr. Kane leaned down next to me. "Chynna, who is Carolyn?"

For the next few minutes I told them who she was and the connection to Pat and DaKota, and that no one had seen Pat for a few days.

"All you know is 'Carolyn'?"

Shit. I never did ask about her last name. "Some detective," I said, feeling a resignation wash over me. "What day is this anyway?"

"Tuesday," said Dr. Kane. There was a quick eye exchange between the doctors and Anders left the room.

"Holy shit," I said. "Now I remember, sort of. I kind of freaked out, didn't I?"

"You could say that, but it's understandable given everything that's going on right now. Dr. Anders was worried that you might go into a deeper shock than you were in already so he's had you sedated for a few days, just to get you back in gear. I have a hunch Detective Douglas will be here shortly with many questions. He's been bugging us since Sunday to come see you but we've kept all visitors away until everything settled down."

"What the hell is going on?" I asked. "I mean all this crap; DaKota, me, Pat?"

"I don't know. What do you think?"

"There's a patented shrink answer."

She smiled, but waited silently.

"I think somebody out there is shuffling the deck and I'm being dealt a new hand of strange cards. It doesn't fill me with a boatload of confidence. I don't mind change but the whole people dying or disappearing thing really sucks."

"How does that make you feel?" she asked, her voice even but not without compassion. She was in full-therapy mode.

"It pisses me off," I snapped.

"Why?"

"What do you mean, 'why'? Kind of obvious isn't it?"

"Is it?"

"Ugghhh," I growled in total frustration. Driving me bat-shit was not going to accomplish anything. If I wanted someone to annoy the crap out of me I'd call my mother and…mother.

I looked at Dr. Kane. "Mother and Dad. It's them all over again isn't it?"

She raised a single eyebrow, prompting me with an unspoken question.

"She morphed into the society queen, Nana Lenox died and Dad offed himself, leaving me alone, which I quickly turned into years of pain-numbing powder snorting. Crap. No wonder this blows."

Dr. Kane clasped her hands and leaned forward on her legs. "People and things that were rock solid are not so stable anymore. I'd say that qualifies for some serious reaction, don't you?"

A brief flicker of relief washed over me. I hadn't looked at it quite that way before. "You're very good at your job, you know."

"Thank you. Tell me what you're feeling right now."

After a quick mental scan I said, "Anxious. Sad. Angry. Hungry. All rolled up together."

"Sounds right to me."

We talked a while longer then she left with a promise of returning the next day. I had to pee. Realizing that I was hooked on either arm I lifted up the sheet in disappointment; the damn catheter was back. Shit. I closed my eyes, hoping all the bad things would just go away. The darkness became sort of comforting, like hiding under the blankets as a kid so the monsters were kept at bay. Monsters can't get past blankets. Maybe if I kept my eyes closed all my current monsters would look elsewhere instead of harassing me.

Twenty

Anders had reached his patience limit with me and was kicking me out with a prescription for two weeks of in-patient physical therapy and weekly visits with Dr. Kane to check on my mental state. I couldn't wait to get the hell out of the hospital, eat real food that did not taste like sawdust and breathe non-conditioned air. On the other hand two more weeks of being locked up in a rehab and not being near Andi was not a thrilling prospect. Missing the daily visits would leave a big hole. What I really wanted to do was just go home but that wasn't on the Anders menu.

Following my farewell session with Carmine, I was to be transported to a rehabilitation facility in Princeton, about an hour's ambulance ride. I could only imagine what that was going to cost and shot a quick prayer to Mom about having no overdue health insurance premium notices sitting in the pile at home. I made a mental note to have Katrina check for me. She had brought me some comfortable clothes, including several changes of underwear. From what I heard, the dress I wore to DaKota's funeral was no longer wearable. I didn't really want to know why.

Armani wheeled me down the hall and I waved my goodbyes to the nursing staff saying I hoped never to see them again.

"We're stopping on five."

"Honey, your ride is downstairs waiting."

"It can wait another ten minutes. Just let them know to keep the meter running."

Andi was sitting up; the bruises under her eyes had reduced in size and turned a lovely yellow-green shade. The skull bandage had been removed showing little more than stubble covering her scalp. She sat, staring straight ahead, a newspaper on her lap and tears running down her cheeks.

"Hey," I said, more of a question, sitting on the bed facing her. She turned her head to meet my gaze.

"I…I can't…" was all she could say. I saw the paper open to the Sudoku puzzle. She had a pen in her hand but all the empty spaces were still empty.

"Can't what?"

She looked down at the paper. "The numbers. They don't make sense."

I gently pulled the pen and paper away from her. "Your brain got a good knocking about. It will come back. Patience."

"I guess," she said half-heartedly. A knot grabbed at my stomach. Dr. Anders explained Andi's injuries to me, a TBI he called it, a traumatic brain injury. Andi was going to have a tough time with memory and possibly other brain functions for awhile. Her rehab stint would make mine look like a walk in the park. I felt responsible and helpless at the same time, which further pissed me off and pushed the guilt meter higher. If I ever catch the son of a bitch that messed with my brakes I'm going to feed his still attached nuts to a pack of rabid dogs.

"You look great," I said going for a subject change.

"I look hideous with these bruises on my face."

"Gay guys and chicks in New York are paying big bucks to have mascara permanently applied to get that look."

"On their eye*lids*, not under their eyes."

"So what?" I said, "You look hotter now than I ever could."

"Pull the other one. Check this out." She bent her head down toward me. "Look at the ugly burr-hole scars I've got now. Mad brilliant, aren't they?"

"Wow," I said looking at the four small red dots, two on either side of her scalp. "I predict you will be the next fashionista and every chick within a hundred miles will want her head shaved with hole marks tattooed on."

"Only the barking mad ones."

"When are you coming home?"

"I'm…I'm not sure. I can't remember what they told me." Another knot for the guilt collection in my stomach.

"You can come stay with me."

"And sleep where? On the sofa? Thank you, no. Besides, I'd like us to remain friends."

After a long hug and a promise to call her every day, I walked out determined not to let her see me either pissed off or upset, but I was plenty of both.

Armani wheeled me through the lobby and out of the hospital. I took a deep breath of hot humid air, it felt heavy and wonderful.

"You do everything they tell you in rehab, Princess, or I come there. Then you be in real trouble," Armani said smiling.

"Thank you," I whispered. "For everything." We stared glassy-eyed at each other. "I know it's not your floor but please keep an eye on Andi for me?"

She ran her thick fingers through my hair. "I'll look in on your friend from time to time while she's here. You have a powerful aura, child. Make sure you take care of it. You know what is good and what is bad. Don't let nobody tell you different."

"You're going to have to teach me how to see auras someday."

She smiled. "It's not difficult. You just have to open your eyes." We fell into an embrace and all of a sudden, I wasn't in such a hurry to leave.

A glance around the entrance of the hospital revealed a two-seater Mercedes convertible and a familiar, beat-up, olive green junk pile with a shredded vinyl roof and a rusted chrome bumper tilting to the left side, which was held up by frayed brown rope.

"Cool. I've always wanted a ride in a two-seater convertible."

The door to the junk pile groaned open and out stepped Spag, death metal incarnate.

"Hey," he said with a slight nod. "Where to?"

Armani spoke up before I could. "Vista Rehab in Princeton. And you mind this one carefully."

He smiled quietly. "Yes, ma'am."

Turning to me he said, "First class or coach?" pointing to the passenger side doors.

"Without a doubt, first class." He held the back door open while I slid in the front. The inside was ugly olive green, worn, but clean. All the dials were analog and each window had its own manual crank. "Most people consider the back seat first class. You know, like a limo. Hope you don't mind open windows," he said once in the driver's seat. "No A.C."

"Works for me. I've had enough A.C. to last me for awhile."

The entire vehicle shuddered as the engine roared to life. The hot air through the window was delicious. I leaned my head out just to feel the impact of the wind through my hair and the sun's heat across my face.

The fastest way to get me to the rehab was via the New Jersey Turnpike. My last experience tooling down that highway was floating through my mind as we chugged the green bomb out of the hospital parking lot.

"Music?" he asked.

"Please. It's the one thing I really missed being cooped up in there."

"You sure? My taste leans toward the harder side."

"Yeah that's a surprise. Play on McDuff."

Hard indeed.

"There's something I've been meaning to ask you," I screamed over the wind and music blast. "Where does Spag come from?"

"Born in Honolulu but lived most of my life in Colorado."

"I meant the name."

He smiled, turned down the music to merely deafening and said, "Ahhh. I make the finest Linguini Carbonara on the planet. Most of my roommates think all pasta is spaghetti so I was dubbed Spaghetti King, Spag for short. The rest is history."

My ears were bleeding by the time we pulled up to a two story dirty orange brick building tucked away on a back alley cul-de-sac across from a truck repair garage. From the outside, the Vista Rehabilitation Hospital looked like a waste management incinerator that was converted into bed space. The greasy first floor resembled a waiting room for truck jockeys complete with scuffed and torn furniture and old copies of Motor Trend magazine heralding the introduction of the Yugo. Fortunately, the second floor looked like a different building altogether, combining a hospital structure with some of the comforts of home. Two clean, bright rooms on either side of an endless hallway reminded me of large restaurant kitchens, without the steel and chrome; more of a Better Homes & Garden photo spread complete with kitchen appliances, bright Formica counters, oak cabinets and matching tables. Following the rooms was a series of "dorms' as the staff called them, decorated to remind the inhabitants not to get too comfy as this was, after all, a hospital complete with the same motorized beds, horrific fluorescent lighting and press board cabinetry covered in wood grain contact paper. The real difference was in window space. Where the hospital had narrow slats in the walls, the rehab offered the kind of window I'd expect in a beach house, letting in gobs of light and fresh air.

I was barely settled in when a wide-eyed young gent wheeled full speed into my room.

"You're Chynna?" His Ukrainian accent was thick and his energy boundless. I could see myself hating him within short order.

"Ivan", he pronounced it *EE-von*.

"Hi," I said shaking his offered hand wrapped in a fingerless black glove.

"Exc-c-cuse the glove. Cuts down on blisters. So, ready t-t-to go?"

"Go where? I just got here."

"Come. I-I show you." He wheeled out before I had a chance to say another word so I followed him back down the hall. At the nurses' station he hung a right and disappeared. I did some hop-skipping to keep up, catching a glimpse of his chair rolling through a door that led to a large room with a mostly glass wall. Inside were several people milling around who all turned toward the door expectedly when he entered. I followed and the people, mostly dressed in white, burst into applause, all converging on me to shake my hand, grab my shoulder and all saying things like "Welcome. Glad you're here. You look great." I figured Spag inadvertently dropped me at a mental hospital. I kept scanning the room, looking to spot Winona Ryder and Angelina Jolie, when a familiar face came into focus.

"Glad you made it," said Dr. Kane.

"What is all this?"

"Let me introduce you to your rehabilitation team," she said taking my arm and pushing me to my prosthetist, occupational therapist, physical therapist (Ivan), staff nurses and medical doctor.

Dr. Kane plunked me in a chair that looked like it was assembled by Stevie Wonder, a cushion-less wooden armchair with a seat extending to the left past the arm and four uneven legs. She handed me a Coke (how quick they learn) and the Doctor, a man named Duggan, approached me with Ivan wheeling along side. Duggan was the antithesis of Anders with his navy blue pin-striped suit, silk jacquard tie and starched white pin point button down. He was deeply tanned; short black hair gelled in-place and would have made a good TV MD.

"I see by your hospital chart that the swelling on your residual leg has reduced way ahead of the norm. You're their star patient."

"Huh? You mean the stump? Yep. That would be the case."

"That's good. That means we can probably measure you for your first permanent prosthesis sooner than expected, assuming you keep up the good work. Ivan here will be in charge of driving you to distraction."

"I can't wait," I said as they both smiled.

Duggan continued. "The one thing we don't want to have happen is…"

"Hip or knee contractures. Yes, Carmine drilled that into my head in the hospital."

"So let's see how far you can lift your residual leg while sitting."

"Sure. Get me drunk on Coke then torture me."

I was able to straighten out my leg to about one hundred seventy degrees. In one quick motion, Duggan grabbed my stump, pulled it up and before the gasp of pain shot from my lips he swiveled the extended piece of wood on the chair around so it rested under my stump. He gently put my leg back down but my muscles and tendons were not happy.

"When you sit, I want you to keep your leg straight as possible at all times. Is that clear?"

"Jawohl, Herr Doktor," I grimaced.

"Oh this is nothing. After two weeks with my friend in the wheel-chair here, I'm going to look like Santa Claus on Christmas morning," he said smiling. The inspection of my scars commenced as he removed my prosthesis.

"Hmmm."

"I hate when Doctors say that. It's never a good sign," I said.

"No, I'm impressed. You've healed incredibly well and your skin doesn't look rough or red at all. You've been taking good care of it. That's a good sign. The compression hosiery seems to have paid off. They teach you how to use the sock donner at the hospital?"

"Yep, but I got to the point where I didn't need it. I can dress this baby without any mechanical aids."

"Excellent. You're up to what, about ten ply?"

"Eleven, thank you very much."

"How's your mood? I hear you've been through some tough events lately."

"Mostly okay," I said. "That lady over there has been shrinking my head on a fairly regular basis."

"She's the best," he said standing up. "I think I'll let you two plot out a strategy. I'll be by tomorrow to check up on you."

Duggan made his way around the room, saying his good-byes and making updates. When he got to Dr. Kane he stood with his back to me so I couldn't see either of their reactions. It was a smooth move but I was suspicious of the reasons. I looked at Ivan who was putting a bottle of Gatorade back in the cup holder on his mobile gizmo.

I said, "This is going to suck, isn't it? That's why everyone is being nice to me now."

"P-p-parts will be tough, I won't bullshit you. What you have to keep in mind is everything we do now will make sure your m-m-mobility and balance will be with you in long run. Without this, you could easily end up with one of these for rest of your life," he said, pointing to his contraption.

"What happened?" I asked.

"L-l-lightning strike. I was playing baseball and lightning struck about t-t-twenty feet away. Surge from electric field stopped my heart, is called a ground current ef-f-fect. N-n-nothing worked when I came to, my arms my legs. Couldn't even talk. I had to learn all over again. That's why I stutter occasionally, but is getting better. Always h-h-happens more when I meet new patient."

I tried not to feel bad for him but it struck me as hugely unfair that this kid got electrically fried into a wheelchair at a young age. "How old are you?" I asked.

"T-t-twenty-eight." He looked closer to seventeen.

"Me too. As far as I'm concerned we're a couple old neighborhood friends hanging out for awhile. Deal?" I put my fist out to him. He wheeled up and gave me some pumps.

"D-Deal."

Twenty-One

"Even though tomorrow is your last day here you need to continue PT on the outside, otherwise all this good work you've accomplished will reverse itself." Two weeks had flown by and Dr. Duggan examined my leg for the last time and gave the usual non-committal "mmm"s and grunts. He rarely smiled but gave off a sense of well-hidden satisfaction. I think he just liked feeling up legs. He pulled a clipboard off the bedside table and wrote the standard doctor-indecipherable notes.

The physical therapy had been grueling; the daily pattern of torture, sweating with Ivan, showering, eating, rinse, repeat. I talked to Andi at least once a day. She was sounding a bit stronger but still disoriented from time to time. This morning, however, she sounded groggier than she had in the past couple of days.

"You okay?" I asked.

"Yeah. Pain in my head. They gave me something."

She was fading fast. After two weeks I needed a fix, just see her long enough to know she was healing. The trick would be conning someone into making the one hour drive to the hospital.

Still no word from Pat either, which felt more and more like something was wrong. This was not like him to just disappear, even if Carolyn's husband was looking for him. He had never shied away from a fight, as far as I knew.

"I think you're ready for your first permanent," Duggan said.

I was about to make a thoroughly stupid comment about my hair when I realized he was talking about a prosthesis.

"First permanent? Isn't that an oxymoron?"

"They do wear out," he said with a trace of a smile, "and your body will change with time as well. Every five or six years you'll have to be measured for a new one."

After one last torture session with Ivan, a tech came in to take measurements for my new appendage, informing me that I'd get a call when it was ready.

"I guess that means I better get a phone," I said after he'd left.

"Th-that reminds me," Ivan said, wheeling over to a far corner and returning with a white gift bag on his lap.

"Happy graduation," he said handing it to me. I wasn't expecting this and I stumbled through a clumsy "thank you". Inside I was stunned to find a new iPhone.

"Ivan, I…"

"Star-two-two-eight and you're g-good to go."

"I love getting new toys. Thank you," I said leaning over to hug him. His muscled arms wrapped around me. His felt good but I wasn't sure he was going to let go.

"Inside box," he said when I stood, "is my phone number. Put in your address book. Call me if you have trouble…about an-anything."

I bent to kiss his cheek. "Thank you for everything. I won't say it's been fun, but I know it's been good."

It had been a long, tough day, physically and emotionally, with the onset of monthly raging hormones sneaking up on me.

I was spent and skipped going to the kitchen for dinner, I had neither the energy nor the desire. After eating, everyone was supposed to gather in the lounge area to watch a movie, "*Mary Poppins*" or "*Deep Throat*" or some other blockbuster but I was not in the mood. I was sitting in bed watching the gray skies grow gradually darker. I really missed my apartment and felt like a kid on Christmas Eve waiting for the next day. I just wanted to be in my own bed, with the fans on, away from everybody and everything.

I grabbed a quick shower. Sitting down in my own private 'Stevie Wonder' chair to bathe had become second nature. Initially, I was a disaster trying to coordinate the hand held shower head and get clean without covering the entire bathroom in spray or hanging myself by the cord. I even explored the fixture's famed multi-purpose uses and committed to installing one at home as quickly as possible.

Walking in my birthday suit from the bath to my bedroom was a normal activity back home; it kept the clothes I was going to wear from getting damp in the steam. Mom, again, proved her worth as the thought of donning the rehab-supplied robe prior to exiting the bathroom appeared out of nowhere. Two hops into the bedroom and I stopped cold, water from my hair dripping on the floor. There sat Gralewski, perched like melted Silly Putty on the windowsill.

"To what do I owe the honor? My guess is your visit is not out of a deep personal concern for my well being."

"Hostility," he said, "That's helpful. Trust me there are a thousand things I'd rather be doing than hanging around this creepy dump."

"There's the door. Try to let it hit you on the way out."

He oozed off the sill; it made me think of unrestrained jello on the move. "You know, just because you had an alleged accident doesn't let you off the hook."

Bracing myself on the wall I stuck the stump out of my robe. "Wow. It looks like I allegedly lost my foot as well."

"Criminal minds come up with strange shit when boxed into a corner. I knew a creep who whacked his whole family, wife and three daughters, with a butcher's knife. After slicing and dicing the kids, he nonchalantly jammed his right arm down the kitchen garbage disposal and switched it on. He was right-handed, see, and he figured if the investigation proved the killer was right-handed, he'd be in the clear."

"That's the most realistic right hand prosthetic I've ever seen," I said, nodding at his arm.

"Very clever. I got the tox report on your pal this morning, but I'm guessing you can probably tell me what's on it. Want to take a *stab* at it?" he said with an undisguised chuckle.

"I've come to accept juvenile remarks like that from you, being a complete asshat and all."

His smile instantly disappeared. "Here's the deal, Sweetheart, your girlfriend had enough different chemicals in her bronchial passages to ice two or three people. Chemicals that are used by spoiled Princeton brats sitting around with nothing better to do but huff and spend Daddy's money."

"Wait a minute. So she was dead when he..." I said, not wanting to finish the thought.

"What?" By his evil grin he knew what I meant but wasn't about to help in the slightest.

The words stuck in my throat and I had to push them out through clenched teeth. "When her tongue was cut out and stabbed to her chest. Bastard."

"You aren't an actress too, by any chance? I'm not buying this shocked act. Especially after obtaining a search warrant for your place and guess what we found?"

My spine stiffened at the thought of Gralewski rummaging through my stuff with his scummy paws. "If anything is missing or damaged..."

"A box full of nitrous oxide poppers stuck in the back of your closet. Surprise, surprise," He said, pleased with himself.

"Oh I'm sure. What else did you just happen to plant, oh sorry, *find* there, your brains?"

He started toward me with a menacing grin and reached into his jacket. For a second I thought he was going to pull out a gun and shoot me. Looking back, that may have been preferable.

"Chynna Lennox, I am placing you under arrest for the murder of Jessica Holt-Gibson."

Stunned, it took a few seconds for what he had said to sink in. "Are you crazy?"

"You have the right to remain silent..." he continued, snapping open the handcuffs and grabbing my wrist.

"Hey. Back off, asshat." I struggled to free my arm from his grip.

"That's resisting arrest. Happy to add that to the list as well."

"At least let me get some clothes on," I said, but not before he had my hands cuffed behind my back. "I can't fucking believe this."

"You have the right to speak to an attorney," his hand on my shoulder pushing me into the hallway, now crowded with fellow cripples gawking in fascination. I tried to shrug off his paw but it just clamped on tighter. "Let go. I'm not going to run away."

The floor nurse made a half-hearted attempt at appeasement but Gralewski waved her away as if she was little more than a picnic mosquito. All I wanted to do was go home, sleep in my own bed and just be alone for awhile. What the fuck.

Twenty-Two

Well, that's it. Along with my narcotics arrest, I'm officially a homicidal maniac in the eyes of the State of New Jersey. I was treated to a night behind bars learning the fine art of filleting a man's penis from a woman named Kill-Mama-G who had the words "fuck" and "you" tattooed on her left and right breast respectively, which she had no reservation in displaying. I performed a subtle scan of the cell looking for broomsticks. One sleepless night and inedible breakfast later, I was led back to the intake section to be met by the shit-eating grin of Captain Suckmaster.

"What are you doing here, Snevley?"

He winked at me and said in a needlessly loud voice, "What? Let my little sister face this all alone? Never."

"Little…what?"

Before he could answer I was whisked into a courtroom to stand next to Jason, looking dapper in a khaki suit that obviously been stored under his mattress.

"What…"

"This is your arraignment. Utter one noise, make the slightest gesture and I will personally escort you back to your cell. Understood?"

I did what I was told. For a change. I didn't even listen to the exchange between the attorneys, just kept praying to Mom to give Jason and the judge the wisdom to get me the hell out of here.

I heard something about bail set at a number with a lot of zeroes and felt my heart sink. Who the hell had that kind of money? I know I didn't. Hopefully Kill Mama kept my bunk warm while I was away.

I was led out of the courtroom but stopped in the hallway; the guards silently removed my handcuffs. Someone yanked my arm and I found myself being dragged through the Police station. I glanced at the Sergeant behind the desk who looked at me as if I just ran over his dog.

Blinded by the hot sun, I focused on the red Boxter in front of me and stopped to look at Snevley. "Wait. Who posted bail? Certainly not you."

"Why not me?"

"Because you don't have that kind of money, and it's a selfless gesture so that lets you out on both scores."

He grabbed his chest and said, "I'm crushed."

"Bullshit."

He smiled, "Ok. It is true I did not personally put up the cash but I did persuade the paper that you were being set up. Needless to say, my ass is on the line here, and if it weren't for your attorney being a genius, you'd still be housed in your deluxe accommodations, stacks of cash notwithstanding."

I slid onto the hot leather seat. "I don't buy it. What are you getting out of this?"

"A crusade for truth, justice and what better be a Pulitzer-winning story."

"Exclusively for you, of course. Jesus. You're going to sleaze up this whole thing to sell a few papers aren't you?"

"This is bigger than selling a few papers, Babe," he said, flashing his victory grin.

"Call me 'Babe' one more time and you'll be shifting gears in this heap using a different part of your anatomy."

I never realized how complicated being innocent could be. Jail, extortion, abuse and all in the name of convincing everybody and their brother that I didn't kill DaKota. At least I don't think I did. Good God, am I doubting myself now? What next?

"Listen, I think I found your funeral mystery woman," Snevley said as we sped northward on Route one.

"Hmm?" I said, "Oh. Yeah. Carolyn. She was seeing my step-brother Pat but she's married so they called it off. Theoretically. What she was doing at the funeral and how she knew DaKota is still unanswered."

Snevley's jaw slackened in disappointment. "I'm out busting my hump for what reason? Why didn't you tell me about her?"

"Excuse the hell out of me," I said, my voice rising. "I've been a tad preoccupied lately what with rehab and getting arrested. What did you find out? How does she know DaKota?"

"Got me," he said in a petulant five-year-old tone I knew so well.

"Well what the hell good is that?"

"Hey, I don't see you paying me for any of this. It's not like I don't have other things to do in order to keep my job other than playing junior detective for you."

"That's your own problem." This wasn't going well. The guy just bailed me out yet all I felt was pissed-off at him. "I didn't ask you to do any of this."

"How about I turn around and take you back to jail? I'm sure the paper would love its money back."

"Up to you. I didn't ask you for that either."

I'm glad seat belts work because Snevley slammed the brakes hard and veered to the highway curb. Given recent events, my body seized in fear. Losing another foot was not part of my immediate plans.

"Jesus, asshat," I shouted.

"You want to walk home?" He said gripping the wheel and staring through the windshield.

"Gladly." I unbuckled, got out and limped up the highway. The Boxter inched its way along side me. Blaring horns, squealing brakes and creative obscenities blasted from vehicles whipping past us.

"Get back in here," he said.

"Bite me."

"Come on. You're twenty miles from home. You'll never make it."

"Get lost," I said, not even looking at him.

Any further comeback Snevley had was drowned out by the quick whoop of a siren from a state police car that now inched along behind the Boxter. I just smiled and kept walking.

In the middle of nowhere, on a three-lane highway, cars jetted by at sixty-five miles an hour as I gimped my way up the road. Who said I don't know how to live? I walked down the Whitehead Road exit ramp just to be off the highway and out of sight when Snevley and his police escort tooled by. After fifteen minutes of sweating from the heat and exertion, I plunked my ass on the curb to have a chat with Mom.

"You know if I had both legs, this would be a no brainer. I could easily make the fifteen miles from here to home, but no. You had to give me this little present. I've got to tell you, Mom, you better start dealing me some good cards quickly because this game is getting old, fast."

A beat-up muscle car covered in red bondo patches cruised by, honking wildly with a hairy male ass hanging out of the window. I just looked up at the sky. "Thanks. Thanks a lot."

I got my ass up to continue walking when I felt something vibrating against my thigh. Scratching it I realized it was my phone, set on vibrate.

"Where are you, Hon? I thought you were supposed to be home today?"

"Katrina. Feel like taking a ride?"

Twenty-Three

"Welcome back," Katrina said, standing next to me in my backyard, once we had dismounted her Harley. I made a mental note of how much I enjoyed riding on a bike and wondered if it was something I would ever be able to do on my own.

"Someone put a thousand more stairs in while I was away," I grumbled staring up the back stairs. Katrina started to help me ascend but I wanted to fly solo. Once at the top I was drenched and felt like passing out, but the thought of falling back down and having to climb it again kept me motivated. I felt like I was dragging a thousand pound weight, on top of which two blisters had formed on my residual leg so each step was a new experience in pain. I couldn't wait to get inside and take the damn thing off.

"I'm off to Whole Foods," Katrina yelled up, "be back in a few."

I opened the door; the place smelled musty even though Katrina had visited in my absence. The mail was sorted and piled neatly on the kitchen table. Eighty five percent junk mail and fifteen percent bills. Katrina had taken it upon herself to get me organized. A hand carved, blonde wood cane was lying on the table as well. A shaft of carved twists led to a two inch brass tip at one end, and at the other a polished redwood knob that fit perfectly in my hand. There was a post-it note stuck on the side that read, "Hope you don't need this but just in case…-Spag". I walked around the kitchen, the brass end of the cane thumping on the floor, and it felt wonderful to be able to take some of the pressure off my leg. The first thing I did was open up the windows, although the air outside offered nothing in the way of coolness.

In the back room sat my drum kit looking lonely and neglected. I tried a couple bass drum and hi-hat beats with the prosthesis.

"Okay. I can see this is going to take some doing." Most of the speed needed for those pedals comes from ankle and toe movement. Using my whole leg was going to slow things down significantly. So much for double bass rolls. Still, it felt good just to sit behind the kit. Thirsty, I went into the kitchen steeling myself against whatever new life forms had taken residence in my absence.

Katrina had gone into overdrive. I was greeted with bright whiteness and a twelve pack of Coke. I poured one in an ice filled glass and headed for the front porch. A hot breeze greeted me; the scent of earth and the trees felt new after so many weeks of industrial air. Sliding into the Adirondack chair, I undid the clasps and straps of my prosthesis and, with great relief, slid my foot off. At one point I was up to fourteen ply but was now back down to twelve. Dr. Duggan felt the swelling was just from pushing too hard.

"Get used to it," I said to the appendage. "This is home until your replacement arrives. Hope you like it. We've got great trees out front and the neighborhood is fairly quiet, except for me, as you've already discovered."

I stood my "foot" on the table next to me so it could look out into the neighborhood then pulled the stool up against the chair so I could keep my stump straight. All that physical therapy brainwashing had paid off.

Feeling more at peace than I had in weeks, I found myself wishing for someone to share it with. I'm not sure what I'm looking for anymore. My personal ad would be more equivocal than a priest in a boy's choir room. "P(ossibly)B(i)WF looking for either male or female depending on her mood". That's sure to attract every desperate lonely male and female for miles around. Just what I need, someone in need of severe care-taking. I can't even walk properly. Plus, the whole 'charged with murder' thing I'd have to keep secret at least until the second or third date. Hell, maybe I did do it and have just wiped it from my mind. Maybe I'll go back and turn myself in just to stop all this craziness. At least I'd eat regularly. Of course, I'd have to work out and get ripped so I don't end up as somebody's bitch. It's called taking the good with the bad, I guess. Maybe I could start an all girl prison band, "The Shank-MILFs", or "Bleeders Behind Bars". It might work.

From DaKota's porch below, wind chimes delicately sang. She was giving her approval to the possible band names.

The first waves of calm coursed through my muscles. It felt so good to be home, even with all the changes. Dorothy Gale knew damn well what she was talking about.

Footsteps tramped up the back stairs followed by a knock at the door. What now? Can't I get five minutes peace anymore?

"Come in," I shouted, not wanting to get up.

"Hello?" A female voice.

"On the porch," I called.

Susan Roche's head popped out of the doorway. "Oh," she said spying my foot.

"Susan. Grab a chair," I said pointing to the other Adirondack chair. The last time we spoke was to plant a wet one on her face after being called a pervert so this ought to be interesting, I thought. She was wearing a starched short sleeve white blouse, navy Capri pants and polished black slip-ons. She sat on the edge of the seat, back ramrod straight and her hands in her lap. She had trouble meeting my eyes when she spoke.

"I heard about the investigation, that the police believe you killed her."

"I'm fine after losing a foot and almost getting killed. Thanks for asking," I said, as tersely as possible.

Susan bristled at my comment but remained silent.

"Some of them believe I did it but I didn't," I said.

"I know what you told them. That you found her that morning when you came downstairs."

"That's true."

She smirked. "No. That's a lie. You were with her the night before."

Okay. That I was not expecting. My spine stiffened a bit.

"What makes you think that?" I asked.

"I saw you. Saw you go into her apartment. I was out back," her head nodded toward the back of the house.

"Spying on us. That's very neighborly of you." The peace I had felt minutes prior to Susan's arrival had evaporated.

"That's not the point."

"So you told the Police."

She smiled, faintly. "No. No, I haven't told the Police."

Algebra was never my strong subject but I can add two plus two as quickly as anybody.

"I'm impressed. You're a devious little shit underneath the Nancy Drew clothing. What do you want?"

"Get all your smart aleck remarks out while you can," she snapped back as if she was going to pounce. She visibly collected herself and continued. "Here is what is going to happen. Within the next thirty days, you will pack up and move out. On day thirty-one if you are still here I will go straight to the Police. If you are gone, you have my word that your little secret is safe."

"Until you think of something else to blackmail me with."

"It's up to you. Think about it." She rose and walked out. The back door gently clicked shut.

"Welcome home," I mumbled.

Twenty-Four

"The therapist will be right with you," said a long-haired, wide-eyed teen wearing skin tight jeans, size negative five. I wanted to force-feed her a cheese steak.

"Hey, what's up?" said a muscular pit bull heading my way. "I'm Bo."

"Why does that not surprise me? Let's get this over with."

Bo was a good physical therapist, which was a double edged sword. Good in that I knew he was going to get me healthy. Bad because he was going to kill me doing it.

After an hour, the muscles in my leg hurt like never before. I thought Carmine and Ivan were tough but they were lightweights.

"Here," he said handing me a twenty ounce bottle of water. "Finish this and drink at least one more bottle before the day is out. You've released a heavy dose of toxins into your body and they need to be flushed out. Sit here and rest for ten minutes or so. Did you bring a bathing suit?"

"Why would I do that?"

"Bring one next time. I want you to spend twenty minutes after each session in the hot tub."

"Yeah," I smiled. "Twist my arm. Do I really need a suit?"

He shrugged with a smirk. "It wouldn't bother me but some of the older folks might get a tad upset."

That night I was cursing Bo out because my legs, arms and back were throbbing from my eyes down. I downed three Aleve and flopped on my bed. Restless, I turned over and stared at the picture of DaKota and me that I had taken from her apartment. That felt like ages ago. I felt like I needed to apologize to her for not having the answers yet. I grabbed the frame, rolled over on my back and balanced the picture on my one raised knee. It wobbled a bit but stayed even though that little voice in my head was saying "It's going to faaaallllllllll......"

DaKota's eyes stared back at me. They were slightly down turned at the outer corners. I never picked up on that before. All of a sudden she seemed sad, even when smiling.

I jumped when the phone buzzed and even though I made a valiant effort to grab it mid-tumble, the frame toppled. I wasn't fast enough; it performed an Olympic trampoline bounce on the bed then crashed landed on the floor. I heard pieces of glass break away.

"Shit." I snatched the phone. Dammit this better be good. "Hello?"

Silence. Then a deep breath.

"Who's there?"

Another breath. Then the line went dead.

I do try to keep my paranoia to a minimum, but the call lit a faint spark. I checked my "Received Calls" list for the number and was not surprised to read "Restricted" for the most recent call. Hitting 'send' to call back or dialing star-six-nine was not going to get me anywhere so I put the phone down. Ten seconds later it buzzed again.

I reached out hesitantly. 'Restricted' appeared in the caller ID.

The same deep breath on the other end. I read somewhere that phone creeps thrive on panic, anger or any sort of emotional response from their victims. I tried to keep my voice even.

"Hello."

Another breath. Then, "Don't push it." Click. The voice was raspy, probably disguised, but unmistakably female.

A chill jittered through me. I looked at the clock; 11:23 PM. I could hear the faint chirp of crickets and cicadas outside, otherwise the air was deathly quiet. I wasn't sure if I should call someone. After fifteen minutes I remembered the broken picture on the floor. I rolled off the other side of the bed and made my way around to the scattered glass on the floor, picking up the larger pieces and heading for the kitchen to get a wet towel for the smaller bits.

The glass cleaned up, I pulled the contents out of the frame to make sure no jagged pieces remained. The backing and cardboard slid out, as did the picture of DaKota and me. What else slid out startled me - another picture of DaKota standing with a woman I didn't recognize. DaKota wore a simple black tank top but her friend modeled a deep emerald corset complete with black string lace running from top to bottom. Over that she wore a deep bronze coat turned up at the sleeves. Shoulder length ebony hair in multiple layers coupled with some serious red-eye from the camera flash and the whole gypsy image was complete. There was something about her that tugged at me but whatever it was stayed out of reach. The picture was taken at night, outdoors and it looked like they were standing on a deck or a porch, as the railing behind them was illuminated, along with what looked like dune grass in the distance. The beach? In the far left corner of the photo the porch railing took an abrupt ninety degree turn back toward the camera. There was a small plaque sitting on a post in the corner. One of those cute beach things owners stick around their houses. It had writing on it but I couldn't make it out. I needed a magnifying glass. A search through one of many junk drawers produced one of those cheesy, clear, plastic letter openers complete with a half inch wide magnifying glass for two year olds. It was almost impossible to see through all the scratches.

"Welcome…to…the…Pay Paynes. Welcome to the Paynes. But who are the Paynes?"

There was a house, somewhere, that belonged to The Payne family. That fact narrowed the possibilities down to a couple million Payne's living in the country. I hadn't noticed it before, but a last look through the magnifying glass emphasized something that made my stomach lurch.

"What the fuck?"

The woman's face. Even without the bruises and with the dark hair, I knew it was Carolyn.

Twenty-Five

I bolted upright in bed at the sound of a large metallic crash, not knowing if it was real or if I dreamt it. A few seconds later, more sounds of metal scraping and that wonderfully soothing beeping sound signaling a truck in reverse. The clock read ten fifteen. I jumped from the bed, grabbed Spag's cane and hopped into the kitchen. Through the back window, I saw large tire tracks in the grass leading up to a large green dumpster, the chipped paint fighting the rust for space.

"It all goes," I heard someone yell. I tied a robe around me and went out on the balcony. Noel Greenstein, the building's landlord was shouting up at the house. To whom I'm not sure.

"Hey!" I yelled. "What's going on?"

"Ah, Ms. Lennox. I got the okay from the police to move everything off the second floor."

"What do you mean 'move everything off'?"

"I need to re-rent. You want this should be a shrine for all time? I'm losing money. I need new tenants."

Move it out? That felt way too final. "What about her parents? Aren't they going to clean it out?"

He shook his head. "I talked with the Mother. She said just throw it all out."

The sentimental bitch. I bopped down the stairs. Two high school football linebackers were starting to walk out onto DaKota's balcony and heave a sofa over the edge slamming into the dumpster on impact. I got past them and went to the back rooms. They would be busy with the kitchen and living room for a while. The second bedroom was still a shambles. My instinct was to grab it all and sift through it but reason stopped me. Did I really want to put myself through all that? Was there anything here I really wanted? I looked at all the clothes still hanging in the closet, lifeless remnants of DaKota.. I knew I couldn't bring myself to wear any of it without feeling guilty or just plain weirded out, yet it was just wrong to throw it all away. Somehow I knew she wouldn't want that. I grabbed everything, hangers and all, and tossed it over my shoulder. The shoes I left there. I hobbled back upstairs and heard the boys on the landing below me. I looked down and caught them looking up through the open stairs at my naked ass, among other things. Pervs. I dumped DaKota's clothes unceremoniously in the living room, then I got dressed, foot and all, and went back downstairs. The boys seemed disappointed to see me with clothes on. Tough shit. My trips up and down the stairs continued as I carried jackets, sweaters, jeans and shirts.

Passing Greenstein in the hallway I said, "What about the furniture? Don't you want to donate it somewhere?"

"Who has time for that? The painters are coming in two days. Everything goes."

What a waste.

Upstairs, I made my way to the bathroom and looked in the mirror. The horror that stared back was, well, horrible. I hadn't been paying too much attention to my appearance lately and apart from blotchy skin and bags under the eyes, my hair had grown out enough that the green side was now red and green. I ran my hands through my hair in a vain attempt at instant styling but nothing was coming together.

That's it, I thought, time for a change. After a quick bath, I grabbed a pair of scissors from the kitchen that looked reasonably clean. I stood in front of the bedroom mirror and held my breath.

By the time I was done the green was gone. Actually, by the time I was done most of everything was gone. I thought it looked fairly hellacious for an instant hatchet job but it saved me a couple hundred bucks for the same results at a salon.

"Damn," I muttered, standing naked in my bedroom and dripping on the floor. Staring into my predominantly empty dresser drawers, and save for one pair of neon pink silk thong panties that just never fit right, I realized there was no putting it off. The Laundromat, scum central. In the bathroom closet sat my garbage bag-hamper engorged with putrid laundry into which I stuffed the dirty clothes previously flung around my bedroom floor.

Staring a DaKota's clothes scattered on my bed, I toyed briefly with putting on something of hers. The jeans would not fit without rupturing some vital organ. I tried on a couple blouses but each sent a shiver through me. It wasn't time yet. Forgoing the thong, I made do going commando with a pair of far too tight jeans shorts and a single remaining t-shirt with a frayed collar and a faded Sabian cymbal logo. As long as I didn't bend over and flash my ass cheeks, I was set.

There are two options while in a laundromat, watching soapy water splash against the round washer window or watching the paint peel off the walls. In an attempt to forestall major boredom I hauled my ancient laptop along for the ride just for something to do.

Inside the Filth-O-Mat, the floor looked sort of clean but if I stood in one place too long my boot and plastic foot stuck to it. It was national laundry day. It had to be. The place was wall-to-wall people and screaming rug rats, most of whom were screaming at each other in Spanish. Princeton has a huge Hispanic population all cloistered in one spot and surrounded by the rich white neighborhoods. Its Princeton's dirty little secret. All the help are corralled and kept out of sight.

An air conditioner hung precariously over the back door with a sign reading "Ou of Ord", the missing letters having long since worn away. Even if it had been operating, the air from that small unit stood no chance against the thousand degree heat of the weather plus the inferno from the clothes dryers. I found one open machine that looked to be mostly disease and dirt free and piled in a white load.

Throwing heaps of colored clothes in a second washer, Nana Lennox suddenly flashed into my head, the image of her stationed in the basement doing laundry. She was forever finding my treasures because she searched pants pockets thoroughly prior to washing and found shells, rubber bands and any other junk I collected through my daily scavenging. Becoming more accustomed to paying attention to random thoughts Mom put in my head, I tossed through the clothes already in the washer, searching all the pants pockets. A whole lot of nothing, until…

I pulled two things from my black jeans pocket: the jump drive from DaKota's apartment and a scrap of paper with the numbers from Pat's restaurant.

I crumpled the scrap of paper and tossed it in the trashcan next to the washers, and then fed the machines with coin. Once they started their sloshing, I booted up my laptop, a beat-up relic with peace symbol stickers on the outside, and plugged in the jump drive. Nothing but picture files with no names appeared in the file listing, just some random number dot 'jpg' for a file name. I double clicked the first one.

What flashed on the screen caught me off guard, I stopped breathing and my legs felt boneless.

Staring back at me was a close up of DaKota's face, half smiling, taken from inside a vehicle. It was taken from her right side so I assumed she was driving.

There were a few more of essentially the same thing; pictures where she was facing the camera and other shots of her staring out what I assumed to be the windshield.

The next two were taken from the same place but at a wider angle revealing tan leather seats that looked expensive. DaKota was wearing a cherry red tank top that highlighted the blush on her cheeks.

I clicked another file.

"Ho-ly shit," I said out loud. I knew I was drawing stares from my laundry mates but didn't care. The picture was taken from the outside looking in on the driver's side. DaKota was still at the driver's seat but she was flashing that killer smile out the window at the photographer. The angle was far enough back to see that it truly was an expensive car. It was a Jaguar. And it was sky blue.

There were four more of essentially the same picture, but the last one showed DaKota staring directly into the camera, lips parted just a bit. I knew what that look was reserved for. I had to turn away from the monitor to catch my breath. Damn her. In my head I knew that being jealous was stupid. All this was before she and I got together. My insides didn't believe what my head was saying. This hurt, as if I had walked in on them under the sheets.

I stared at the screen. All I heard was the hum of the computer. A voice was telling me to get up, walk out, go home, close the door and turn on the TV. Isolation sounded damn good right now, but I knew that's not how it would go. A cold drop of sweat slithered between my shoulder blades sending an involuntary shiver across my body.

Eight jpgs remained. I wanted to see them but I didn't, because deep down I knew what I would find as much as I tried to deny it. I took a deep breath and tried to block out the sloshing and spinning of the machines, looking for some direction, hoping Mom would give me a sign. The list of unopened files stared back at me. Maybe if I snuck up on them slowly, I thought, and changed the screen view from file details to thumbnails.

The first thing I noticed is that the previous pictures were now reduced to little DaKotas smiling back at me. The next thing was that the remaining eight were considerably darker; I thought I saw outlines of people. Two people. Shit. Two naked people. I double clicked one of the darker pictures.

They were not hard-core, more porno-chic with the soft lighting and moody atmosphere. It was definitely DaKota, it was definitely Carolyn as the witchy brunette from the frame, and they were definitely more than good friends. I heard DaKota's voice say "significantly older." This must be her, which was cold comfort against the ache thundering through me.

I thought two of the shots were quite beautiful once I was able to detach for a few seconds. The one that caught my eye over all the others was taken in a mirror. DaKota stood in front of the woman who had one arm draped between DaKota's breasts, her hand landing on her waist. In the other hand a remote release cable for the camera. The two of them, naked, were staring into the mirror with the camera off to the left. Nearby table lamps provided an orange glow around them. In the back was a low dresser with a larger attached mirror. The effect was striking, hundreds of replicated images pushing out to a vanishing point in the distance.

There was a palpable intensity to the picture. They were both staring right at me. I felt drawn into them. They were both beautiful and in an odd way, perfectly matched. She definitely looked older than DaKota by ten or fifteen years.

"Mommy, that lady's naked!" I hadn't noticed the two preadolescent Hispanic kids hanging over my shoulder. I closed the laptop with a heavy blush under the angry glares of a couple Moms who were screaming something in Spanish, probably something like 'get away from that white devil'.

Anger and longing were duking it out in my brain so I walked out of the Laundromat to get some air. A warm breeze caused the leaves to softly rub together, a late summer sound. I wondered if all this had a point, if it would ever end. Leaning against the building, I let the sun soak into my skin, not the smartest move for a redhead but right now it felt good.

Who is Carolyn and what the hell is she up to? It felt like I was looking for two different people, the dark-haired DaKota partner and the blonde Pat girl-toy. The married girl-toy. Had she been married when she and

DaKota were together? I needed to find her, but everyone connected to her was either dead or missing. Shit, I didn't even have a last name. How the hell was I going to find her? The only thing I had going was the "Payne" sign. Somewhere in the world there was a house with that sign. Maybe that was her last name? Maybe not. With my recent good fortune, her last name was probably something more unique like Smith or Jones. Someone at the restaurant might know, even though she and Pat were keeping it a secret, he had to tell somebody besides me. With luck, somebody would have a last name or better still a phone number would turn up but I knew that was a long shot.

I slumped against the building, my hands in my pockets. A car packed with laughing high school kids and thumping bass lines blasting from the windows passed by the laundromat. How easy life was then. All that mattered was music and a ride, none of this life complicating shit that never seems to end; for the kids in the car adult responsibilities were an eternity away. My thoughts wandered back to high school, threading through classes, friends, teachers and romances.

I don't know if this happens to you but when my mind drifts on about inconsequential trivia, that's the time when synapses that need to come together usually do. No amount of force could have made it happen otherwise.

"Shit!" I screamed and ran back in the Laundromat. A man in green coverall was standing next to the washers, just starting to pull the green bag out of the trashcan.

"Stop! Stop!" He looked at me as if he were deaf. "Halto." My Spanish is severely lacking.

He stopped moving and I tried to grab the bag from his hands. He pulled back in a whirl of Spanish invective, a United Nations tug of war ensued without the benefit of a translator. Women in the place were gathering their children around them as the crazy white women appeared to have lost it and would pounce unexpectedly like a rampaging bull.

I stopped pulling and put up my hands in surrender. The man was still cursing at me, I was fairly certain. I sat, put away my laptop and waited for my laundry to be done. The man closed up the bag and four others that were in separate bins and headed out the back door. The sounds from behind the back door of the dumpster lid slamming down made me smile.

Twenty-Six

I was fairly certain that what I was looking for was in one of the four green trash-bags I pilfered from the dumpster. After three round trips on the back stairs to get the bags and the laundry inside, my leg was screaming for a break. I removed the prosthesis then spread a sacrificial sheet on the living room floor and ceremoniously dumped the garbage from the first bag on it. The contents were not too skeevy, mostly empty soda cans and sandwich wrappers, a snot-rag here and there but that was okay. Newspapers, plastic wrappers, a wad of something I hoped was only dryer lint, but no small crumpled piece of paper with numbers in red ink. I shoved all the crap back in the first bag and was in the process of unloading the second when there was a knock at the door.

Sure. Why not. Nothing like having folks over with a trash-strewn living room. It was sure to make a lasting impression.

I cracked the door using my body to make an attempt at blocking the view. "Detective Douglas. To what do I owe the honor? Let me guess. It's the annual Policeman's Ball and you're selling Girl Scout cookies. No thanks. I'm trying to cut down."

His hand came up quickly to keep me from closing the door. I thought about making an issue of it, but Douglas was half-decent to me on that wonderful day DaKota was killed and I had no cause to give him the same attitude reserved for Gralewski.

"Mind if I ask you a couple questions?"

"Look, the investigation is over, you guys already have me facing murder charges what else could you possibly need?"

"It's just that I've never seen anyone carry four loaded garbage bags *into* their apartment before, so curiosity got the better of me."

"How did you…have you been spying on me?"

"Let's just say I happened to be in the neighborhood."

"Do I call my lawyer now and have you sued for harassment or wait until morning?"

"Okay, okay. Can I at least come in?"

I hesitated, staring into his face. It was a nice face, smooth with just a trace of crow's feet at the corner of each dark eye. But Simon Cowell has a nice face too. What the hell. How much worse could it get? I pushed open the door and let him inside. He stopped at the entrance to the living room, surveying the bag of trash piled on the sheet.

He looked at me and was about to say something when I threw a hand in the air to stop him, and then hopped back to the garbage heap.

"I threw away a piece of paper when I was at the Laundromat that I really didn't mean to throw away." I told him about my interaction with Mr. Maintenance Man.

"Must be something pretty important," he said, still eyeing the garbage suspiciously.

"No, I rummage through trash on a lark. I'm thinking of making it a full time hobby. Now, why the hell are you stalking me?"

"No choice. Detective Gralewski was none too happy about your making bail and convinced our Captain that you were a flight risk. So I got the night babysitting shift."

I knelt back on the sheet and resumed my picking through the trash. "Well if you're here you might as well be useful. Get down here and look."

He did a double take. "You can't be serious."

"Got anything better to do?"

"Yeah I could be home enjoying a bowl of Jambalaya, a beer and my wife. Not necessarily in that order." I let the silence hang. He finally asked, "So what are we looking for?"

After I told him he started lifting things out of the pile with two fingers as if each piece might leap out and bite him. A half an hour later I had refilled the second bag and dumped out the third.

I sighed. "I'm starting to feel really stupid."

"Only now? I passed that feeling twenty minutes ago."

"Tell me something," I asked, "what are you doing here? I mean I'm the bad guy, you're the good guy. Aren't you supposed to be making my life hell? If Gralewski were here he sure would be. So, what are you doing here?"

"Look," he said pushing off his knees and sitting on the floor, "I may be out of my mind but I've done most of the interviewing and background work on you. I've talked to neighbors, your band and other merchants in town. I know you had drug issues in the past but appear to be working that through. I checked your phone records. Even though you live here and the vic...um, Ms. Gibson lived downstairs, there were lots of phone calls sent and received from her number up until two weeks before she died, but not a single call after that. On the surface the evidence and motives are not in your favor, but how this whole thing went down, it isn't you. At least it's not the 'you' everyone perceives. But I don't think you're that good a con."

I was torn between wanting to give him a hug and hook him up to a lie detector. After Gralewski, knowing a police type who didn't think I was a complete lunatic was nice. Letting my guard down completely, however, was another story.

"What are you, an amateur psychologist?" I asked.

He shook his head. "Don't need to be. I married a real one who also happens to provide criminal profile consulting for the North ROC in Philly."

"Mind translating that into English?"

He smiled. "The north side regional operations command of the Philly police force. It's a fancy name for the homicide detectives in the city's north side."

"So Mrs. Detective Douglas thinks I'm not the criminal type."

"That may be a bit too broad, but from what I've told her about the case and you, which is also subject to question, she has doubts that you would react the way the killer did."

The knots inside me eased ever so slightly. "She's a smart lady. So how about you? Do you still think I did it?" I murmured.

"The actual killing? No. I'm not ruling out you were involved. I'd be a total idiot if I threw all the possibilities out of the window based on a hunch. But Sabina is rarely wrong, as she will gladly point out."

After fifteen minutes of silently sifting through more garbage Douglas held a scrap of paper in the air and said, "Is this it?"

"You might actually be a good detective after all," I said looking at the red numbers on the paper.

I looked again at the red numbers again and counted. One…two…three….ten numbers. As I suspected. Ten numbers. A phone number. Carolyn's phone number? Possibly, but wouldn't Pat have it memorized or at least programmed in his phone? I dialed the sequence on my cell.

"The number you have reached is not in service…"

"Damn. Douglas, I need you to look up a phone number for me."

"How do you know it's a phone number?"

I handed him the slip of paper and said, "Ten numbers. What else could it be? The first three numbers though, 484, don't sound like an area code."

"Western Philly up through Bucks County," He answered without hesitation.

"Since when?"

"Do I look like I work for the phone company?"

"Asshat," I said with a smirk. "Can I get arrested for calling you that?" I asked after realizing what I just said.

Douglas smiled. "It's a misdemeanor but I'll let it slide. This time."

Twenty-Seven

My dreams were filled with tornados, long thin black fingers scratching against a sick greenish sky, a heavenly claw ripping the ground's skin. I headed in their direction on a train, watching them in the distance through the windows. I have never seen one for real but my subconscious was in control, composing all the out of control aspects of my life into vivid apparitions of violent destructive force.

I woke at 7:30 in the morning with all those loose ends spinning in my brain, and my nostrils filled with the scent of DaKota. I had simply pushed her clothes to one side of the bed rather than find a spot for them or take them to a clothing drop box. During the night, I had rolled into the pile and woke up clutching a couple shirts and sweaters.

I rolled over, not having the energy to crawl out of bed, and stared at the ceiling and let my mind wander. Maybe our relationship was just a…convenience for DaKota. We never spoke about being a couple; we just kind of were. We never talked about marriage or long term commitments. It was always day by day. I guess that was my fault but it never seemed all that important. Jesus. What else didn't I know?

To shake the funk, I eventually stumbled into town heading for Grace and Alpha Bagel, where it was still possible to get just plain coffee flavored coffee, a bagel and a newspaper. It was more like an extension of my own kitchen, fortunately there was more food there than at my house. Grace, the owner, gave me a perfunctory wave from behind the cash register as I opened the refrigerator case and grabbed a Coke.

There was no place to sit at Grace's as the store was just wide enough for a service counter with coffee urns, baskets of fruit, goodies and enough floor space for a single line of buyers to queue up at the register. Grace had a single wooden stool in front of a metal counter that was part of the sink but doubled as her bill paying desk. I sat until she freed herself from the front of the store. She was a small, slender Grecian Goddess who did just enough business to stay open and pay the bills. She peered over her Ben Franklin's when she reached me.

"So let me see," she said in a Motherly voice with a kick to it. I had not seen her since the accident but there was no doubt she knew all about it, as there was very little in town Grace didn't know.

I stuck my leg out and pulled up my pant leg to allow a complete inspection. There wasn't anything to see except a plastic molded foot, a steel rod and a sock covered cuff. She nodded and said "um-hum".

"Here. You sit. I'm fine," I said getting up from the stool.

She grabbed my shoulders and gently eased me back down. "I'll tell you when you're fine. Sit." She returned a couple minutes later with a lightly toasted and buttered cinnamon raisin bagel. Since the hospital I'd been stuffing my face with comfort food. Mashed potatoes, cupcakes and Ben and Jerry's Cherry Garcia with all of it going straight to my ass. The bagel was also on that list. If I didn't get back to exercising and drumming soon I'd look like Violet Beauregard, just paint me blue and roll me down the street.

"How's business?" I said between mouthfuls.

"Yesterday, great. Today, lousy. Tomorrow, who knows? I just keep doing what I do every day. Sometimes lots of people show up, sometimes they walk by like the store has a condemned sign in the window. Who can tell? What about you? What is this crazy business you're mixed up in? I'm not liking what I'm hearing. You lose a friend, God rest her soul, and then you lose a foot. This is bad business."

"I wish I knew. I really do."

"What do the police say?"

"Officially? They're working on it. I do know that what happened to me wasn't an accident. The car was tampered with. As for DaKota, there is something, or was something, going on between her and a woman named Carolyn. The odd thing is, Carolyn was also seeing my brother, Pat, who no one has seen lately and I assume is hiding out somewhere from Carolyn's husband."

"Of course it's no use me telling you to let the police handle it because you are the only one who can figure all this out, right?" she said giving me a hug then holding me at arm's length. "You're exhausted."

Just saying that made my shoulders slump. She was right, I just didn't want to admit it. I sort of fell back into her arms.

"I'm exhausted," I breathed into her shoulder. I closed my eyes and wished to stay right where I was forever. "Thank you for the food in the hospital. It saved my life."

After a few seconds she patted my back and pulled away.

"Here," she said digging in her purse and producing a key on a brown leather key ring. "Take Gregory's car."

"I can't do that. He'd kill me if it got a scratch on it, plus I don't even have a driver's license on me."

"He won't know and I know you'll take care of it. It's just sitting there and I don't always remember to turn it over like he asked me to so you'd be doing me a favor." Gregory, her son, was currently on a tour of duty in Afghanistan. Maybe the car was a constant reminder of his location. "It will help you get around and don't tell me getting around is easy."

"I love you," I said hugging her again.

"I better go lend a hand. There's quite a line brewing. Look, go home. Rest. Take some time to heal, and I don't mean your foot. Let the police handle this."

She kissed my forehead and strode up front. I knew she only said those things to give herself the necessary ammunition to scold me later after I didn't follow her advice.

Gregory's car was a stick. "Oh this will be interesting," I muttered getting behind the wheel of a refurbished 1967 fire engine red Volkswagen Beetle Convertible with tan top. I pumped the clutch a couple times; it felt odd, not unlike first sitting behind the drum kit after leaving rehab. I started it up, shifted into reverse and almost died from whiplash as it bucked and stalled. Pumping the clutch was easy. Getting the feel of where the clutch engaged was something different. It took a couple more tries and two more thoroughly embarrassing red light stalls to get the hang of it.

I think Grace wanted me to take this car for another reason. It was the first time I'd used my new apparatus for something practical other than walking. The truth was I really did like this car. Sure it wasn't luxurious but it was hot in that *look-at-me-I'm-a-hot-chick-driving-this-hot-car* way, which was never a bad thing in my book as long as I was the hot chick in question. If it was some other chick driving by I'm sure I'd make some snarky comment out of sheer jealousy.

While I was out, I decided to start rebuilding the pieces of my life left scattered on the turnpike. Between the bank, DMV and the library, five hours had flown by. Once home, I took a bath then put on my blue running shorts and an old white button down shirt that belonged to Snevley at one time. Just about the only worthwhile thing that came out of that relationship. The summer humidity had returned and I put the standing oscillating fan on high to try to cool the place off. I flopped down on the sofa, turned on the TV and slipped a copy of "*Casablanca*" in the DVD player. I half paid attention until Rick took the letters of transit from Ugate, and then turned it off. Opening the fridge, I realized I had consumed just about everything Katrina had brought for me my first day back so grocery shopping was now added to my list of things to do. I pulled the last dill pickle from the jar and scarfed that, putting the empty jar in the sink. I walked down the hall to my bedroom, realized I had no purpose for being there, and then went back to the kitchen to grab a Coke and a handful of pretzels. Plunking down on the couch in the living room I just stared out the front window at the humid gray day.

My brain spun with questions I couldn't answer but I couldn't focus on any one thing long enough to make any headway. Even when the phone started yelling Pythonisms at me I didn't want to answer it. I wanted to talk to no one but I couldn't sit still. Like Grace said, just rest awhile without any intrusion. I guiltily checked the voicemail after it stopped ringing.

"It's Katrina. Geoff and I wanted to know if you were up for playing. I know it's not going to be easy right off but we thought the sooner the better. Spag is chomping at the bit as well. We still have The Phang tomorrow night and the gig at South 26 in Philly this Saturday. Let me know what you're up for. Call me, Hon."

The band. Did I even care anymore?

Twenty-Eight

Around midnight, I slumped onto the decrepit brown couch backstage at the Phang. Drained and pissed from a really sucky one hour set, I alternately chomped on orange slices and chugged water from a gallon jug, thinking that maybe it was time to give the whole band thing up. DaKota was gone, I couldn't play for shit and I just didn't have the energy to give a rat's ass.

"Not bad for the first time out in awhile," Spag said coming into the room with the rest of the band.

"You guys were fine. I couldn't do dick."

"Give it time," said Katrina. "We still have to rearrange some of the songs for only a single guitar. It will take practice and patience."

"Rearrange them for one guitar and a lame drummer. That'll make for a great sound."

"It really didn't sound bad," Geoff piped in.

I shook my head. "I don't know. It'll never be the same. Everything I tried to do tonight sucked. I clammed every song and blew out three sticks. I sounded like..."

Geoff cut me off. "A one-legged drummer?"

I snapped at him. "Not fucking funny, G-man."

"Chill. Cut yourself some slack. For not practicing since the accident what did you expect?"

He was right but I didn't want to hear it. I wanted someone to make it all better and have all the bad stuff go away.

Back home, I washed the stink off my carcass, set the bedroom fans on high and passed out.

I awoke the next morning with DaKota, once again, in my nostrils, making my stomach clench with want and sadness. A voice in my head, which had to be Mom, told me it was time to get DaKota out of my bed. I piled all her scattered clothes in the living room. My logic was that by having the clothes there, I would be forced to look at them, which would give me the push to get them out of the house altogether. I stubbornly tried to take everything from the bedroom in one trip which left several items sliding off the pile and onto the hallway floor. I went back to pick up the clothes I dropped, one of items being a denim jacket, and as I picked it up a white business sized envelope fell out of it. The outside was blank but it was stuffed with a dozen or so folded pages of expensive looking bonded stationery.

A quick scan of the pages caught my breath in my throat. "Oh my God..." I said aloud. This had to be something the Police missed when they searched the place or I would have heard about it.

Right then, my plans for the day were set. I was heading to Connecticut.

Hurling in Gregory's car was not the most polite thing to do but as I made my way up the Turnpike for the first time since the funeral and the accident, that's what my stomach was suggesting. A morbid curiosity had me clogging the ninety mile an hour left lane by strolling along at sixty-five trying to spot the exact place of the wreck, and as I got closer, I almost rear-ended someone because I wasn't paying attention. Like I needed another reason to sweat. I let it go and sheepishly stayed to the right for the rest of the trip.

New Canaan Road in Wilton, Connecticut is one of those quaint, back country two-laners overgrown with ancient trees hiding an arrogant amount of money; one trip to Google maps confirms this fact. The telltale sign to look for are driveways that extend into the overgrowth that keep the houses hidden. Trailer parks are an unheard of commodity 'round these parts. The Holt-Gibson driveway fit the mold perfectly. The curved driveway led me through huge maple and elm trees that eventually opened up on a colonial monster consisting of a series of white clapboard buildings attached to one another, each topped with a weather-veined cupola. The compound perched on the shore of a mini-lake with ducks and two white swans. They probably paid to have the swans trained to stay put. All this was so not DaKota, at least the DaKota I thought I knew. How the hell did she survive all...this?

Not ten seconds after ringing the bell I was greeted by a familiar and unwelcome sight.

"Oh great," I murmured.

"What do *you* want?"

Filling the front door was my good buddy Nicholas from the funeral parlor, replete in casual wear and blue blazer that bulged slightly on one side. I thought it best to play it straight as something told me my usual wit and good manners were not going to help me.

"I need to speak to Mrs. Gibso…um..Mrs. Holt-Gibson. Please." Okay. So I was laying it on.

"Are you expected?" Remember Lurch from The Addams Family? Yeah. That voice.

"Honestly, no. This is kind of a spur of the moment thing but I need to ask her a very important question. I don't even have to come in. I'll just stay right here."

"That's right. You will stay right here," he said closing the door. It wasn't so much a suggestion as a command.

Up close, the outside of the house needed a paint job. I peeled a piece of cracked and curling paint off the door jamb, crumbled it up and let the flakes fall like latex snow to the flagstone porch.

The door swung open, "Follow me," he said with a look of complete disapproval.

Some houses are filled with warmth and life regardless of their decoration. This house was stone cold from room to room, each being expensively appointed and furnished but without an ounce of life. The wood floors, oriental rugs and expensive oils hanging throughout held no sense of happiness, history or purpose. They were truly inanimate things.

An expansive glass-enclosed solarium looked out upon levels of lush green backyard. DaKota's Mom sat in the far corner in a Rattan love seat staring out the window, a cigarette burning in one hand resting on her knee, and a half empty rocks glass on the table next to her. As I approached her I looked to see what she was watching and saw a group of men on a shaded patio next to the built-in pool. I recognized Mr. Gibson in a tacky Hawaiian shirt and khaki shorts. Three other men wore severe blue suits.

"What did you want to ask me?" Her voice was controlled, slow, trying desperately to keep her speech from slurring.

"Was DaKota adopted?"

It took a second but a grave smile curled the corners of her mouth. She picked up the tumbler, held it in the air and jingled the half melted cubes. Nicholas took the glass from her and left.

"DaKota," she said, as if spitting something unpleasant to the floor. "What an absurd name." Still facing the window, her eyelids fluttered closed.

The silence hung between us until Nicholas returned with a replenished glass and placed it on the table without the woman acknowledging his existence. I repeated my question.

"What difference does it make?" she said with a deep sigh and took a deep gulp from the tumbler.

"I found paperwork in a jacket of hers from an internet site that helps people find their birth mother or father. Why would she have this if she wasn't adopted? Did she ever find her real mother?"

Another deep breath. "I have no idea."

"But you know who it is, don't you? You could have told her. Why didn't you?"

"I was never asked," she said. I couldn't tell if it was anger or pain that shone in her eyes. Maybe it was a combination of both. "You see we didn't speak much the last couple years she was here. She was a difficult teenager, kept to herself. Wanted no part of all the things I could give her. She turned away from me. As a child, I gave her everything, the best schools, the best tutors, new clothes, trips to Europe. Things most children can't even dream about. She wanted for nothing. Then the teen years hit and she withdrew, shut me out of her life, after everything I'd done for her."

My spine stiffened has her words sunk in, words I had heard my own Mother speak. "You didn't do it for her. At least be honest about it."

Her eyes shot me with a cold glare. "What could you possibly know about it?" she said and took another shot from the glass.

I knew denial when I saw it. Hell, I'd mastered the art during my drug days. The booze was just a crutch to keep the denial intact, keeping whatever pain that plagued her mind at bay temporarily. No matter which way she turned, sober or using, she was going to walk through a lot of hurt to get to the other side. This is when the program tells me to pray for this person to have everything that I have, to put aside all the anger and resentments.

Her eyes glistened as they returned to gaze outside, she sat silent and motionless. The house was starting to make sense. Lots and lots of stuff meant to fill the void of an emotionless existence, a quiet hell for anyone to experience as a child. I remained lost in my thoughts of DaKota, trying to imagine her spirit, trying to conform to a life without fun, happiness, and the closeness of a Mom and Dad that genuinely gave a shit. I could relate to some degree but certainly not to the level that must have been the Gibson household.

I snapped out of my reverie as a wave of sadness coursed through me. Mrs. Holt-Gibson was still gazing out the window, her eyes glistening with tears. She hadn't moved a muscle which, suddenly, seemed odd.

"Hello?" As I stepped closer I realized tears weren't showing at all. Her eyes had rolled back in her head, the outside light reflecting off bloodshot whites.

"Are you okay?" I said, gently shaking her shoulder.

Nicholas suddenly body-checked me out of the way and scooped the comatose woman in his arms as if she weighed no more than a down pillow. Her head lolled to the side and rested on his shoulder. "It's time for you to leave," he said and carried her from the room.

I followed Nicholas back into the house. He was murmuring something I couldn't hear as he carried her upstairs. I took a deep breath and looked around. If there was any sign that DaKota had once lived here there was no immediate evidence. There were no personal pictures or mementos anywhere. Sure it was set up like House Beautiful but had I stumbled upon it without knowing where I was, identifying the owners would be near impossible.

For some insane reason the thought entered my head that Mr. Gibson should know what's going on with his wife. Reaching the table out back, everyone fell silent but only the three guests glanced in my direction.

"Sorry to interrupt but Mrs. Gibson needs some help."

"What are you doing here?" he said without looking at me. "We are busy at the moment."

"Your wife just had some sort of seizure. I thought you might..."

He snapped, "Is Nicholas there?"

"Yes, but..."

"It's being handled," he said.

Across the table, a stocky but fit man with a shaved head was staring at me, or rather staring at my chest. "Is this?" he said pointing the large cigar in his hand at me.

"Yes," said Mr. Gibson.

"I see," said the man bringing the cigar to his lips. The way his gaze bore into me I might as well have been naked.

"What are you looking at, asshat?"

He took a puff on the cigar then rolled it around in his mouth, his eyes slowly inching their way up my body until they met mine. He wore a starched, white button-down shirt with the initials "LHJ" monogrammed on the sleeve. "I'd watch your manners if I were you," he said returning the cigar to his mouth.

"Said the man sucking on a big brown dick," I said with more than a touch of anger.

The two other gentlemen jumped at my remark but they were waved back in their chairs by cigar-man who gave me a greasy smile.

"You're a hell of a guy Gibson," I said. "You really don't give a shit about anybody or anything do you? Between a self absorbed dwarf for a dad and a drunk mom it must have been a swell house for DaKota to grow up in. Pretty sad, especially since she was adopted in the first place. My guess is that you're shooting blanks or possibly can't get it up to begin with."

Grabbing a cell phone off the table he pressed a button and set it back down.

"Calling your hired goons to come get me? That's okay. I can't stomach being here much longer. I'll leave you little boys to your super-secret conversation."

I met Nicholas coming down the stairs responding to the electronic call of his master. "I'm leaving, I'm leaving" I said. As I reached the door I turned back to him and asked quietly, "Is Mrs. Holt-Gibson okay?" For a brief second his face softened as his gaze looked toward the stairs.

"Yes. She is resting."

"I'm sorry." I really didn't know what else to say.

Twenty-Nine

I was tired and sore, even before driving to Philly and playing a forty-five minute set.

The South Street block looked like a war zone; the only lights shining in the darkness belonged to South 26 Upstairs. The boarded up store fronts surrounding the club all had signs that announced "Improving Philadelphia. A Joint Venture Project between the City of Philadelphia Planning Commission and FamilyFirst Development." What a load of crap. It should have read MoneyFirst Development. The rumor was the whole block was going to be leveled to make room for the city's first casino.

South 26 Upstairs was a black-walled, hundred foot long, six inch wide, venue on the second floor above a standard Philly bar complete with three pool tables and shredded dartboards barely visible through the cigarette smoke. Of course there was no elevator so all the gear had to be carried up a flight of stairs. At least I didn't have to make six trips lugging an entire drumkit. One of the benefits of playing some clubs is that all the bands on the bill share a house drum kit, so each drummer just brings cymbals and sticks. The downside was playing on a beat-up kit, well past its prime, with foot pedals having little spring action, drumheads covered in duct tape to muffle the sound and stripped hardware, especially hi-hat stands, that any self-respecting scrap metal dealer would reject. Such was the case tonight. The first couple songs were god-awful; I felt totally out of sync. My new foot was not cooperating on the rickety hi-hat or bass pedal.

After the set, Spag nursed a beer sitting at the bar while I gulped a large glass of water and a 6 ounce fountain Coke, that was more seltzer than syrup and cost seven dollars. Geoff was supervising the equipment change on stage to make sure none of his stuff got ripped off and Katrina was explaining the metaphysics of being an asshole to two half-drunk guys attempting to entice her into wild sexual escapades.

The sound guy was blasting The Ramones through the sound system while the next band set up, four guys dressed in Ivy League tweeds calling themselves Dirty Sperm. It was sure to be total crap but club etiquette held that sticking around for the next band was the sociable thing to do.

"Not bad. Better than last time, anyway," Spag said yelling and leaning close to me.

I nodded in semi-agreement. I really wasn't in the mood to have a conversation that required screaming over the sound system. I could feel the onset of a headache reaching out to grab me from deep inside. Dirty Sperm screeched into their first song in a cacophony of sludge that was designed to sever spinal nerves and sterilize small animals. I looked at Katrina who was pretending to hurl by jamming her finger down her throat, offering her critical review of either the band's performance or the half-drunk guys, I didn't know which.

In the midst of the roar I felt a deep, dull thud shake the floor, which I would have taken to be part of the noise coming from the stage if glasses and bottles from the bar had not toppled and smashed on the floor. The band stopped mid belch. Screams and raised shouts came from the first floor. People rushed to the stairs only to be met by an ascending crowd trying to escape a mass of flames licking at their heels.

Smoke alarms started wailing as the room filled with thick, choking clouds. The screams from below grew louder. I pinballed my way through scrambling bodies toward the closest visible Exit sign, under which two guys were frantically pushing and pulling at the door.

"It's painted shut!" one of them screamed.

I heard glass smashing and looked back to see that someone had thrown a chair through a thick glass window in the back. That someone turned out to be Detective Douglas. The heat in the room had doubled as the smoke thickened. Screams were still coming from the first floor. People were either hugging the floor or bulldozing their way through the crowd to the broken window, stomping and tossing aside anyone who got in their way.

"What the hell are you doing here?" I shouted once I threaded my way to Douglas. It was a two story drop to the pavement below.

He looked back at the crowd. "Stay here. Don't let anyone jump yet," he said and climbed out of the window.

"What are you doing?" I screamed but he had let go of the ledge and was falling. I saw him hit and roll, clutching his calf and rocking back and forth.

"Douglas!"

He slowly got up and started hopping on one leg around the corner of the building.

"Where the hell are you going?" I shouted. Was he just leaving us here? The crowd behind me was pressing hard. If I didn't move I was going to be pushed out the window as there was nowhere else to go. I climbed onto the window sill, thinking that if I landed with most of my weight on my left foot, the worst I could do was break the prosthesis. Wrapping my fingers around the inside of the window to avoid slicing my hands on glass shards, I gingerly slid myself through, lowering myself slowly until I was hanging. It looked a lot higher from this position. Maybe this wasn't such a good idea. I tried to pull myself back up but the entrance was blocked by a human wall. I had nowhere to go but down. I held my breath and let go.

The fall took longer than I thought. I braced myself for the pain of hitting the concrete. It felt…soft. It didn't hurt. I opened my eyes to see a dozen or so people holding me aloft. They put me on my feet and went back to the window. Douglas stood off to the side like a stork, yelling at people to get in there, organizing the crowd to catch the window jumpers. This went on for fifteen minutes until the firefighters arrived with their nets and ladders. Spag, Geoff and Katrina had jumped after me and the four of us helped Douglas over to an EMS truck where they braced his leg in a board and inflatable cast. Geoff had a streak of blood running from his head. Katrina and Spag looked relatively unscathed.

I said to Katrina, "Find one of the EMS guys and get his head looked at." Geoff reached up to feel the blood on his head. "What the hell?" he said staring at his bloodied fingers. "What is it with being around you and getting my head smacked around?"

As Katrina led Geoff away, Spag headed back into chaos to offer his help. I climbed in the back of the ambulance. "Good thinking there, Dude," I said. Douglas just smiled at me.

"Well, I couldn't let us burn up in there now could I? How would that look?"

"Which begs repeating the question, what are you doing here?"

He started to say something, hesitated, then came out with "I wanted to hear your band play."

The hair on my neck rose, a sure sign that something was amiss. Douglas impressed me more as the Black Eyed Peas type, certainly not an aficionado of Frank Zappa.

"Bullshit. You're here to keep an eye on me, aren't you? Jesus. Will Gralewski ever lighten up? Afraid I'll skip town before the trial? I can't believe this shit."

"You're welcome for saving your life."

He had a point, but that still didn't make me feel any better–knowing I had a shadow following me everywhere. "You performed heroically," I said, "and I'm glad someone here was thinking but come on. Are you going to be my watchdog from now on?"

"I do have an ulterior motive if you will calm down for thirty seconds. That phone number you gave me? I did some checking, just out of curiosity," he said with a kid-in-a-candy-store grin on his face.

"And?" I said impatiently.

"Carolyn Hill." Hill. At least I had a last name now. "What's her address? Did you talk to her? Has she seen Pat? Did you arrest her husband? Come on, Dude, give."

"I've graduated to 'Dude', huh? I guess that's better than 'asshat.'"

An attendant spoke from outside the ambulance. "Ma'am we've got to take him now."

"Ma'am," I said to Douglas, and then turned to the attendant. "I'm going with him."

"Are you immediate family?"

"No."

The attendant shook his head. "Then I'm sorry, you have to come out."

"I'll follow you," I said and watched the ambulance pull away, then realizing I had forgotten to ask what hospital they were going to. "Shit," I muttered.

I tracked down Katrina and Geoff. Geoff was holding a thick gauze pad on his head.

"You okay?"

"I'll live," Geoff responded with a wave. The EMS attendant tending to Geoff's head told me most of the ambulances were headed for the University Hospital on Spruce. I told Katrina to stay with Geoff. I hobbled down the street away from the chaos. News media vans started pulling up to the police line, all jockeying for position. I avoided the lot of them and flagged down the first cab I saw. It was faster than getting back to my car parked six blocks away.

At the hospital, I went to the ER admissions desk to check on Douglas. I needed to know the rest of the information he dug up about Carolyn. At the registration window sat a prim, tidy-lipped woman with a starched nurse's uniform so thoroughly bleached that it garnered its own UV index rating.

"Name?" she said in a clipped tone.

"Douglas."

"Please fill this out Ms. Douglas, and sign all the forms, here, here and here," she said flipping through the pages and pointing a bony finger at each line where I was supposed to sign.

"No, that's not my name..." But before I could protest further the phone had rung and she was on to her next task. What did I know about Douglas' information? Hell I didn't even know a first name other than Detective Sergeant.

"Yes, can I help you?" she said as if she'd never seen me before.

"Hi. Look, I don't have any of this information ..."

"Just do the best you can, Ms. Douglas."

"Look! I am not Ms. Douglas. Try being human for a second and listen to me. They just brought in a guy whose last name is Douglas. My name is Chynna Lennox. We are not related. I have no friggin' clue what his health care numbers are, where he lives, his blood type, his heart rate or sperm count. I'm just here to make sure he's okay. You want more than that...go ask him!" I threw the clipboard with the forms on the desk and heard it clatter to the floor. Stupidity makes me nuts.

I marched past the admissions desk into the ER, searching in all the curtained cubes. Finally, one of the floor nurses told me he'd been lucky. His leg was broken in three places but he was able to go right into surgery and it would be a couple hours before he would be in post-op.

My choices were simple. Drive all the way back to Princeton and then all the way back to Philly when Douglas was awake, or hang out in a quiet spot in the hospital for a few hours. It's a hospital, there had to be an empty bed somewhere. After snooping around a couple floors, I found an empty, dark surgery waiting room with a decent sofa upon which I curled up in one corner and promptly passed out.

* * *

Crusty. That's how I felt when I woke up, and in serious need of a toothbrush. I found a restroom and made a brave attempt at not looking like a complete skank by sticking my head under the large faucet and washing my face with that god awful hand soap. I half-dried my hair by blasting it off my head with the wall mounted hand dryer. Checking the mirror, I decided to spend the next three weeks sleeping; it was the only thing that could improve my appearance.

Douglas was asleep when I found him, his leg propped up and in a cast from knee to ankle. Sitting next to him was a tiny black woman I assumed to be Mrs. Sergeant Douglas. "How's our hero doing?" I asked quietly.

"Loaded on Demerol at the moment. He started having some pain this morning so they gave him something. The surgery went fine. Hopefully, he'll be coming home later today."

She was dressed like someone who dashed out the door in a hurry; a head-full of ebony curls pulled back in a tight pony tail and mismatched sweats. An unmade round face the color dark caramel smiled down, jet black eyes showing contentment at watching Douglas' deep breaths.

"He saved many lives last night. Including mine."

A smile grew across her face. "There will be no living with him. He was giving the nurses grief about letting him go home last night. Kept saying it was no big deal. Then the anesthetic started wearing off. He'll try my patience wanting to get back on his feet sooner than he should."

"The sooner the better," I said. She looked at me with a questioning expression. "He's my buffer, keeping me from setting his partner on fire."

"You'll have to take a number for that event," she said. A second later she made the connection. "You're the young woman who was arrested for that murder," it wasn't an inquisition or a judgment, just a statement of fact. "I have something for you."

I certainly wasn't expecting that.

"I'm Sabina Douglas, his wife. He wanted me to give you this in case you showed up," she said handing me a slip of paper.

"I guess I should thank you for not profiling me as a mad killer." She looked at me with a questioning glance, one eyebrow raised. "He told me," I said nodding at the snoring patient.

"Hmmm," she said, not unkindly.

"All right," I said, smiling, as I read Carolyn Hill's address. "Tell him I said a hundred thank yous. And if he gives you any trouble while convalescing, just call me and I'll help you tie him down."

Laughing, she said, "Honey, I got him to the altar. Everything after that is a piece of cake."

She rocked.

Thirty

The western suburbs of Philadelphia, the old "Main Line" towns such as Ardmore and Bryn Mawr, once housed the sprawling estates of the Philadelphia elite, their summer getaways during the nineteen thirties and forties, the playground of the Tracy Lords of the world. "*The Philadelphia Story*" Tracy Lord, not the porn star. Maybe I'd see Cary Grant or Jimmy Stewart hitchhiking along the road after an all night social bash. Nah, they all had chauffeurs.

I drove through Ardmore in search of Carolyn Hill. After twenty minutes of turns, and back tracks, I found Rose Lane. I had to take it slowly as house numbers were not in large quantity and the ones that did exist were well hidden on ivy covered security gates.

"Bingo," I steered through an opening in a twelve-foot hedgerow, went a hundred feet and was met by black wrought-iron gates enclosed by thick brick columns on either side.

"Yes?" a voice bellowed out of built-in speaker lodged in the column.

"Carolyn Hill, please?"

Silence. More silence than was comfortable. I had the urge to throw the VW in reverse and get the hell out of there.

I was debating whether to speak again, my hand on the gear shift, when the gates slowly pulled back, sliding on their tracks into the hedges.

The driveway curved to the left and became enclosed in overhanging trees trimmed to come together at the top as if driving through a forest cathedral. A single yellow house light appeared ahead illuminating a heavy wooden door with a small roof overhead. Large rhododendron bushes in full bloom stood sentry on either side of the door.

"Servant's entrance?" I said, cutting the motor.

The backdoor to the house opened and a tall, white haired man dressed in a dark suit emerged and stood in front of the car, his hands clasped in front of him, waiting patiently. He looked gaunt and worn with ruddy skin the color of old plaster.

"Please follow me, Ma'am," he said matter-of-factly after I got out of the car.

Ma'am? That's twice in two days. I'd almost rather be 'Babed'. Almost. He led me into the house, up a small set of stairs that emptied into a kitchen bigger than my apartment. Recessed lighting in twelve foot ceilings gave off a warm glow. More than anything, it was clean and perfectly ordered. No dirty dishes in the bathtub-sized double porcelain sink or in the chrome prep sink in the black granite-topped island.

"Dude, does Architectural Digest know about this place?" I said.

"Oh, yes Ma'am," he said, smiling. "They've been here. Twice."

I followed the man through a swinging door into a small space lined with counters and trays. On either side, glass cabinet doors trimmed in white showed hundreds of plates stacked to the ceiling. A serving area. Oh, sure, everyone has one of these, I thought. We walked through another swinging door and into another world.

"Wow," I said under my breath. The first things I noticed were the arches. Everything was arched, the floor to ceiling windows, the two sets of glass French doors at the far end, even the ceiling was sculpted to give the impression of looking up into a dome. I could have sworn we walked into the dining room of an old European mansion, complete with thickly framed oil portraits of elite men and women in late nineteenth century dress. A scrolled arch marked the entrance to a walk-in fireplace that was built into the far wall. In the center of the room, an enormous mahogany dining room table sat under matching crystal chandeliers at either end, composed of thousands of hanging jewels.

"I bet those are a bitch to clean," I said.

"We contract out for that service. Oh, before I forget, please give me your keys and cell phone."

"Excuse me?"

With a small smile and soft-spoken manner he said, "Trust me. This is the easy way. You will get them back, I promise."

I stepped back away from him. "What if I just turn around and walk out the door."

"You won't get very far I assure you." A tired spirit was vaguely showing through his attempt at being tough. There wasn't any feeling behind his mild threats, just rote recitation.

"Look, I just came to see Carolyn Hill. What the hell is going on here?"

"Your cell phone and your keys, please."

"Not a friggin' chance." I protested.

My arms were suddenly pinned behind me. I struggled to break free but the grip only tightened. Turning to see who was holding me was impossible.

"Let go," I said, trying to thrash.

"That's not necessary," said the man.

A voice behind me growled, "Take them."

The man reached into my jeans pockets coming away with what he had requested. The grip loosened and I flipped around quickly, my right fist smashing the nose of the face behind me. I don't care what you see in the movies, a move like that hurts the puncher as much as the punchee.

"Aw shit, you bitch," he said, doubled over clutching his face. I was hopping around shaking my hand trying to ease the pain.

"Well, it didn't do my hand any good, you idiot."

The stinging started to subside and I looked up to see a blood spattered face topped with blond curls starting for me. I moved away as the old man interceded. "Let's attend to your nose."

"You're dead, bitch."

"Bite me."

He continued to claw at me as he was dragged back towards the kitchen entrance.

"Wait here, please," the man said, calling back over his shoulder. He turned and exited back through the swinging door. What the hell was all this and who was the owner of this quaint accommodation? My hand still throbbed and I desperately wanted to rest my burning leg. I shifted my weight to my good foot for a moment, but the ache continued.

"Enough of this shit," I said. I pulled out one of the Edwardian dining chairs with upholstered cushions and sat, pulling another chair across from me to rest my leg on the seat. It didn't help much so I unclamped my foot and placed it on the table, adjacent to a glistening china place setting for one, which sat waiting for food and a diner. The relief in my leg was a massive improvement.

At that moment, one set of glass French doors at the far end flew open and a barrel-chested man in a starched pinpoint blue shirt, silk tie and navy blue suit pants swaggered in. My jaw hit the floor.

"What the…" I said

"Who said you could sit? Mark, let's move it," he yelled across the room. Instantly the swinging door flew open and the old man who led me in hurried to the table with a sterling silver tray and began serving the cigar chomping sleaze-bag from the Gibson's house. Carolyn Hill's husband? He looked like the type to smack a woman around. The loathing I felt before became instantly cemented.

"Get your god damn foot off the chair. Where the hell do you think you are? This isn't a sleazy dive where all your freak friends hang out, and get that fucking thing off the table."

I was too stunned to even reply or move my leg. I didn't move a muscle. I watched Mark serve eggs and toast and pour coffee in a bone china cup and orange juice in a crystal goblet.

"Why sure," I said, "I'd love to have something to eat. Tea instead of coffee though, please. And you can skip the cigar altogether." Mark stared at me wide-eyed, and then turned to leave.

"Mark these eggs are fucking runny. Can't you get this right? How many times have I told you? Dry. That's the opposite of wet. Look it up if you can't figure it out, Idiot." Mark inched back to the table and attempted to take the plate back.

"What are you doing?" he yelled. "Get the hell out of here. I don't have time for this. Go. Now." Mark slunk, red faced, out the room. The bellicose man started slurping his food and coffee in rapid succession.

"Think you're fucking cute, don't you? You aren't shit. You're lucky to even be fucking breathing at this point."

"Yeah, well, you're really living up to all my expectations, Mr. Hill."

"I'm not impressed. Even a stupid bitch like you can figure out what's going on here."

"Wow. Real ladies man, aren't you?" I knew I had to stay calm on the outside, even though my instinct was to reach across and fillet this bastard. Just the same, I knew what he was capable of doing. I'd seen his handiwork. "So tell me, did you personally abuse your wife or did you pay that inept moron who just attacked me to do it for you?"

"What the fuck are you talking about?" He downed his orange juice in one gulp. He wiped his mouth on a linen napkin and threw it on the table. "Hank!" he called.

"Just one question. Where's Carolyn?"

"Downstairs until I get back," he said pointing at me and looking at the bloodied Hank. "What the hell happened to you?"

Hank sucked in some air and glared at me. Hill cracked a small smile.

I said, "Are you going to answer my question, Prince Charming?"

He jumped around the table and kicked the chair holding my leg out from under me; my stump hit the wood floor sending bolts of shooting pains up my leg. He lifted me up by my shirt, grabbing handfuls of my boobs in the process, until my face was even with his and my legs dangled in the air. It felt like my skin was ripping off my chest.

"Listen, you nosy bitch. I ought to cut you up into chum and go shark fishing, or better yet, take you apart a piece at a time."

"Let go of me." I said through clenched teeth.

"You and I are going to have some fun when I get back. Well, I'm going to have some fun anyway." He pulled me to him and slowly ran his slimy tongue up my neck. If I had anything in my stomach I would have done my Exorcist imitation. Instead, I pushed it all down. He held me away. I could smell the bitter coffee on his breath. I gave him a sly smile, licking my upper lip, and then, as hard as I could, kicked him square in the balls, which sent us both to the floor.

"Oh, God. You bitch! Oh God." He was wailing, doubled over. "You're dead you fucking bitch!" That seems to be a common reaction I'm getting lately.

Hank grabbed my foot off the table, grabbed my shirt and dragged me down a long flight of stairs at the bottom of which was a heavy wooden door. Unlocking it, he threw me into the darkness. It was cold. I was already shivering from the exchange with Hill and the damp chilly air wasn't helping. A single hanging bulb clicked on and I saw row after row of wooden racks holding hundreds of wine bottles fading into the shadows in either direction.

"I'll come for you when he comes back," he said with a sneer.

"You've got to be kidding me. How about a jacket or sweater or something? I'll catch pneumonia down here. What if I have to pee? How long is he going to be gone? "

"Shut up. God, do you ever stop fucking talking?"

"I suppose you think your boss is an okay guy?"

"He'll be back in a couple hours. Grab a piece of floor."

"What about a bathroom?"

He gave a thin smile. "Hold it," he said, "Oh, and one more thing." He chucked my prosthesis at me causing me to duck which gave him time to charge in and drive his fist into my gut.

I collapsed to all fours gasping for breath but nothing was coming in. I was dying. He yanked my head up by my hair so our faces were inches apart. I was going to black out from no oxygen.

"I owe you some pain," he snarled and cocked his arm back, fist clenched. I had nothing to ward off my face getting smashed in. Just then, a distant sensation crept up then exploded through my leg.

"Shit! Ow, God, stop. Stop!"

"What the…" he said, confusion on his face. "I didn't even touch you."

Thrashing and grabbing for my thigh and the jagged lightning coursing through it he finally let me fall into a heap on the floor. I rocked back in forth on agony.

"Hank, Mr. Hill wants you…" Mark stopped and looked at me wide-eyed. "What is going on here?"

"She's insane. I didn't touch her."

"Mr. Hill wants you upstairs. Immediately."

Hank sneered down at me, "We're not through yet."

I would never wish phantom pains on anyone, especially myself, but they just saved me from Hank pummeling me into ground chuck.

"Mom! Come on!" I screamed. The pain was not letting up, my face drenched in sweat.

Suddenly I felt a pull on my leg, a release of pressure. Heat. Heat on my stump. The pain subsided gradually. Hesitantly I exhaled, waiting for the next jolt, the next spasm, the next hot steel needle jammed through my leg. I opened my eyes to see that Mark had my stump wrapped in a hot wet cloth.

"Hope you don't mind," he said quietly.

The pain was there, fading further, but I still braced myself for another round, just as it had done in the hospital. Mark squeezed hard as if trying to squirt toothpaste from a dried out tube. Still, it was preferable to the phantom pains.

"How's it feeling?" he asked.

"Better. Better. I'm just waiting for round two."

"With any luck you won't have one."

I waited. The sensations receded further. I started breathing evenly, a rush of relief swept through me. Mark kept the pressure on, squeezing the cloth tightly and even though it stung from outer damage, the phantom pains continued their retreat.

"How did you know?" I asked.

"Past life experience." He left it at that and I didn't press. "You should be out of the woods now. Just stay here and relax for awhile. I'll try to come back later and see if you are okay." He stood, with a sad smile, and shut the door behind him.

I was tired, hungry…and scared. How did I get here? One minute I'm running a CD store and playing in a band and now I'm missing a foot, people are disappearing from my life and I'm trapped in a basement waiting for…well, I didn't want to give Hill the satisfaction of thinking about it. I started thinking about everyone I knew, and whether or not I would see them again.

Thirty-One

A stinging cold in my cheek jerked me awake. Exhaustion had unconsciously turned into sleep, and my face was pressed to the cold cement floor. The hum of the cooling units was the only sound. I didn't know how long I had been asleep; it could have been ten minutes or ten hours. The thick slog in my head was unwilling to clear, I felt nauseous and had to pee like nobody's business.

There were no windows, no clocks. The room was large and curved as if part of a huge circle. My leg was lying on the floor next to me. All the plies had fallen out at some point so my stump was going to scrape against raw plastic and wobble loosely in the cup. Gingerly walking back and forth between the racks I thought of downing some wine, at least it might warm me up a bit. Or was that brandy? It didn't matter. I'd take anything right now. The problem was drinking wine would do two things: make me sluggish and stupid and make me have to pee worse than I did already, not to mention it tiptoes on the addiction border for us druggies. Drinking is technically permissible but is usually the first step down a road best not taken.

A new humming in the air kicked to life. I assumed it was another cooling unit, but something else caught my ear. This hum sounded a lot rougher than the smooth air conditioning units. I followed the noise around the left curve of the room. With only a single light fixture back by the door, the darkness thickened at each curved end of the room. I waited for my eyes to adjust and continued following the noise. It was coming from the far back corner where no light shone. I took careful steps toward it, inching forward with my good foot so I could at least feel something. Suddenly, the floor gave way and I pulled my foot back in time to keep my balance. I knelt down and felt with my hands. The floor did give way. In fact, there was a hole in the floor about two feet in diameter with something running in the middle of it. A sump pump. Of course. Hill certainly would not want any water in this room.

Well, at least I solved the problem of having no place to pee. With any luck I'll short circuit the motor, I thought smiling to myself.

Feeling a bit better, I started to think about my options upon Hank's return, if Hank returned. Maybe Hill would want to keep me down here. I tried to make mental notes of what I had going for me and came up with only two: dark corners and heavy glass bottles. I imagined how the scene should play out, or at least how it would play out in the movies. I hopped around the racks, looking for the biggest bottle I could find that also felt comfortable to wield. A hefty champagne magnum was perfect. I sat in a dark corner and tried not to think, tried to stay calm and get my adrenaline pumping at the same time.

Sometime later, a loud click at the door shot a charge through me. I could hear footsteps shuffling in.

"Okay. Come on out. I know you're in here," Hank said. I felt lucky that it was Hank. There was another click and suddenly the room was bathed in incandescent light. Damn, I thought, why didn't I think of looking for another light switch? So much for luck, and darkness. Time for plan B, I thought. It made me wish I had one.

"Come on. You're not going anywhere." He came around the curve and saw me standing there with the bottle in my hand. His face sported an x-shaped bandage over his swollen nose. It wasn't lost on me that his blond curls may have been the ones tearing out of my apartment the night DaKota's place was trashed. But why?

"Right. You were going to jump out of the dark and hit me over the head with the bottle. What am I, an asshole?"

"Actually, yes you are," I said and threw the bottle at him as hard as I could, it just missed him, but smashed on the concrete, a fizzy puddle spreading across the floor.

"Shit," he shouted. By reflex, I grabbed another off the nearest rack and heaved it. He ducked between two racks, this bottle also shattering on the floor.

"Knock it off, you dumb cunt!" he yelled. "The "c" word. That pumped my adrenaline another sixty notches. I threw another bottle at the rack he was behind. Then another. They hit hard sending glass shards and wine spray through the rack.

"Shit, God damn it!" I chucked another one at the same spot. "Christ!" He moved away, down further rows. I couldn't see him move anymore. I grabbed another bottle but silently stayed where I was, listening.

I moved to my left down the row as quietly as I could. I thought going this way would at least bring me up behind him. I peaked around the corner of the rack just in time to see him move out of one row and down another, about five rows away. Now what? I looked down. All the racks were freestanding and entirely movable. Grabbing the rack I found I could jiggle it without too much trouble. I knew I only had one shot at this. I put the bottle in my hand quietly on the floor and moved back to the center of the rack. With both hands I grabbed a shelf high enough to give me some leverage without taking away my arm strength.

I pushed. The rack was heavier than I thought. It gave a little but wasn't about to give up easily. I closed my eyes and put everything I had into it, putting my good leg against the wall and balancing on my prosthesis which hurt like hell. The skin on my stump felt like it was splitting. My arms were just about to give out when gravity took over and the rack went tumbling, taking me with it. I felt it hit the next rack and slowly give way into the next one. Then the next one. The domino effect, crashing bottle after bottle, on the cement floor.

"Aw shit!" I heard a yell. More racks fell until it reached the top of the curve where there was enough space to let the last one fall without hitting anything else. The stench of alcohol filled the room. Chunks of glass were scattered all over the floor, sitting in large, growing puddles of purple liquid.

I tiptoed around the puddles to see Hank lying unconscious, trapped between two racks. I didn't know if he was dead or just knocked out and, frankly, didn't care. I just wanted to get the hell out of there.

On the floor was a bottle with the bottom missing, leaving only the neck and the jagged remains of the body. It would do nicely. I picked it up and headed up the stairs.

Each step out of the cellar felt like salt in an open wound on my leg. I cautiously opened the door at the top of the stairs and listened. Silence. I poked my head out. Lamps were lit here and there; I had a feeling that it was dark outside. I had to get the hell out. There was no doubt in my mind that Hill was more than capable of smacking me around, or worse.

I made my way down the hallway toward the glass double doors leading to the dining room. Pressed against the wall, I inched my head forward to look inside. The lights were dim. The table was clear. I could see a light shining under the swinging door to the serving area. Maybe Mark was in there. I thought I could probably take him if I had to.

I pushed open one of the glass doors and crept inside, closing it quietly behind me. It took forever to get across the room, pain shooting up my leg with each step. I put my ear to the swinging door. Nothing. Inching it open I saw an empty serving room. The same held true for the kitchen. Empty. A quick limp across the kitchen led down the stairs to the back door. My car had been moved further down the curved drive. Favoring my good leg I hopped toward it, hoping it was unlocked, praying the keys were in it. Looking through the driver's window did not bring good news...No keys. Now what? I didn't know anything about cars so hot wiring, however that's done, was out of the question. If only I still had my cell phone. The sky was dark with only a couple stars visible through the thick tree branches as I stumbled down the drive. The air was still thick and hot.

I wobbled as quickly as I could toward the wrought-iron gates, the skin on my leg scraping away. The darkened yard on either side of the drive was scattered with lightning bugs, which took me back to the farm when I was a kid. We all had empty peanut butter or mayonnaise jars filled with grass pulled from the lawn and holes punched in the metal tops, running around catching fireflies. My jar sat on the table next to my bed at night, the bugs flashing their tails as bursts of energy, or panic, hit them. A wave of guilt washed over me for trapping them. I now knew how that felt.

At the gate at the end of the drive I looked for a switch box on either side, hoping to find some way to get the damn thing open. If there was a way to do it manually, I couldn't find it. The gate was about eight feet high on the sides with the posts increasing in height toward the center so the top had a curved look to it. There was one cross piece at the bottom and another one at the eight foot mark so if I wanted to climb over I'd have to shimmy up the wrought iron posts to pull myself over.

I tossed the bottle into the bushes, grabbed one of the iron posts and started pulling myself up. My feet were useless as they kept slipping off the posts when I tried to gain some traction. The wrought iron was rough and digging into my palms. I placed my feet on two different posts, my butt sticking out, and ascended in sort of a half assed crab walk. Pain coursed through my leg with the pressure of each step. Even so, I made significant ground. The top crosspiece looked to be within reach. I lunged at it, grabbing just enough to hang on. Pulling myself up, my stomach knotted up at the thought of escape.

Suddenly I was blinded. Half a dozen spotlights flashed on. From the shadows of the yard I could barely see a silhouette moving toward the gate.

"You definitely get an 'A' for effort."

Hill. My heart sank. He stood in the drive, looking at me. I was hanging on the gate, like a fly caught in a spider's web.

"You wouldn't want to leave just yet, though. The party has barely started. Come on. Get down."

"How about helping me?"

"You can't expect me to believe you need my help at this stage of the game, can you?"

I shimmied down the posts, landed tentatively on my good foot and furtively looked for the bottle in the bushes.

"Let's go," he said. "After you, of course."

Thirty-Two

Back in the dimly-lit dining room, I asked, "Okay. So now what?"

"Sit over there," Hill said pointing at a straight-backed chair next to the fireplace.

"Why?"

He grabbed my arm to lead me to the chair but I quickly yanked it away. "Don't even think about touching me, asshat. Remember this morning? Want more of the same?"

"You're not in a position to demand anything. No one knows you are here. If you disappeared forever, no one would know where to start looking, so you can cut the tough bitch attitude. Now sit the fuck down."

"Bite me."

For his bulk and size he was fast. He caught me with a backhand across the face. The sting rose quickly, my head swam for a second. I told myself crying was not an option as I brought my head back to face him without reacting or bringing my hand to my face.

"Don't think for a minute that I can't, or won't, do anything with you I fucking feel like," he said stepping closer, trying to use the twelve inch difference in our height to intimidate me. I stood my ground.

"Feel like a big man now, hitting a woman half your size? Takes guts to tackle that, huh? Coward."

He raised his hand again. I closed my eyes but did not turn away. I wasn't about to give him the satisfaction. The blow didn't come.

"You bitch," he said and stepped behind me, lifting me up by my arms.

I squirmed and kicked. "Put me down." His grip tightened, squeezing my arms until I thought they would break. He spun me around and slammed me into the chair.

"Now sit there and shut the fuck up for five seconds."

Even in the dim light I could see his face turning red. I had to catch my breath plus I needed any amount of time to figure out what to do.

Continuing to give him lip would not last forever, at some point my luck was going to run out.

"Can I ask you something?" I said.

"No. Shut the fuck up. Hank!"

"He's a bit indisposed in the basement."

Hill snickered. "What the hell does that mean?"

"When I left him he was catching some Z's in the wine cellar. Of course he happens to be pinned between some racks that somehow managed to tip over. Shame about all those broken bottles, though."

His face slackened, staring at me. I just smiled in return. After a few seconds he shook his head, seemingly in disbelief.

"You're a one man wrecking crew," he said.

"If I was a man, I'd take that as a compliment."

"Don't be too pleased with yourself. I can always collect on the insurance saying it was a burglar, and then sue the security company saying their system was compromised. I'll make twice what that junk down there was worth."

"Yeah, I don't see you as the wine connoisseur type, which brings me back to my question. What the hell is going on? Where's Carolyn? What the hell are you up to with that shithead Gibson? And while we're at it, what have you done with my step-brother and he better be alive!"

Suddenly his nose was an inch from mine. I heard a metallic snap and felt something sharp digging into my chin. I moved to grab his arm and he pressed the blade harder into me, breaking the skin near my jawbone.

"You've got a lot of balls coming here and asking for Carolyn Hill," he growled, his eyes boring into mine. "I ought to skin you alive right now."

I arched myself back in the chair to keep the knife from going any further. My aversion to anything sharp blasted images of steel slicing through the tips of my fingers, which sent shock waves of panic to every nerve in my body. Uncontrollable shudders coursed through me while I tried not to imagine his other suggestion. He broke into a maniacal grin, seeing the fear in my eyes.

"Yeah," he said slowly. "I think you'd look real good strapped to a table. Oh, the things I could teach you. Stuff you've never even dreamed about. You wouldn't know whether to beg for more or beg for death." The pressure of the knife subsided, but he trailed the point down my neck and the top of my chest. Sweat jumped to my skin. I started to kick out with my leg, but he quickly moved his leg to crush mine against the arm of the chair then slammed his beefy hand to my throat, squeezing.

"Oh, no. We certainly aren't going to repeat that. Which reminds me, I owe you."

I had to stay conscious. He was squeezing hard enough to keep me from breathing. I had to do something. With his other hand he sliced my shirt down the front with one tug. Another hard tug, my sports bra opened. I struggled in the chair, trying to move anyway I could to get out of his grip.

"No, you're not going anywhere," he said his grip tightening. "Not until I'm done." The light was getting dimmer. Dammit, I was not going to black out, I thought. I was not going to let him rape me, or worse. Everything started swirling in my head, getting hot, close. I felt a hand groping me, pressing hard against my breasts, kneading and pinching me, followed by cold steel pressed against me. I tried to scream, but I couldn't make a sound. Getting darker and darker.

He pressed his full weight against me and I tightened every possible muscle to brace for the assault. Then his hand loosened from my throat and suddenly, the weight was gone. I gasped, coughed, trying to suck in more air. I pushed away from the chair, falling on the floor. Light was returning but my throat felt raw. I was on all fours gasping, sweating and engulfed in panic and fear.

I quickly looked up to see someone standing there with some sort of stick in his hand. My eyes tried to focus. I sat up on my knees, checked my breast, which appeared to be in one piece and pulled my torn shirt around me for cover.

"I'm sorry." It was the old man, Mark, standing there with the spear end of a wrought iron poker in his hand, the heavy bulbous brass end at the other. I glanced at the floor. Hill laid there, blood running down his face, pooling on the floor.

"Don't be," I said. "Thank you. Again."

Mark threw the poker on the floor. "Come with me," he said extending a hand to help me up. I stood but almost went right back down. I was shaking hard. My legs felt like rubber.

"Are you okay? Do you want me to carry you?"

"I'm alright and you've been chivalrous enough for one day. Just give me a minute." I steadied myself on the back of the chair. Mark left the room and came back with a black zippered jacket.

"Here," he said handing me the jacket. "I'm sure it's monstrously large but…" He turned his back to me as I took off my shredded shirt and bra, climbed into the jacket and zipped it up. The sleeves were about four inches too long and the coat's waist fell just above my knee, but it was lined and the warmth felt good.

* * *

EMS carted Hill out on a stretcher while the police sequestered Mark and me in separate rooms to give our stories. Among other things, I learned Hill's first name was Lucas and that Hank was merely knocked unconscious. Damn shame. Following my statement, I was left alone in a room that was somebody's office, probably Hill's, if the evergreen and mahogany décor was any indication. The only things missing were stuffed animal heads protruding from the walls. The desk held little in the way of personal items, a large flat screen monitor, wireless keyboard and mouse, a pile of files to one side and a single picture in an acrylic frame. It was a studio portrait of a man, taken a long time ago, like the nineteen forties or fifties. The face was serious, the eyes dark, hairline receding. He wore gray tortoiseshell glasses, very corporate-geek. The jaw was rounded although it didn't give off an air of being heavy. The creepy part was the man's eyes. They were Lucas Hill's eyes. The image was too old to be Lucas but there was no mistaking the cold emptiness.

I nudged the mouse but nothing flickered on the monitor. The stack of files was calling my name like a Hershey Bar calls a diabetic. A flicker of guilt spoke in my mind saying, "This is private stuff. You shouldn't be going through it."

Thanks for sharing.

There was no noise outside the office so I quietly thumbed through the pile of folders. It all looked like letters and legal documents for different business deals. Nothing registered until I saw what looked like a presentation in a clear plastic binder that was labeled FamilyFirst.

FamilyFirst. Where had I seen that name before? It was rattling around in my brain just on the other side of a gray fuzzy wall. I knew it was there but I just couldn't grab it through all the slog. I thumbed through the presentation that was mostly spreadsheets with numbers until I hit a rendering of a massive glass and steel structure that twisted halfway up what had to be forty or fifty stories. The drawing was labeled 'South Street Project–West elevation'.

South Street. FamilyFirst. That's where I saw it. The signs on all the boarded up buildings on either side of South 26. South 26-that was the last holdout on the block and was now a pile of ashes. Holy shit. I heard footsteps coming down the hall and quickly pulled the presentation out of the pile and shoved it under my armpit inside the jacket, which, hopefully, Mark wouldn't ask for before I left.

I shuffled the pile of files to straighten them out before putting them back in their spot when a small black book fell out and hit the floor. Out of reflex I shoved it in my back pocket and pulled the jacket down to cover my ass just as Mark came into the room followed by one of the police officers.

"You'll need these," he said and handed me my keys and cell phone.

"Can I ask you something?"

"I borrowed a large sum of money from him years ago and couldn't pay it back. He threatened to kill my sister and her children unless I worked off the debt," he said, eyes cast down from either shame or sadness for the lost time in his life.

His hand felt calloused and rough as I grabbed it. "I think you've more than made up for it. Just by what you did today. Thank you."

He gave my hand a squeeze as a weary smile crossed his face. "I have to go to the Police station," he said, "but there's one more thing you should know."

"Do I want to?"

"Oh I believe so," he said. "You asked for Carolyn Hill when you arrived. Had you asked for anyone else you probably would have been spared all this but you piqued Mr. Hill's curiosity."

"I noticed he wasn't especially thrilled that I mentioned Carolyn. What's that all about?"

"There is no Carolyn Hill, at least not any more. She died five years ago."

Thirty-Three

Silence and darkness greeted me when I got home. On the way I had stopped at Dominic's and got a large cheese steak with mushrooms and sauce, a side of onion rings and a mondo Coke to go, quenching a need for some comfort food.

I turned on all the lights in my apartment, pushed the piles of mail to one end of the table and sat and stuffed my face. I raced through the first half of the sub as if it was going to disappear if I didn't eat it fast enough. Then I finally started breathing. After gnawing a bit more sandwich and most of the onion rings, bone weariness took hold. I grabbed my drink, headed for the bathroom, closed and locked the door then turned on the spigot in the tub as hot as it would go. Once undressed, I looked at the mess in the mirror. The cut on my chin wasn't too bad, more of a puncture wound than anything. There were some faint blue marks on my neck where Hill had squeezed. Hickeys I'll tell everyone. The mirror fogged up quickly which was just fine. I didn't want to look anymore.

I sat in the tub, turning the temperature down just enough to keep it scalding, but tolerable. The water stung but felt good. Submerging to wash my hair I then soaped my body from head to toe. Then did it again. I still felt dirty. I washed again. All I could feel was his hands against me, groping my breasts and choking me. The feeling wouldn't go away no matter how much soap I used.

I finally got out of the tub and put on a white terrycloth robe I usually don't break out until December at the earliest. The apartment may have been ninety degrees but I didn't care. I crawled into bed and wrapped the covers around me without removing the robe, still shivering, wishing Nana Lennox were here to make it all go away.

There was a black ball twisting in the pit of my stomach. I wanted to fight it but the harder I fought the larger it got. Mom, please make this go away. I choked it down as long as possible, but the eruption would not be stopped.

Flinging myself across the edge of the bed, I snatched a trash can in the nick of time as dinner came rushing back in muscle tearing spasms. The first wave subsided leaving me panting. As my breathing slowed the muscles in my chest tightened again.

"Oh God," I moaned and wretched again, feeling like my insides were trying to escape. Coughing, spitting out the last bit of bile remaining in my mouth, I sat back on the bed, sobbing hard and feeling the anger, grotesquely large. Anger at the creep Hill for violating me. Anger at DaKota for leaving me, my foot for leaving me, Pat for leaving me.

The gates to dangerous and familiar territory cracked open. Little sparks flared in my brain, reminding me how good doing a line would feel right now. It was how I dealt with anger in the past, or at least how I pushed it out of the way. I just wanted all the anger and hurt to leave me alone. I wanted to feel better right now. I knew a coke connection in town; she would be easy to find.

Every nerve in my body was throbbing, responding to the euphoric recall of getting high. All the memories were in full bloom, all the energy all those good feelings. The voices urging me on were stronger than the voices pleading with me to stop. I jumped out of bed and started to get dressed. One time wouldn't hurt me and with everything going on I deserved it. I would just do it once and be done.

I bounced into the kitchen to find Zenobia sitting in the middle of the floor, back to the door as if guarding it, staring me down, daring me to walk past her. Her mustard eyes regarded me with more of a question than a judgment as if to say, "So. What's it going to be?" As I looked back at her, a shiver ran through me and suddenly I saw DaKota in Zenobia's face. And Nana Lennox, Pat and Andi. All the people I cared about were facing me down.

"Damn it," I mumbled and forced myself to dial Andi's number

"Hey," said a groggy voice. I glanced at clock and it was nearly two-thirty in the morning. I told her where I was standing and what I was planning on doing. Her response surprised me.

"Go ahead," she said.

"Excuse me?"

She cleared her throat and said, "Go ahead. Use. Go score some blow. What's stopping you?"

"At the moment, the fucking cat," I shouted.

"If you want use, go ahead. You'll be dead in a year."

The silence hung between us. I knew she wasn't trying to scare me like some school teacher; she was just talking about facts. She was talking about events that were guaranteed to take place. We had both seen it happen with others who forgot, for just a moment, that they were addicts and the rules for addicts who want to live in recovery are different.

After a few minutes of sponsor talk, the urge that had filled me had dissipated. I could still feel it scratching at my soul but I sent some prayers Mom-ward to keep myself steady.

At some point, I crawled back in bed and leaned against the pillows, eventually falling into a restless sleep with every light in the house still blazing.

Around mid-morning I woke up feeling like shredded dog meat, wanting to pull the covers over my head and not come out. Ever. My stomach ached from lack of food and the blow I took from Hank, my head throbbed and I was drenched in sweat.

I sat at the kitchen table and examined the stuff I swiped from Hill's house, flipping through the brochure again to find an address for Family-First on Spruce Street in Philadelphia, not that I was planning on paying a visit there anytime soon. The small black book turned out to be a phone book, containing entries of last names, cities and phone numbers. The listings revealed contacts scattered across the country but almost all were major cities, New York, Chicago, Dallas, L.A., San Francisco. The one that made me stop was listed as 67 High Point Drive in Loveladies, NJ. The last name was Payne. Loveladies. That's Long Beach Island. The picture in the frame of DaKota and the brunette Carolyn, or whoever she was. "Welcome to the Paynes." The number listed was the same as the scrap of paper with the red numbers. Carolyn Hill's phone number listed at the Payne address? What the hell…

A quick internet search pinpointed High Point Drive in Loveladies and showed it as a little cul-de-sac off West 85th street. Maybe it was time to take a day off and relax. At the beach, of course.

Thirty-Four

I put the top down on the VW and headed south on Route 579 through the Pine Barrens, which were becoming less and less barren in Jersey as real estate developers scrambled over the remaining build-able land like pumas over a dead deer carcass. Our state motto should be 'Home of The McMansion'. If I had a million to spend on a house it sure wouldn't be in a desolate horse farm in the middle of nowhere.

With roof-less sun exposure I should have put on sun-block on my shoulders as they were bound to be burned by the time I reached the beach. Redheads don't tan, we parboil. Halfway there, I put on my green baseball cap that had stitching in the front that read, "Beware: Norman Bates' Sister". I glanced at myself in the rearview mirror. Yeah, I looked really hot in the cap and Ray Bans, DaKota's hunter green tank top, which was a bit snug on me, and frayed jean shorts.

Route 72 and the Manahawkin Bay Causeway was the only automotive way in or out of Long Beach Island, an eighteen mile stretch of land surrounded by the Atlantic Ocean to the east and the Manahawkin Bay to the west. Driving over the Causeway has the same effect on me as swallowing a handful of Valium. The first whiff of salt air hits and every muscle in my body unwinds. On the bridge the air turns instantly cooler; completely breathable.

Hunger churned in my stomach and having lunch on the beach sounded perfect, and truth be told, I really didn't have any idea how I was going to approach the Payne household. Maybe the waves would provide inspiration.

The first twenty feet of the sand was blazing hot, not to mention a bit awkward with my foot. I was more concerned with not burning my good foot than looking like a total spaz until I got to the cooler sand near the water. I found an empty patch of sand in between the clusters of vacationing families, sat my ass down and dug into a roast beef and Swiss, with lettuce, tomato, roasted peppers and oil and vinegar, a Vanilla Coke and a bag of sour cream and onion chips. The tide looked to be low and calm as the ocean was filled with people. Kids tumbled through the water on their boogie boards, a few skimming their boards across the shore into the waves and somersaulting into the surf upon impact, always ready to come back and do it again.

With lunch devoured, I closed my eyes and listened to the waves. The sound washed over me, and with each low rumble on the shore, my body adjusted its rhythm to the rolling surf. There was nothing better.

Relaxed, but uninspired, I headed for the Payne house, which stood on a relatively new cul-de-sac about three miles north of the causeway on the Bay side of the island. It was a Wedgewood blue, three story behemoth with white trim and almost no windows on the driveway side. My guess was the front of the house, or back depending on your point of view, was solid glass, as it sat with an unobstructed view of Manahawkin Bay. The red paving stone driveway was short leading to a two car garage; one side was empty, in the other port sat the blue Jaguar.

My leg hurt from the walk on the sand so I leaned on Spag's cane as I hobbled up to the oak stained door and knocked.

No answer. I walked around a bricked paved pathway leading through a well landscaped garden to the front of the house, which was fully surrounded by an elevated white porch deck. In the corner at the top of the stairs, there was a flower pot with blazing red begonias and a small blue sign on a post stuck in the dirt that read "Welcome to the Payne's." The dune grass in the picture turned out to be patches of water reeds in the bay. Four sets of French sliding doors lined the house along the deck, two of which were open.

"Hello?" I called through the screen door. Again, no answer. Towards the bay was a dock without any inhabitants; only the cries from a couple of passing gulls broke the silence in the air.

The screen door slid open easily and I stepped in. "Hello?" I said, more softly than before.

The main living area covered the width of the French doors; a showplace to watch the sunset over cocktails and cheese dip. Fake wooden beams across decorated with masses of hanging plants ran front to back below a fifteen foot vaulted ceiling. The furniture was beachy-wicker, but not cheap. Large, low pile rugs covered blond hardwood floors. The off white walls displayed beach artwork but not the typical stuff that was found in art bins throughout the island. It was abstract, original and expensively framed.

Standing still and just listening, there was not a breath of movement in the house. If someone had answered I don't know what my explanation would be for standing in the middle of their living room uninvited. I was trying to ignore the fact that I was breaking and entering.

To the right was a massive Food Network style kitchen, sporting cutting-edge counters, cabinets and appliances. It was also devoid of any sign that it had ever been used. Everything was spotless and perfectly arranged.

The hallway to the left of the living area had half a dozen doors, all closed. The outside doors were all open to create some circulation but the inside doors were all closed. What was up with that?

I climbed the wide staircase at the rear of the house to the second floor. Again, all the doors were closed. The ones facing the top of the stairs were a storage closet and a bathroom. Making a u-turn to either side of the stairs led to carved oak doors, a little excessive, I thought, for a beach house. The door on the left was locked. If I was tall enough I would have felt around the top of the doorframe for a key.

Expecting the door on the right to be locked as well I grabbed the knob and was surprised to find it turning in my hand. I slowly pushed the door open and poked my head in.

"What the…" Even though the heavy drapes covered the windows, slivers of daylight shone through to reveal a room decorated in black. Not just in color, but also in energy. The blackened walls were covered with posters of hideous images from the recent spate of torture/gore films such as "*Hostel*" and "*Saw*." Artwork of rotting zombies was interspersed among a score of medium-sized little girl dolls nailed to the wall with ten inch spikes; some of the dolls were spattered with red to simulate the blood and some had their heads cracked open. Each one still showed painted smiles through the damage.

Garbage littered the room. Broken pieces of furniture, torn up books, fragments of CDs and dozens of take-out food wrappers and containers were scattered everywhere. Fist-sized holes dotted the walls on all sides.

This was total carnage, the likes of which I had not seen since…

"DaKota's apartment," I said out loud. I decided I didn't want to meet whoever occupied this room.

As I made my way back down the stairs I saw someone in a white two piece suit, showing off full breasts and curvy hips walking toward the house from the bayside dock. The suit caused her sun-bronzed skin tone to radiate. I wasn't far enough down the steps to see a face.

I backed up the stairs and darted around the corner to kneel down in front of the horror room as she came through the screen door. Saying a quick prayer to Mom that whoever this was did not come upstairs, I peeked around the corner but she had vanished from sight even though I could hear bare feet slapping the tile floor below. Just how I was going to get out of the house without being seen was still a mystery. Simply running down the stairs and through the door was not an option as ninety year olds using walkers could run faster than me these days. Maybe she's just getting something to drink and will head back outside, or maybe she'll take a nap in the living room and I'll end up peeing on the floor.

A cat's meow floated up the stairs. I didn't see, or smell, any sign of a cat when I came in. The meowing continued until it was abruptly cut off by the woman's voice, "Hello?"

Damn ringtones. Like I should talk. "Yes this is Jennifer Payne."

What the hell was I doing here? Maybe the picture I found was taken at a party, or somebody else just rented the place. This was a bad idea and I could ill afford another arrest. If Gralewski got wind of it he would crucify me and I'd be back in a jail cell faster than a Kardashian divorce.

"Asshat," I mumbled.

Bare feet gracefully slapped the floor again and the sound was getting closer until I realized she had started up the stairs. I silently pulled myself back into the shadow of the door and shut my eyes, like that game babies play thinking they are invisible with their eyes closed. Early denial at its finest.

The sound of a door unlocking on the opposite side of the stairs caused me to crack one eye open just in time to see a blonde pony tail, just like Carolyn's, enter the room and shut the door.

In the second that the door remained open, what I saw, or thought I saw, made me shiver. A single, five-by-seven acrylic frame on the dresser containing the same picture of the man that was on Lucas Hill's desk. At least that's what I thought it was. Could that possibly be? Maybe it was a different picture that just looked sort of the same. How could there be a connection between that scumbag and this house? Well, the address was in his book wasn't it?

I bolted from the premises as quietly as possible, but it made no difference to me whether Jennifer Payne heard the chugging VW engine as I gunned the motor and sped out on squealing tires. What the hell was I thinking anyway?

Thirty-Five

It was the third week in August and the year's crop of freshman were nervously making their way around campus and town. This meant a new collection of amazed faces at the store and a handful of kids who didn't even know what a 'record' was; if it wasn't digital it was old-school. It was the first crack in the summer wall; like robins in the spring, the "frosh-corps" was the first sign of impending autumn. I didn't want to think about it. I'm a spring/summer person and not a cold weather lover. What I was doing in New Jersey was beyond my comprehension but that's the way of things.

As I left the apartment, I called Andi who was due home from rehab that afternoon, assuming I didn't forget to pick her up.

Walking to work, my long jeans and a black t-shirt garnered suspicious looks from passersby; while completely inappropriate for the steaming humidity, I was dressed perfectly for the store as Geoff was running the show today.

The faint strains of "*We're Knights of the Round Table…*" sang from my jeans pocket. "Hello?"

No answer. I pulled the phone away to look at the number. 'Restricted'. In front of the store my phone rang again with the same readout, 'Restricted'.

Persistent bastard, I thought. Something told me not to answer and something told me I had to. I can live quite happily without adding to my growing list of complexities.

"Yes?" I said.

"That's the first delivery. There are more to come. You better hurry." It was the same voice as before. Harsh, but definitely female. The line went dead. What did that mean, the first delivery? Just for kicks I dialed star six nine. As I suspected, a recorded voice saying the number was restricted and could not be accessed.

Geoff did a double take upon my entrance, glaring at the purple blotches on my neck. "Whoa. Tell him or her to ease up a bit."

I smiled. "I had a date with Edward Cullen."

"I don't see any glitter."

"I'm sparkle resistant," I said striding back to my office. I was able to get through a couple boxes of records and let Geoff know what to offer the customers for their collections. At least that cleared a little bit of space for me. Katrina had already tossed most of the junk mail for which I was eternally grateful. The last pile of mail was stuff addressed directly to me or anything that looked like a bill. On top of the pile was a plain brown box, about four inches square and just as deep. The address was hand written with no return address. I shook it. Something softly rattled inside.

I grabbed the box and all the remaining mail that was probably junk, thinking I would look at it after I got Andi home.

Her hair was slowly growing back in, the burr holes were no longer visible, but the color was almost white blonde. She walked purposefully as if the sidewalk was going to race up and smack her in the face and there was still a glossy fog behind her eyes. I just wanted her to get back to the way she was, which I was determined to see happen, if only to keep the guilt from making me sick. I knew deep down that one hundred percent recovery was not possible but keeping that in a little box labeled "Denial" felt so much better. During my visits to her in rehab I told her that she had no choice, I was going to move into her place and be her temporary roommate. I didn't get the objections I thought I might as she had miles to go in her work to get her cognitive abilities functioning and welcomed having an interim flat-mate, as she called it.

Once she settled back in the house, I found her in the kitchen standing at the gas stove, turning the dial until the electronic clicking turned into a blue flame, then turning it off and repeating the process. She was fully focused on what she was doing and didn't notice me watch her go through the on-off cycle about ten times.

"Umm…what are you doing?"

Startled, she said, "I have nightmares of leaving the stove on and not being able to figure out how to turn it off until the house goes up in flames. I'm just retraining my brain on some basics."

I let out a big sigh.

"You are not going to stay here," Andi admonished, "if you continue to make those noises. No guilt feelings allowed."

"Yes, ma'am." I consented, but knew I was far from letting the guilt go.

After I hit the grocery store and stocked her shelves and fridge with things that were way too healthy, I sat down with a Coke and sorted through the mail retrieved from the store. Andi was sleeping, breathing peacefully in bed. She told me naps were now a frequent occurrence during her day. On the windowsill in the kitchen sat a row of plastic orange bottles. A twinge in my gut made me wonder how someone in N.A. recovery handles prescription medicine and, what is more important, does it trigger old behaviors? Andi was big into vicodin, which is what got her into NA, and almost fired from her job. A discussion, perhaps, for a later time.

As I sorted the envelopes I decided to start a printing business and get the credit card mailing concession, I would be Paul McCartney-style rich within a year. Seven different applications in the store pile. No wonder everyone is in debt up to their eyeballs. The last thing to open was the rattling box in plain brown postal paper and a Princeton postmark. Inside, crumpled white tissue paper was modestly packed. I removed pieces until I found something wrapped in red tissue paper. Pulling it out I slowly unwrapped it.

Then I realized the tissue paper wasn't originally red.

Inside the white tissue paper now soaked red with blood, was a finger. A human finger. A human finger with a ring still attached. A gold ring with the initials B.P.M.

Thirty-Six

I couldn't breathe, which was good, as screaming would wake up Andi. I dropped the box and the finger on the table and backed away, shaking in a mix of pain and rage. Running outside with no direction, just to get away and catch my breath, I let out a wail that shredded my throat. It was enough to unblock the dam and I sunk to the ground sobbing.

I tried not to think of how the finger was taken, or what Pat was going through. I just wanted him to appear, right now. Most of all, I wanted to butcher the bastards who did this to him. I don't remember anything else until a hand shook my shoulder.

"Are you all right, ma'am?"

Through blurry eyes the blue uniform was visible as if underwater.

"Are you okay?" he said.

I don't know why, but all I could say was "Douglas."

"Excuse me?"

"Detective Douglas."

"Yes, I know …"

I pleaded, "Please get him here. Now. Please."

The officer stayed with me until Douglas pulled up and hobbled out of his car sporting a walking leg cast.

Before he could say a word I said, "Inside."

He helped me up and hung on to my arm as we climbed inside. I just pointed to the table. "Please," I said, barely audible, "get that out of here."

Quickly moving to the table he looked down. He grabbed the scattered white tissue and used it to pick everything up and put it back in the box.

"How did this get here?" he asked.

"Mail. At the store."

"May I have this?" he said grabbing the box with a clean tissue. I nodded.

"I am taking this over to the station. Will you be okay?"

I nodded and sat, trying not to let tears of white anger spill out of my eyes. Andi stumbled in from her bedroom. "What's up?"

Douglas turned to her before I could answer. "Keep an eye on her. She is not to go back to the store today."

Andi looked bewildered but said, "Okay."

Douglas grabbed the box. "I will call you later," he said and left. Andi grabbed my hand and I told her what had happened. We stood there for what seemed like hours, two damaged people hanging on to each other.

Every muscle in my body clenched when, out of nowhere, the phone call popped in my head. *That's the first warning.* I called Douglas and told him about the phone calls.

I wanted to run, run fast and hard. Run away from everything. Just run and keep on running so all of this would be left behind. Andi saw that I was rammy and about to freak-out.

"Go swim, cool off. Then let's get a nosh somewhere."

"Are you up for that?"

"Be off."

I just nodded in response and broke out of the door.

I swam with difficulty, partially because I was hyper-charged with energy that was making me push too hard and partially because I still could not get used to swimming with one foot. The chlorine stung at the scrapes of my stump but I figured it would kill any lingering bacteria and that was a good thing.

Somewhere, out there, Pat was in pain. I tried to erase the image of his finger in the box and keep from imagining what he went through as some twisted shit cut it off his hand. My brain produced images of him screaming in pain, which may or may not have been the case but it made my body shake with fear and anger. The harder I swam the less I moved, which just fueled my anger further. I stopped and sat on the bottom of the pool, reveling in the isolation. The cool water enveloped me, protecting me from everything and everyone that was…out there. I was running out of air but didn't want to emerge. I wanted to stay cocooned, stay protected. The tightening in my chest grew until I burst to the surface with a screaming gasp, which garnered a few looks from others and the lifeguard.

After showering and changing, I picked up Andi, who was carrying a slim brown paper bag, and had decided Karen's Chinese Restaurant on Witherspoon was the destination. It was a small, spare place but the food was always good and Karen, who not only owned the place but also prepared food in the kitchen and waited on tables, was one of the nicest shopkeepers in town.

She took our orders and brought us two wine glasses and a corkscrew.

"Is this allowable? For either one of us? I'm assuming this won't mess with your meds?" I said to Andi who was pouring the wine.

"As your sponsor I will consent to this, I can tolerate a glass and I'm not trying to get into your knickers. So put a sock in it. Cheers."

We both sipped cautiously. I'm not a big wine person. I can't tell a cabernet from a kitchen cabinet but whatever this was tasted excellent.

"Who would do something like that?" I said breaking the silence. "Why disfigure Pat and send it to me?"

"What about that woman he was seeing? Did you find her? Would she know?"

Karen served our food and I brought Andi up to speed on Carolyn and her connections with Pat and DaKota, the Lucas Hill incident and my visit to the Payne house on LBI. By the time dinner was over the wine bottle was empty and my teeth were starting to hum as I spent most of the time drinking and talking. I remember leaving Karen's and stumbling down the two steps landing flat on my ass on the sidewalk, laughing hysterically while people walked around me. After that, I'm just not sure.

Thirty-Seven

In my mind I was in a hospital bed, and then realized that was impossible. At least I hoped it was. Opening my eyes made my eyelashes hurt. Someone had stuffed a wad of cotton gauze in my mouth. The gauze moved and I jumped, and then figured out that it was just my tongue.

I turned over but it felt like my stomach stayed where it was. The consistent blur slowly cleared to just a general unpleasant feeling in my eye sockets and revealed some strange furniture. I panicked for a second only to finally recognize Andi's sofa. How did I get here? A nauseous wave rolled through me by way of reply.

I sat up. Big mistake.

"Oh my." Andi sat on the coffee table next to the sofa and handed me a cup of something hot. She was dressed in gym shorts and a T-shirt. I was dressed for death.

I tried to say 'Thanks' but it sounded more like a chorus of croaking toads. I sipped the liquid and felt the heat but certainly couldn't taste anything.

"A bit squiffy last night, eh? I guess the wine was a bad idea. Here, pop these," she said handing me three pills. I started chuckling but quickly stopped before my eyes exploded. "I don't know. First my NA sponsor gets me trashed then hands over some pills. Seems a bit random to me."

"It's just Tylenol." It could have been crack cocaine for all I know, but I was willing to try anything at this point. My hair was throbbing.

"I'm going out for a walk."

I nodded and said, "Is that allowed?"

"It's required. I have to walk at least a mile a day."

"Need company?"

She stood, smiling. "I think I can handle a solo run."

"That's good. I don't think I could do it anyway."

As she was leaving I growled, "Just one question. Do I owe anyone an apology?" She laughed out loud. It was good to see her laugh again.

I took a couple more sips of tea, groaned and lay back down. Did she really just say 'squiffy'? What the hell does that mean? I tried to remember the last time I was hung over. I think it was my cousin's bachelorette party about six years ago. Somewhere in the world there is a picture of six topless women poking through the sunroof of a stretch limo. These thoughts were not making me feel better.

Reaching for the tea mug I promptly knocked it on the floor.

"Typical," I muttered. As I stumbled into the kitchen for some paper towels, some evil schmuck kept tilting the floor back and forth.

"Let's try this again," I said post cleanup.

There was one message on my phone, from Douglas, making sure I was okay and asking me to call.

The pounding in my head was begging me to ingest some caffeine, just something to get me going and take the edge off. Since I stocked it I knew Andi's fridge was of little help, so I braved the outdoors and the blinding sun. With any luck my car would still be parked at the store. I felt fairly skeevy, still wearing the same clothes from yesterday; hopefully, I could steer clear of anyone I knew as I stumbled between Andi's and the store.

Then I felt my skull split open at the sound of a blaring car horn.

"Need a lift?"

"Aw, shit." Red Porsche Boxter. Snevley.

"Come on. Where are you headed?" he yelled through the car window.

Of all people. Well, I guess it could have been worse. It could have been someone I wanted to impress, although no one came to mind at that instant.

"You're not looking so hot," he said once I was inside.

"Bite me. I'm going to the store and you don't have to be concerned with how I look. Plus I'm still pissed off at you, even more than usual. Can you turn the damn radio off?"

We traveled East on Witherspoon Ave, heading into town. "I was on my way to see you anyway, to find out how you got involved with that slime bag Hill."

"You've met him?"

"Not personally but I've covered enough news conferences and Hill Building Grand Openings to last me the rest of my life. Condescending ass."

"So you found your soul mate."

"Nice. Good job putting him in a coma. Glad to see you're okay."

I think it was a veiled attempt at being sincere but I didn't want to go there. Nor did he need to know I had little to do with Hill's present state.

Snevley said, "Come on, tell me how you hooked up with him."

"Why should I?"

"Because, Babe…" He didn't get a chance to finish before I seized a handful of his button down shirt and yanked him forward. Not the best move to the driver of a moving vehicle. "Alright, alright," he said in a panic and jerked the wheel to the side to avoid the parked cars, "I'm sorry. Chill."

We turned down Tulane Street and I could see Greg's bug still parked behind The Slipped Disc. He pulled up next to the red VW waiting like a faithful dog for its owner to come home.

Snevley turned to me, "Look, I'm stuck and I need your help."

"Said the spider to the fly."

"What do you know about FamilyFirst?"

I nodded. "Some big construction project in Philly, right?"

"Any idea who FamilyFirst is?"

"I know Hill was involved."

"Hill and a deep-pockets money partner, a company by the name of Grasslands Associates. They've been quietly spreading money around, not all legit, to get the approvals and variances they need. Not to mention making sure the block is cleared of existing occupants."

"And I care because?"

"Think about it."

Thinking hurt, but I gave it a go. "Wait a minute. Are you saying Hill was responsible for fire at South 26?"

Snevley grinned at my conclusion. "Indirectly, and by the way it was more than a fire. Don't you read the newspapers? I'm mortally offended."

"And I'm Natalie Portman. What the hell are you talking about?"

"Witnesses have come forward saying they saw a flaming object being tossed from a car into South 26. Speculation is some sort of sports car. A blue sports car."

"The jag? Someone threw a Molotov cocktail from the blue jag? Was it Hill?" I said.

"That's not what I said," Snevley replied, "that's your word for an airborne flaming object. Did he personally throw said bomb? Doubtful. He's too smart for that, but was it his idea? Probably."

It finally sunk in. "Why do it when it was packed with people? Why not just burn it down when no one was around?"

"That would be like throwing a rock through somebody's window with no note attached. Hill was sending a message to the owners. If it cost a few lives, so be it."

All those people, just out to have a good time, now maimed or dead. I didn't think it was possible to loathe Hill any deeper. "Why don't the Police arrest him?"

"Good question. Politics and gobs of money greasing the right palms is my guess. That and no real evidence that connects him to any of it."

"Who's the money partner?"

Snevley got quiet, which was unusual. He was like a gossiping old lady when he thought he had juicy tidbits to share. He shifted his gaze to stare out of the windshield.

"What?" I said, trying to read his face.

"One of the principles of Grasslands is DaKota's step-father, Parker Gibson."

After a minute of silence I calmly said, "That makes sense."

Snevley's expression of disbelief didn't need words. I told him about seeing Hill in a meeting with DaKota's Dad at their house.

"So where are you stuck?" I said.

"Right there. I have all these pieces of information that don't seem to fit together, especially DaKota's death and your accident. It doesn't make sense."

I agreed with him but wasn't about to let him know, so what I said next sort of spilled out. "Here's something to add to the puzzle. Remember the mystery woman? Carolyn Hill? Was dating my brother and was at the funeral?"

"How could I forget?"

"She also dated DaKota for awhile, before she dated me. And one other thing, she doesn't exist."

He stared at me, not comprehending, until finally he said, "Excuse me?"

"Whoever Carolyn Hill was, she died five years ago."

Snevley may be a pain in the ass narcissist, but he wasn't stupid. His eyes betrayed the energy in his brain, trying to put two and two together. In the nineteen forties he would have made one hell of a private dick. Now, unfortunately, there was nothing private about him.

"So let me timeline this. DaKota gets murdered, and then you have your accident, which wasn't an accident. Hill burns down the club, then comes after you for snooping around about a woman who dated DaKota and doesn't exist, but is now dating your brother who himself has pulled a vanishing act."

"Let me add an additional little tidbit." I told him about the package in the mail.

"Jesus, this is getting strange," he muttered.

As I got out of his car he said, "Thanks. That gives me something else to dig through."

"Be careful where you put your shovel," I said through the window.

The award winning smile that lured unsuspecting prey to their shameful doom flashed across his face. "I'll take that as a compliment."

"Asshat."

Thirty-Eight

A shower, a Coke, three Advil and I still felt only semi-human. It was close to 2 p.m. and the brain-fog had mostly lifted, which meant I had no excuse for not getting dressed and going to the store.

Virginia Woolf said, "There is much to support the view that it is clothes that wear us and not we them." My mood was clearly reflected in my outfit from a black tank top and black jeans to black bra and thong panties.

Geoff was trying to keep cool in the store by setting the air conditioning to sub-atomic frost.

"I'm sending you this month's electric bill, G-man," I said pushing the thermostat out of the fifties and into the high sixties.

"Come on, it's a b.o. funk day." For some reason bathing was an option for a sizable group of our regulars. When it got hot, the store took on that special locker room atmosphere.

"If it gets too ripe, we'll deal with it," I said.

Geoff was perched behind the counter as a very well endowed young hottie, between the ages of twelve and twenty-seven, approached the counter with three CDs in her hand. Wearing a pink camisole top with spaghetti straps and a white bra with wider straps, she was obviously affected by the cold temperatures in the shop. Geoff took his sweet time checking out her items, as well as her CDs.

Once she left I said, "Dude, you're a perv. What is it about guys and boobs? Half of humanity has them and you horndogs act like they're the keys to the kingdom. What is the big deal with two sacks of fatty tissue?"

He smiled, blushed and said, "They're cool."

"Sure. Keep in mind that chick you just visually molested will be sixty years old someday with wrinkled, stretch-marked tits that hang to her knees."

His eyes widened. "Mmmmm. Tasty."

"Strangeoid."

Before I reached my office Geoff called, "Hey, some guy named Bo called and said not to forget your one o'clock appointment."

I looked at the clock. It was twelve fifty. "Crap."

Top performance under rushed conditions is not on my list of positive qualities. In fact, just the opposite. For the sake of time I skipped stretching before tracking down Bo, which is about as dumb as playing a drum solo without warming up. All the weights felt twice as heavy and I was unable to get into a groove. Taking all my frustration out on Bo was another mistake. It's like telling the person whipping you that they're a fucktard. He pushed me hard and gave me well-deserved grief for not keeping up with physical therapy. I just silently took it, boiling inside, but it didn't matter what excuses I had as far as he was concerned, the bastard.

He pushed the resistance up to where I could do about fifteen leg lifts before my leg gave out.

"Nope. Not good enough. Ten more."

"If I could do ten more, don't you think I would?" I said, snapping back.

"You can and will."

By the seventh lift I was screaming with each movement. It hurt like hell. I thought every sinew and tendon in my leg was going to snap. The end of my stump felt like it was being jammed into street gravel.

"I can't!" I broke down. I was in pain, but I was pissed off that I let him get to me, let him get through. He held a towel out to me and I snatched it from his hand.

"Chynna, listen to me," he said, his voice soft, "you have to keep up with your therapy. What you don't realize is that you are still healing on the inside. If you don't keep everything loose and pliable it will shrink, harden and you will lose the use of your leg from the knee down. That means a cane, at a minimum, forever. No prosthetic, no nothing will ever bring it back once it goes. Eventually you'll need a walker and, in the long run, a wheelchair. I don't see you there. You're too strong for that, but I can't help you if you won't help yourself. If you're not willing to do that, then we can stop wasting each other's time and call it a day right now. It's up to you."

Knowing he was right didn't completely quell my anger, but it softened it enough to realize lashing back any further would be a mistake. Maybe Mom was helping me to keep my mouth shut for a change. I half-grinned thinking Andi would be proud of me.

"You're what, about a size ten?" he asked.

"What's that got to do with anything?" I said, in an unflinching sneer.

He went to a cabinet and pulled out a plastic bag with a Sears logo on it. I looked inside and there was a black one piece swimsuit. "I knew you wouldn't remember to bring one. Go sit in the hot tub for twenty minutes. Then go home. I expect to see your ass back here tomorrow at the same time. Your leg will hurt like hell tonight. Keep an ice pack on it."

"I don't have any ice packs." My internal five-year old was still being petulant.

He smiled and headed for the door. "Use bags of frozen veggies. Peas seem to work the best."

Bastard. Why is it so much easier to feel sorry for myself than listen to the people trying to help me?

Thirty-Nine

Bo was right on both accounts. My leg was killing me and a bag of frozen peas made a great ice pack. I had just settled on the sofa when the Pythons sang.

"Thank you for keeping in touch."

"Douglas. I'm sorry. It's been a brutal day. What's going on?"

"An interesting development."

"About Lucas Hill blowing up the club to grab the land?"

Silence on the other end, then Douglas said, "No, I don't want to know how you know these things. Your friend, Mark, provided the Philadelphia police quite a list of past deeds guaranteed to keep Mr. Hill occupied for some time, if he ever regains consciousness."

"Be a shame if he doesn't," I said, "but if he does I hope he has all the intelligence of a kumquat."

"I knew you would be heartbroken about that. It seems the Hill Real Estate Empire makes a decent amount of money from its many holdings, but certainly not enough to justify the lavish lifestyle. Besides a mansion here and one in the Bahamas, he owns a hundred foot yacht docked somewhere in Maryland used for entertaining clients."

That didn't surprise me with all his references to fishing bait and feeding me to the sharks. I asked Douglas exactly what sort of "entertaining" occurred on the boat.

"Whatever the clients wanted," he said, "everything from drugs to booze to sex, and each with their own specific preferences, some of which are thoroughly felonious in nature."

"So, I assume you are going to talk to a number of these clients."

He hesitated before answering. "Some of them. In order to talk to all of them, we would have to contact the Army Corps of Engineers and have them dredge nearly fifty square miles of the Atlantic Ocean, according to Mark."

I was starting to realize how lucky I was. This guy was easily capable of squashing me like a bug. In some very bizarre way I was glad he wanted to jump my bones instead of just break them. "Maybe I should pay a visit to Mr. Hill in the hospital. Just to ensure he doesn't wake up."

"There's probably a waiting list. Finding people who hated this guy is like finding people who want to win the lottery."

I felt a blast of ice run down my spine. "Pat. Did Mark know if Pat…"

"No. Not a clue. I do have other news for you, though. Your friend upon whom you showed the joys of a wine rack avalanche? He made bail and while the kidnapping and assault charges are still part of his life, he's out and about."

That was unnerving, knowing that Hank was running around loose somewhere. "Just swell. Who put up the bail?"

"Apparently some corporate entity put up the cash."

With Hill in a coma it couldn't have been FamilyFirst, unless someone else held the purse strings. That left one other possibility. "Let me guess, Grassland Associates?"

"Why do I bother? How do you know all this?"

"Son of a bitch. Why the hell does that asshat care about Hank?"

After I explained who Grassland was and the connection to Hill, Douglas said, "I should just get you a desk here. Look, my guess is that Hank is not all that happy with you so be careful. Try not to spend too much time alone. Maybe take a couple weeks off."

"He doesn't want to come near me. Trust me. Any news on…my package?"

"Just that it's the real thing. I'm sorry."

I was having trouble breathing. That empty helpless feeling was creeping up on me again. My brother was out there and some maniac was hacking him to pieces, while I sat waiting for…well, I didn't really know what I was waiting for. Maybe I was waiting for the answer to slap me in the face. I felt like all I was doing was sitting around. Pat would be the first one to tell me to get off my ass and do something. But what? If Hill didn't have him, where was he? And what, if anything, does it have to do with DaKota?

"Douglas, one other thing. Why don't your records show Carolyn Hill as deceased? If what Mark says is true, and I happen to believe him, she died five years ago. How is it there is no record of her death and an active phone in her name still exists?"

"The property is still listed in the tax assessor's records as being owned by the two of them, Carolyn and Lucas, and the Pennsylvania Vital Records office has no Carolyn Hill listed in their death certificate archives for the past thirty years. Whoever she was and whatever happened to her has been kept quiet, which in itself is worth a second look. As for the phone, that's no mean feat given the right IDs and good credit."

My head was spinning and ice water from the quickly thawing peas was dripping down my leg. Throwing the bag back in the freezer, I put ice cubes in a plastic bag and wrapped that in a dishtowel. Voila. Instant ice pack. The apartment was just too hot to stay inside. I doused all the lights and headed for the front porch in an attempt to catch even the slightest breath of cool air. As I plunked my butt in my Adirondack chair and settled my stump on the dishtowel I looked up to see flashes of red moving through the darkened leaves. I stared at it long enough to realize it was a red car parked across the street and the shadow of the streetlight through the trees was dancing across it. As far as I could remember nobody has a red car that parked on the street. In fact, there wasn't any parking allowed on the other side of the street, all the meters were on my side. Where are the parking Nazi's when you need them? Makes my blood boil when some arrogant prick gets away with something. Okay, it has more to do with being jealous that I can't get away with it and someone else can. Some clown like Snevley, I chortled. He's just the type to park where ever he wants without any consequence. Him and his red Porsche...

My stomach clenched. Red Porsche? Snevley?

I went inside, grabbed my phone and dialed his number. No answer. I walked back out to the front porch and dialed it again. I heard it, very faintly, his ringtone. Van Halen. *Jump.* What the fuck was he doing, spying on me? Bastard.

The flames inside were growing as I marched down the back steps, with every intention of blasting his ass.

The tinted windows of the Boxter were lowered about an inch but not enough to see inside.

"Asshat, what the hell are you doing here?" I yelled from the middle of the road. "I don't need a babysitter." I yanked open the driver's side door and Snevley rolled out of the car in a heap on the road, his face covered in bruises and blood that had spotted and streaked his blue button down.

"Aw, shit," I gently straightened him out and leaned forward. He was breathing, but not heavily. I said a quick prayer of thanks that I brought my phone with me. I dialed 911 and then looked in his car for something to put under his head and came away empty.

"What the hell." I peeled off my tank top and folded it under his head. One of the few times I was wearing a semi-normal bra. Thanks again, Mom.

"Don't die on me dammit. You're staying right here with me." There was matted blood on the top of his head. Somebody had worked him over completely.

"Where the hell are they?" It felt like weeks before I heard the sirens in the distance and the police and EMS arrived. The attendant gave me back my shirt and I slipped it on, even though it was spotted with Snevley blood.

DaKota's death broke my heart. Pat's finger frightened me. Now I was pissed. I didn't think it was possible to work up this level of emotion for the Paperboy but it was there and growing by the minute.

Forty

I woke up the next morning sweating from head to toe with a bag of soggy defrosted peas squished under me. Crawling out of bed and pouring a glass of orange juice, I put on the *Melting Pot* CD by Booker T and the MGs and plopped my ass on the front porch to watch the day begin on Vandeventer. I called the hospital to check on Snevley who was out of ICU with his jaw wired shut and covered with stitches and bruises. I called Andi to see how she did on her own last night and all was well there. I promised to stop by later, hung up and called Douglas. He hadn't heard about Snevley's attack but would talk to the officer doing the paperwork. A distant voice whispered to me that Snevley's mangling was Hank's doing, the savage nature of the beating with the body 'left on my doorstep', so to speak–knowing that the odds were high that I would be the one to find him.

I made a quick stop in town then pulled up at the hospital. Snevley's face was a swollen mass of purple and red interlaced with sutures and steel mesh holding his jaw in place. It hurt just to look at him. He had to be doped to the gills if the pain he was in came close to how he looked. I was about to turn and leave when I saw a swollen eyelid make an attempt at opening.

"Turnabout is fair play," I said, placing the chocolate milkshake I brought on the table next to him. "My turn to bring you gifts and since I heard chewing was out of the question for a spell, I improvised."

He barely nodded his head in agreement when his face winced in a mask of pain.

"Don't move or do anything. Here." I plunged the straw into the shake and brought it to his lips. He was able to take two small sips then had to stop to catch his breath.

Forget about communicating what happened to him or whether he saw his assailant. Breathing was Snevley's primary focus but I needed to know why he was jumped, what was he into and who had he talked to.

He made a small grunt that broke me from my thoughts and with his eyes, motioned toward the shake cup.

"Oh," I said giving him another sip. Putting the drink back I said, "It would be really helpful if I knew whose buttons you pushed to cause all this. How about if I ask you some yes or no questions and you can, well, is there any part of you that doesn't hurt that you can move?"

One would have to know the Paperboy to pick up the slight curl at the corner of his mouth and the sudden light in his eye.

"Jesus. Even in pain you're a pig. Come on, help me here."

Slowly, he extracted his cast-encased right arm from under the sheet and gently wiggled his fingers.

"Okay. One finger for 'yes', two for 'no', right?"

He raised one finger.

Fifteen minutes later Snevley struggled to stay awake but I had gleaned that he was digging into Grassland's history, Parker Gibson's past financial dealings and that Snevley had been jumped in the parking lot of the newspaper office by a single person, male, and then driven to my house.

I left him to his undoubtedly lecherous dreams and, keeping my promise to Bo, went through the motions of physical therapy but my mind was elsewhere, moving too fast to allow me to relax, even in the hot tub. Whatever loathing I had felt for DaKota's Dad was blossoming further into a full shit-storm of hatred. Yet, everything that had taken place in the past couple months had the same missing piece, the same blank spot; who the hell was the woman saying she was Carolyn Hill? No matter how many potential answers I rattled through my brain, I came back to the one possibility left to shed some light. Jennifer Payne had to know something. The picture of the gypsy-Carolyn and DaKota kept popping up in my brain, the two of them on the Payne's porch on the bay.

A light bulb went off in my head. What was it Douglas said about property records? The tax assessor's records? Maybe I could bluff my way to an answer. I thought it through then dialed 411, got the number I needed and made the call.

"Long Beach Township Tax Assessor's office," said a gravelly voice in rote recitation.

"Hi. My name DaKota Cassidy. I'm working with the Mercer County Homicide Squad tracking down some background information and I need to know the owner of a certain house in Loveladies. 67 High Point Drive."

"Block and lot?"

What the hell did that mean? "Excuse me?"

"What is the block and lot number of the property?"

Damn I didn't know that and it wasn't something I knew how to fake without blowing my cover.

"Um, I'm sorry I don't have that information. All I have is the address."

"Then you'll have to come to the office and identify the property on the tax maps. We don't list by address," the voice, exasperated, hung up.

Fine.

I made a quick stop at The Slipped Disc to make sure everything was under control and found Geoff and Katrina behind the counter in a heated debate that abruptly stopped once I walked in the door. Both of them silently stared at me as if I were tarred and feathered. Now that I think about it that might have been preferable.

"What's going on?" I said. They quickly glanced at each other and Geoff said, "Don't look at me. Go ahead, but I think you're nuts."

Katrina grabbed my arm and led me back to the office. Without either of us saying a word I stopped cold. On my desk lay the day's mail, and another box in a plain brown wrapper. The silence was broken by my phone sounding off. The display read "Restricted". I pressed Send and without uttering a word put the device to my ear.

"You better hurry. Soon there won't be much of him left." The connection went dead.

Anger and fear physically shook my body. Katrina was about to say something but I cut her off.

"Call Detective Douglas. Tell him what is here. Don't touch it or move it. Just call him."

"Where are you going?" she called after me.

I didn't answer as I stalked out to the car.

A rainy day on LBI made for ugly traffic as everyone was shopping instead of getting burned on the beach and there was a traffic light on every other corner of the main drag. After crawling for an hour, I spotted the brick ranch that housed the municipal offices for the island. Sitting behind the high counter of the tax assessor's office was a round faced woman with red shoulder length hair streaked with royal purple. Without looking up from reading her paperback book she said, "Help you?" I hesitated for a second, not expecting the gravel voice I heard on the phone.

"I called earlier, about looking for the owner of 67 High Point…"

"Maps," she said pointing to the blueprint sized book on the on the counter.

The book held dozens of pages, each a street map section of the island with individual properties designated by a block and lot number. All I had to do was find the page with 67 High Point Drive.

"Here it is," I said after ten minutes of searching, "Block 1009, Lot 7." At that the woman behind the counter disappeared, as if the floor underneath her gave way. I was about to say something when I saw her walking toward a desk in the office. She couldn't have been more than four feet tall. She climbed up on a chair and started typing at a computer, stared at the screen through a couple mouse clicks and then wrote something on a slip of paper.

When she climbed back on the stool at the counter she handed me the paper and resumed reading her book.

"FamilyFirst," I said reading what was on the slip, the address was Hill's house in Philadelphia. Out of nowhere a piece of the puzzle clicked into place and parts of this whole mess started to make sense.

"Thanks," I said, "I like your hair."

For the first time she looked at me, with an expression that was somewhere between shock and alarm. "Oh. Thanks."

"I used to have green in mine but I chopped it out recently. The purple is good with the red."

"I can see where the green would work," she said cocking her head to one side like a golden retriever.

"So what do you get more crap for, your hair or being a little person?"

"The hair. They wouldn't dare make any comments on my size. I'd sue them until smoke came out of their ears. I'm Tonks," she said extending her hand.

"Chynna." Tonks. Now the purple and red hair made sense. "Harry Potter fan, eh?"

She turned her back and lifted up the bottom of her sweater to reveal a tattoo that ran from one side the other, portraits of Professor Lupin and Tonks.

"I would say so," I said. Nice."

She half smiled but with pride beaming. "Had that done about six months ago."

I didn't have all afternoon to discuss obsessions. "Let me ask you something; is it normal that companies own houses?" I said motioning with the slip of paper.

"More often than not, especially with the expensive monsters being built these days. Normal people can't afford to live here anymore. What's your interest in this property?"

"I'm not sure. Yet."

"Be careful with that one," she said.

Her comment caught me off guard. "What do you mean?"

"Not my place to say. Just a lot of talk about those folks."

She jumped off the stool as a phone in the office rang.

It occurred to me that I had absolutely no clue how to go about what I was scheming. Humphrey Bogart always made playing detective look easy, but staking out the house in a 1969 red convertible VW might seem a tad obvious. I'd be easier to spot than Sarah Palin at a Metal festival. I thought about parking the car and renting a bicycle at Faria's rental shop, but a woman with a prosthetic foot peddling a bike in the rain might tend to stand out just a tad. Then another possibility dawned on me and I knew I had my answer. I didn't know how I was going to pull it off, but the details would work themselves out. Hopefully.

It was about four in the afternoon when I found what I was looking for on the Manahawkin side of the bay, just before going over the bridge leading to LBI. I passed several new metallic pre-fab buildings and after twenty minutes of bouncing the car slowly along rut-strewn dirt paths,

I found an old shack, weatherworn and a little moldy around the edges from age and moisture. I pulled into the weedy gravel drive under a faded, lopsided wooden sign, cracked and ready to fall to the ground in splinters. The writing on the sign was barely discernible: "Pete's Bait and Tackle". Under that sign a small piece of wood dangled from a single rusty eye hook reading "Rentals". Whoever Pete was, if indeed he still existed, chances are he had lived here all his life.

The once white paint on the front door was yellowed and chipped, the metal door knob almost black with age. I had to push the door with my body to get it unstuck. Inside the smell of old fish was dense. Dingy glass cases held remnants of fishing lures and accessories that were pushing fifty years old. A few good sized striped bass were mounted on the walls, trophies collecting dust from long ago expeditions. The dirty floorboards creaked as I stepped gingerly inside expecting the whole building to collapse sideways like a house of cards.

"Hello?" I said. I didn't hear or see any movement throughout the place. There were no back rooms. The wall behind the counter held two old windows, long painted shut in a thick glossy dark emerald green. Through the crusty yellow panes I saw that what once was a sturdy dock, was now a twisted mass of gray weathered boards reaching for the sky. At the end of the dock was someone in a baseball cap kneeling down trying to untangle a mass of ropes knotted into a ball. I walked around the counter and through the back door of the place to a short gravel path that traversed through long beach grass toward the dock. I took a step on the planks and felt the entire dock move from side to side. No way was I going out there. I'd end up in the drink as sure as Mom made little white seashells.

"Excuse me," I called to the person on the dock. I was expecting Pete to be about six foot seven, five hundred pounds with a perpetual three-day growth, a white T-shirt covered in fish guts and bleary, bloodshot eyes from a nightly battle with the bourbon bottle. So I was somewhat surprised when the person at the end of the dock wearing a denim work shirt stood and appeared to be about five foot six. I was even more surprised to see the work shirt unbuttoned and a black two-piece swimsuit underneath. She was deeply tanned, wore white sneakers and walked down the shaky dock like it was solid concrete.

"Yeah?" Her voice was a combination of leather and grit. I put her somewhere in her forties. She had a little bit of a pooch but was solidly built, thick-waisted with well-muscled legs. Even through the tan there were traces of acne scars on her high cheeks. Her eyes were almost black. She was not a drop-dead fox but she was pretty in a tough way.

"I doubt you're Pete," I said.

"Who's askin'?" She stayed on the dock, pulled half a pack of filter-less Camels out of her shirt pocket, lit one and blew out a plume of smoke. I got the hint that being cute was not going to work here.

"I need to rent a boat for a couple hours," I said.

"Got a license?"

"Nope."

"Can't help you," she took another long drag on the cigarette and then flicked it into the water. She turned and started back down the dock.

I called out, "I'll give you a hundred bucks over the rental fee if you take me out."

She slowed and stopped, looking back at me. She thought for a minute then stuck her hand out wiggling two fingers.

"All I've got is two hundred in cash and you sure don't look like you accept Master Card."

Her full lips thinned out in a humorless grin. She slowly made her way back towards me.

"What, exactly, do you want?"

"I need to go out in the bay and just sit for a few hours."

"And?"

I knew I'd have to tell her something of what was going on. The question was how much.

"Look," I said, "I'm helping out a friend. I need to keep an eye on a specific house for a couple hours. That's all."

"Drugs?"

"No. I will not be doing anything but watching the house. Bring a fishing pole if you want."

She chuckled and shook her head more out of disbelief than thinking anything was funny. "Fishing pole. Right. Okay, Aunt Polly, let's see your cash."

I handed her a bunch of twenties. "You know where the house is?" she asked stuffing the bills in her shirt pocket.

"Of course."

"From the water?"

Hmmm. I hadn't thought of that and she could see it on my face.

"Better come in and show me on the map." She passed me headed for the house.

"My name is Chynna."

She turned at the door and looked at me from top to bottom. "Uh-huh," she said and walked into the shack.

There was a yellowed map of LBI tacked to the wall. Each corner of the map had dozens of little holes and tears in it. I scanned the North end of the Island knowing that High Point Drive would not be there, but then neither was West 85th street. I pointed to a blank spot on the map.

"It's right about here," I said.

"What street?"

"High Point Drive. It's a cul-de-sac off West 85th."

"House sits on the bay?"

"Yep. Big old blue thing with lots of glass facing the water."

"Uh-huh. So does every other house facing the bay."

We headed outside. "Want me to close the door?"

She tilted her head down and looked at me as if to say, "You really didn't just ask me that did you?", then headed out to the dock.

"Okay…" I said under my breath and followed her.

I stopped after every step on the dock, waiting for it to stop shaking back and forth or for me to slip on the wet boards. I had my arms out like I was walking a high wire. Toward the end of the dock I heard a motor turn over. It seemed to shake the planks even more. With each step I felt invisible hands pulling me off the dock into the brown gas-soaked water below.

"I think I hate this," I called out.

I finally reached the cracked wooden ladder nailed to the side of the dock leading down to a creaking tub that looked old enough to be a lifeboat for Noah. It wasn't huge but it looked reasonably maintained, a white hull with room for about four or five people to sit or stand in the back. A homemade wood covering was built over the wheel so the ship's captain could stand looking through a salt-crusted windshield and be protected from the elements.

I wasn't sure how this was going to work with the prosthetic foot. I got to the bottom rung and realized I had to step down and over two feet of water to reach the edge of the boat. Common sense dictated that I call out to her for some help but, one, I didn't know her name and, two, I didn't want her to think I was completely helpless. Probably more the latter than the former. I had this image of having one foot on the ladder and one on the boat while it drifted away producing a cartoon-like split and a butt-first topple into the oily water. I decided boarding was going to be best accomplished in the same manner as removing a Band-Aid, fast and in one motion. Holding my breath, I put my good foot on the edge of the boat and semi-jumped.

The boat rocked a bit but I was still standing somehow. Before I could catch my breath she said, "Throw off the aft line."

I looked around. "Do what now?"

With a sigh she said, "The rope tied to the back of the boat. Untie it."

"Got it," which I did and stood there holding it. "Now what do I do with it?"

I saw her head slump forward. Without a word she gunned the motor. The boat started moving forward. Now, I had two choices: hold on to the rope and get my ass yanked overboard or let go and stay on ship. I quickly settled on letting go.

I sat on a wooden bench, out of the way, as she piloted the boat out into the choppy bay. We bounced across the breaks at a steady pace. Occasionally a jet ski or sleek racing boat would go flashing by, rocking us in their wake.

The coastline along the island was little more than a series of monstrous houses. Older, smaller homes were in the process of being demolished to make room for new mansions. Each house looked like it had enough room for twenty or thirty people. What do all these people do for a living that they can afford these multi-million dollar ashrams? It had to be something illegal.

I stood, checking my balance, and walked over to the wheel. "So, do I call you Pete?"

"Only if you want me to turn this tub around and kick your ass once we get back," she called over the drone of the motor. I waited for further information.

She said, "J. C."

"What does J.C. stand for?"

She shook her head and pointed to a piece of paper barely hanging on the wall, a yellowed boating license issued to a "Jaycee Craddock". I accepted this information as a huge first step and let it go at that. In front of the wheel was a series of six wooden cubbyholes with everything a good boat captain needs on the water: binoculars, empty pack of smokes, assorted matchbooks, a couple Bic lighters (probably empty), yellowed envelopes dating back to the pony express, and on the far side what looked like the handle of a gun.

"Run into many pirates out here?" I said nodding towards the gun. The resulting glower warned of being thrown overboard.

I remembered something about getting sea legs and figured standing was the best way to do that even though I only needed one leg acclimated. According to the cracked directional compass, we were heading north/northeast up Manahawkin Bay. That made sense to me. Jaycee pulled out her pack of Camels. Her hands were tough and weathered with several jagged scars cutting across the surface just below her knuckles. I'm glad I had not been on the business end of whatever caused those marks. She shook the pack until a single butt popped up and she grabbed it with her lips.

I grabbed one of the Bics as she was stuffing the pack back in her shirt. Surprisingly, it lit on the first try.

She looked at me a bit suspiciously but said, "Thanks."

She pulled off the baseball cap and a blonde streaked ponytail tied with a rubber band fell down her back.

We cut through the water in silence for another fifteen minutes until Jaycee pulled back on the throttle, cutting the motor to a low burble.

"Is that the one?" she said, nodding to the shoreline. I had only seen this side of the house once but it looked to be the Payne house. "I think so."

"Be sure. I don't want to sit out here for my health." She handed me the binoculars and I focused in time to see someone walk out of the porch door and around to the garage side. That someone made me flinch.

"Jesus. What the hell is he doing there?" Hank crossed the back patio then ducked inside one of the sliding doors. The horrible images of the room inside that house flashed through my mind. I hadn't made that connection before but now it made sense in a disturbing fashion.

"So?" said Jaycee.

"Oh, yeah. That's it."

"How close you want to be?"

"This is good for now. I really don't want them to know I'm here." The rest of the house looked quiet. Jaycee cut the motor completely and climbed out to the front of the boat. I heard a splash and quickly looked up thinking she'd jumped in, but she was walking back to the wheel. "Anchor," she said climbing back in.

"Oh."

We sat, bobbing along in the small break of the water. Jaycee smoked in the back of the boat while I kept watch. Hank did not reappear and all remained quiet. I could see a sleek white and green powerboat tied up to the dock in front of the house.

After half an hour, my eyes started to tire and I sat down with my back to the house, rubbing the soreness out of my eyelids and letting out a groan.

"Not what you expected to see?" Jaycee said.

"I don't know what I expected to see," I sighed. It was the truth. What was I trying to accomplish floating around in the middle of the bay?

We sat listening to the gulls crying overhead and watching the skies darken, partially from thickening clouds and partially from the approaching twilight.

Jaycee said, "What's your interest in these nut jobs anyway?"

"It's a long story…" Then I realized what she just said. "You know The Paynes?"

"That asylum belongs to one Courtney Payne. Lives there with her punk of a kid."

"Hank."

"Jack. Excuse me, Jackson. Real asshole. The cops are pitching in to buy a gold plaque with his name on it to hang in one of the Long Beach Township jail cells. Mom keeps pretty much to herself. Usually only comes out to bail the little bastard out. She apparently has stopped firing on all cylinders."

I sat there trying to soak it all in and make some sense out of it. "Know if anybody has seen any other women coming or going in the past couple months?"

"Got me. No one pays me to baby sit that bunch. Rumor has it that some very bizarre shit goes down there."

"Like what?"

"Let's just say people seem to think they are a very close family. Closer than most people would feel comfortable being with their immediate family."

I wasn't sure I wanted to know much more. I trained the binoculars back on the house. Two lamps in the main living area had been lit but I still couldn't see anyone. I had missed whoever had turned them on unless they were on a timer or electric cell that flicks them on when it gets dark.

The rain started again in earnest. Jaycee moved under the protection of the overhang next to the ship's wheel. "Seen enough?"

"Why?"

"Have to turn back. It's getting dark and the lights on this tub need fixing. I don't want to be running through here in the dark and bust the hull open on some rocks or garbage."

"I need to stay," I said.

"Nope." There wasn't much room for discussion in her response.

She started up the motor and walked up to the front of the boat to pull up the anchor. What now? Just walking away felt stupid, like wasted effort and money. I needed answers and I was frustrated with waiting. Jaycee returned just as I was peeling off my tank top. She stared at my empty shoes and un-strapped prosthesis now lying on the deck. I took my cell phone out of my pocket and put it in my shoe. She looked me up and down, and then regained her balance. "What the good Christ are you doing?"

"I need to know what's going on in there. One of the people in that house is responsible for me having this," I said holding up my foot, "among other things. I'm not going home until I get some answers."

Before Jaycee could respond I climbed on the edge of the boat and dove in the water. It was cool, but not cold. As I broke the surface, I heard Jaycee scream, "Get the hell back here, you idiot."

"Will you shut up?" I said, and then started swimming for the house. I focused on keeping a constant motion and breathing pattern, trying to get into a groove where I wouldn't wear myself out too fast. I was fairly certain I could make the pier but didn't rule out the possibility of drowning either.

When I stopped swimming and started treading water, the house appeared farther away than I thought it should be. I figured I was close but I still had at least a couple hundred yards to go.

I finally got to the end of the dock, trying not to audibly gasp for air and alert anybody to my presence. I looked back out into the bay and Jaycee's boat was gone. My grip on the slick piling was tenuous while I listened to the water slap against the wood of the dock and waited for my lungs to stop aching. Rain, colder than the water, poured from the skies and churned the oily bay around me.

Quietly paddling through the water toward the powerboat in search of a ladder, I realized that hopping around the house half naked without cane or foot would not be the quietest activity in the world. I needed to find something to lean on, quickly. Finding some sort of dry clothing would be a bonus.

Grasping the ladder and placing a foot on the second rung, I used my arms to pull myself up, and jump up to the next rung. After hopping up half a dozen rungs, I poked my head just over the dock to look around. No one in sight. I crawled off the top of the ladder onto my hands and knees. Thankfully this dock didn't wobble back and forth but the rain made it slick. Rising gingerly, I hopped toward the house as delicately as possible, slipping and falling only once. My heart was pounding in my chest, in part from the swim, but more so now from trying to stay alert to any movement; I didn't know what I'd do if someone suddenly came around the corner, but I tried not to think about it. In that sense the rain was playing in my favor. I leapt up the wooden staircase leading to the patio, leaning on the handrail to keep the noise of my bare foot slapping against the wood to a minimum.

All looked quiet on the back patio. The lamps that were lit were large, sand colored ceramic jobs with pleated shades. Going through the patio doors might be a bit obvious, I thought. Maybe I could get lucky going through the garage instead.

The smell of gas and oil was strong as I entered the cold damp room and flicked on the lights, two bare bulbs hanging from the ceiling. A black BMW 325i and a blue Mercedes 560 XL convertible sat sleeping, content to be out of the pouring rain. No blue Jag but the little sports car was a close replacement. The left side of the garage was large enough to store the usual garage junk, bicycles, lawn and garden tools, tennis rackets and hold a solid looking workbench, complete with all manner of hand tools. Next to the workbench was a small set of stairs leading to a door that had to open into back into the house.

There was no handrail on the stairs leading into the garage and rather than make seal noises hopping from one step to the next, not to mention the risk of falling on my ass, again, I sat on the top step and lowered my butt down a step at a time until I hit the cold concrete floor. I quickly brushed away the memory of the basement floor at Hill's house.

The place was immaculate. I looked around and there was not a spot on the floor or walls: no dirt, no oil, no grease. The entire garage was pristine. The cars were showroom clean, not a spot of dirt, nick, ding or scratch anywhere. All the car windows were tinted so it was tough to see inside but I imagined the interiors were just as spotless. The side where all the garden tools and toys were stored was just as ordered. Everything had a specific place, everything was spaced equally. It was like looking at a carefully orchestrated still life painting. The work bench, identical. All the tools hung on a pegboard resembling a completed jigsaw puzzle. I felt like I had stumbled into a museum showing some bizarre time slice of life in OCD America.

I looked around for something I could use as a cane and spotted wooden poles stacked neatly against the wall, the type used to stake garden plants. Those would work except for the noise of wood against hardwood once I got inside. I needed something to muffle the sound. I found tennis gear and pulled out what I was looking for, a new tennis ball. At the workbench I found a matting knife and sliced a small "X" through the ball and slid one of the garden stakes through the "X" opening, which was just small enough to grab the pole without slipping off and create a good cushion on the floor. The pole was about a foot taller than me but for now it would serve the purpose.

Making my way up the stairs, I looked to the left just before opening the door; a security keypad blinked its red and green lights. I thought that if Jennifer really valued her privacy, as well she should, there probably was not an audible alarm attached to the system. It was more than likely a silent trigger to some security firm. Jaycee's comments about Hank/Jack made me think it was not a link to the local police. The worst that could happen was a phone call from the security company to check the door. I checked the door handle. It turned. Holding my breath I quickly jumped through and closed it quietly. The temperature was about a hundred degrees colder inside causing instant goose flesh on my arms. I was standing in a small mudroom with a work sink, washer, dryer and a door leading to a lavatory big enough for a john and a sink. Another door at the far end I assumed led into the house proper. I was glad it was closed. Above the washer and dryer was a shelf with a neat row of boxes; detergent, bleach, and dryer sheets. The open washer was half full of clothes yet to be washed.

From somewhere in the house I heard a phone ring. Someone would be here to check the door in a minute. I rummaged through the clothes in the washer, all whites, and found a T-shirt. By the size, probably Jennifer's unless Hank was cross-dressing, which I guess was possible. I snapped off my drenched bra, threw it in the washer and slipped into the T-shirt. It hung down to my thighs and as she was skinnier than me, it clung more than I really wanted it to, especially given the temperature of the house.

The ringing stopped. Either someone answered it or no one was home and an answering machine got it. As two cars were in the garage, the boat was docked and it was pouring rain, I suspected they weren't on the beach getting a tan.

Now what? If I went back in the garage to hide I'd have to come back into the house and trip the alarm again. Not good. Walking into the house now was too risky. No place to hide in the bathroom. A rat couldn't hide in that closet. If I went in and closed the door that would just create suspicion. I looked at the front-loading dryer.

Sometimes it pays to be small.

Forty-One

From inside the dryer, the click of the door opening was muffled as were the footsteps in the mudroom. I couldn't tell from the sounds whether the investigator was male or female. Whoever it was I hoped they would speed things up because my neck was about to break.

Another door opened. It had to be the one leading to the garage. A small beam of light shot through the glass front door of the dryer. Shit. I left the light on when I came inside. I held my breath and prayed for two things. Whoever was in the garage would finish up quickly and two, the metal rib of the dryer drum would not snap my spine in half. Oh, yes, and Mom, while you're at it, prevent them from looking in the dryer please. I closed my eyes and waited, starting to sweat from fear and from being entombed in a metal cylinder with limited breathing space. It was at that precise moment my brain thought it proper to imagine how much pain I'd be in if someone turned the dryer on. There is a recovery phrase, "When you're in your head you're behind enemy lines." No shit.

A half century later I heard a door shut. I was waiting for the other one to close when I heard the slam of the washer door closing. I tensed. My stomach was in my throat. There was silence that seemed to last forever. Finally, a quick grating sound that made me stiffen followed by a rush of water. The washer was on. Not the dryer. Oh, please not the dryer.

The dryer door opened and I pressed myself against the back wall as hard as I could, closing my eyes and praying to become invisible.

From inside the house, the phone rang.

"Damn." Jennifer's voice. I heard her walk out the room without closing the door. I quickly and quietly unfolded my body out of the dryer and immediately collapsed like a rag doll on the floor. The circulation in my legs had been cut off making the good one numb and useless. I grabbed my makeshift stake/tennis ball cane that I had hid behind the bathroom door, pulled myself up and willed my leg to keep me that way. The growing pins and needles let me know the blood was re-circulating but just putting weight on the one good leg felt like real pins and needles piercing my skin and muscle. I decided I had to get moving anyway and stumbled my way into the house.

The glass doors to the patio were on my left. To the right, a dining area with an entrance that led into the kitchen where a female voice was saying, "No, everything looks to be fine. The lights were on in the garage but the doors were closed and nothing looked disturbed." Except for the people living here, I thought.

I quietly hobbled across the living area looking for a place to regroup. Going upstairs was out of the question, especially if Hank was up there torturing small animals. I headed for the hallway where I had seen all the closed doors during my first excursion in the house.

"Thank you," I heard the woman say and hang up. Ducking into a full bathroom on my right I climbed in the shower enclosure and pulled the mottled glass door shut. The prickling in my legs was forcing me to move around. It was impossible to stand still. Quietly, I hopped on my good leg in the enclosure which brought some relief.

In mid-jump, the bathroom light came on. I froze, tried not to breathe, and hoped no one wanted to take a shower. I didn't dare move my head but shifted my eyes toward the glass. A distorted figure rippled across the glass back and forth and I assumed it was Jennifer moving around. A wooden cabinet slammed shut, every nerve in my body twitched. The pins and needles were starting to fade, thank Mom. If I wanted to I could have jumped out of my skin.

A rustling sound, like she was changing clothes. Maybe she had a hot date? Whatever she was doing I wished she'd hurry up and get the hell out of the bathroom. More rustling, then walking…toward the shower! I closed my eyes. Then I heard a click. I cracked open my eyelids and saw muted darkness. She was gone.

"I can't take much more of this," I muttered to myself.

I crept out of the bathroom, making sure the coast was clear. All was quiet. Sneaking down the hallway, I poked my head into a room filled with a pig sty of wires, electronics, strewn clothing and food, but no human life forms. A door on the opposite side of the hall opened up into another bedroom. Ice white walls offset a black metallic bed frame with a sheer white duvet and pillows. The remaining furniture was a deep mahogany, all of it squared off and angular. It reminded me of a sparse and sterile hotel room. A large frameless rectangular mirror hung on the wall over the dresser. Two sets of French doors made up the bayside wall, each covered in thick white draperies, hanging like frost in a freezer. No dust, no dirt, everything was beyond perfect. No magazines or books on the bedside tables, no array of perfume bottles on the dresser, no clothes draped over chairs. Just a single item on the dresser, the man I'd seen on Hill's desk and upstairs in Jennifer's room stared out at me. I examined it and on the back of the picture, through the acrylic, it read "Dad, 1951." Dad? What the...? Jennifer and Hill had the same Dad? How could that be?

Back in the hallway, there was another small bedroom, just as sparse and well ordered.

Footsteps were making their way toward me. Needing to disappear fast I tried the first closed door within reach. A fully stocked linen closet. There wasn't time to figure out how to squish myself in there. There was another door next to the closet. Inside was darkness and...steps. A basement? I nearly leapt in and quickly, but quietly, closed the door. The footsteps passed by. I was about to climb back out when a rustling in the darkness below me caught my ear. Where did the steps lead?

Wait a minute. There were no basements on LBI. Everything was built on pylons or concrete. There were no lights down the stairs and judging by the depth of the darkness, no windows allowing daylight in. I froze and listened.

There. Something was there. Could have been a mouse. Or a cat. Or some other animal. Maybe Hank had a guinea pig. No, he was more the snake type. I wished I hadn't thought of that. There was a crack of light from underneath the hallway door. I hobbled down a few steps until I was stopped by a wall. Groping along it I discovered the staircase took a ninety degree turn to the left. I continued feeling along the walls, searching for a light switch. Nothing.

Then again, maybe turning on the lights wasn't a great idea. What if it was Hank down here? Maybe he used the basement as his little play room? If only I had a flashlight, or some matches...My hand went to my shorts pocket. Jaycee's Bic lighter was still there.

The rustling sounded again. I pulled the lighter from my shorts and hoped my swim in the bay hadn't messed it up. I flicked it on quickly and it lit first time. There were about three more steps until I reached the floor.

I released the switch on the lighter and stood quietly, letting my eyes adjust to any degree they could. The room had a closed-in moldy smell mixed with something strong. It took me back to the hospital, that same rotten/clean smell, trying to mask the scent of decay with antiseptic cleansers. It was pungent enough to choke in my throat. I held my right arm straight out to the right side of my body with the lighter in my hand. I snapped it on. It wasn't much illumination, but enough to see a mostly empty space. A flat concrete floor with unfinished walls showing studs against solid stone. I exchanged my make shift cane for the lighter and repeated the process on the left side. Not much difference, except for a large furnace. Against the wall I saw a small window with the glass blacked out. So it really wasn't a basement, the room was still above ground. However, this room was kept dark for a reason. I rose my arm and almost hit one of the beams of the unfinished ceiling that wasn't more than six feet high.

My thumb was heating up so I took it off the lighter and let the flame go out.

I heard the rustle again. It was on the left side, far back in the corner. I took a few small steps into the room, listening. There it was again, only now there was another sound; metallic. Metal on metal.

I didn't know how long the lighter would last. I didn't want to waste the fuel but without it I was blind... Blind. That's the answer. I balanced on my leg, pointed my stake at an angle to the ground in front of me and waved it back and forth. Inching forward a half step at a time, I waved the cane back and forth across the floor, repeating this motion with each step. The rustling continued and grew louder directly in front of me. I knew I was heading in the right direction.

After fifteen minutes of inching forward my leg was starting to tire. I leaned on the cane for a moment to rest. Even in the cold and damp I was sweating, half from exertion, half from fear. I didn't know why I was drawn to the noise. I just knew I had to find out what it was.

I resumed my process. After two steps I hit something metal. It sounded like a pole, a steel pole. It had a hollow ring to it.

I flicked on the lighter. The brightness blinded me for a second.

I looked down, and then I screamed.

Forty-Two

The lighter flew out of my hand and clattered across the floor to the right. It wasn't what I saw. Please Mom, let it not be what I saw. Panic, fear and revulsion coursed through me. My breathing was jagged. Letting go of the stake, I fell on all fours, searching with my hands for the lighter.

"Come on. Where is the damn thing," I said out loud. There was a muffled moan to my left.

"Here, let me help you," said a voice to my right.

A bare bulb sitting in a short lamp on a table clicked on. Sitting there in an old wooden dining chair, half smiling, was Hank.

I looked to my left, and cried out.

Pat. His arms and legs were handcuffed to an iron rail bed. A blind-fold wrapped around his head. Duct tape wrapped around his mouth. His one hand, with only four fingers, was neatly bandaged. One of his toes was missing as well, his right foot sporting the same bandaged condition as his hand. He was naked. A catheter was inserted in his penis leading to a bag attached to the bed. An IV drip was attached to the bed and stuck into his arm.

I jumped to his side trying to remove the blindfold.

"Don't touch him," Hank screamed.

I was successful and Pat started blinking quickly, trying to focus.

"I said don't touch him." Hank grabbed my T-shirt and yanked me away from the bed and tossed me, sprawling across the concrete. Pat was trying to shout under his gag. He knew it was me but still couldn't focus. The roll across the hard floor rattled my brain, but I put all my will into scrambling back up and confronting Hank, who stood in front of the bed, his head and shoulders hunched to keep from hitting the low exposed beams of the ceiling.

"Move," I growled.

"Make me." My eyes shifted to the floor. I dove back to the floor for my makeshift cane but Hank was quicker and stood over me holding the pole.

"Not this time, bitch." He pulled the tennis ball off the end. "Cute." I stood back up, balancing on one leg.

"Come on," he taunted. "Come get me, hot stuff. Come on, bitch, show your brother how tough you are. Show him that even on one foot you can kick my ass." I glared at Pat. The single bulb reflected off his watering eyes. He shook his head, pleading with me not to do anything.

"Yeah, I didn't think so. See this, Little Bro?" Hank said, pointing to the line of stitches on his hand where broken wine bottles had left a calling card when we last met. "Your big sister gave me that."

"Not to mention the stitches across your cheek," I said with a smile.

Hank's face darkened. "You didn't give me those. You're not that good. Still, not bad considering I never expected you to show up at all. It's an odd thing about cars without brakes. You just can never tell how they're going to react, can you Little Bro? The little cunt here just got real lucky. I thought for sure they'd have carted her away in pieces."

I wanted to jump on him and rip his throat out, just eviscerate the bastard with my bare hands.

Shuddering, trying to maintain, I said, "How? You weren't at the funeral."

"Got that right. Wouldn't catch me at a dyke funeral."

"With Jennifer, or should I say Carolyn, being chief dyke in residence."

"Shut the fuck up," he said, softly taking a step forward, his hands turning red clenching the stick.

I had to keep him talking. I had to get to the lamp, it was the only way I was going to have a chance to get out of this with my skin while keeping Pat alive.

"So who gave you the new threads in your face? Try to steal some cookies from a sixth grade Girl Scout?"

"Guy got lucky is all. Trust me, he got the worse end of the deal, which he deserved," he said, an evil grin showing yellowed teeth. "But, you know all about that."

I quickly looked at Pat. Nine fingers, nine toes but all his other body parts appeared intact. "What the hell..." I gasped. "Snevley. You twisted prick. What did he ever do to you?"

Hank shrugged. "Snooping around, asking the wrong questions of the wrong people. Fellow can get hurt that way."

It wasn't possible to hate one person any more than I hated Hank in that moment, but how could I get him off guard, just for a second, to go after him? "Can I have the stick back? My leg is really getting tired."

He smiled. "What am I, fucking stupid? You need to sit? Here..."

He moved fast, swinging the stick like a sword, sideswiping my leg out from under me and sending me crashing to the stone floor. Pain from solid wood hitting bone finally registered in my leg. I grasped it and rocked back and forth, trying not to cry out. I could hear Pat scream behind the tape and struggle against his bindings.

"What's the matter, Little Bro? Oh, don't work yourself up. It's not good for you." Hank walked over, straddled my body and with one swift blow speared the stake down on the end of my stump. I must have screamed but the blinding pain was all that I sensed, a searing white mass of agony that would not stop.

He squatted down and hauled me up with a fistful of T-shirt so we were face to face. "Not so tough now, huh? You couldn't leave it alone. You had to keep pushing and pushing. And now, it's all going to come tumbling down around you."

Reality started to come back into focus. Everything was still blurry but the white-hot pain was slowly fading. Each of my legs throbbed. I was exhausted, I hurt and I didn't want to play anymore. Mom, is this really what you wanted from me?

Hank pulled me closer so the neck of the T-shirt was stretched out, giving him a full view of my chest. "Huh. I've seen better. Still, that won't prevent us from having a little fun first."

I gasped. Lucas Hill's words. Rage started boiling in my chest. I was not going to go through that again.

"What do you think, Little Bro? Think you'll get off watching me do your big sister? Maybe we'll do one of those dyke prison movie scenes using a broom handle, although all we got is this splintered stake she brought with her. Well, we'll make do. I'm sure she won't mind. In any case I won't, which is the important part."

"You couldn't get it up anyway. Jack," I said. His jaw tightened, but before he said anything I smiled, and then spit in his eyes. His grip eased enough for me to pull away and shove him back on his ass.

"Bitch," he screamed.

I scrambled to the table and swiped at the lamp just as he grabbed the back of my shirt and flung me backwards. The lamp tumbled and the bulb shattered into a thousand pieces, sending the room back into darkness. I rolled to one side and sat up on my knees, moving as far away as possible from where he thought I sat.

"Where are you, bitch? I will find you..." I heard a solid whistling through the air. He was thrashing the stick back and forth. I stayed still. He was moving to my left.

A loud 'bang' echoed through the room as he clubbed the side of the furnace. I rolled to my right, in what I thought was the direction of the stairs, stopping after three or four rolls, trying not to breathe.

"Think you're cute, don't you? You stupid cunt. You can't get out of here without me hearing you, and with one leg I don't think you'll be outrunning me anytime soon."

He was swinging the stick again. Good boy, I thought, keep telling me where you are. I rolled again and stopped.

"Tell me where you are right now, God damn it or I'm walking back and smashing your fucking brother's skull in with this stick. You hear me, bitch?"

I was about to roll again when the basement became flooded with light. We batted our eyes at the brightness. Hank was about ten feet to my left. From the top of the stairs a calm female voice said, "Hank? That's enough. Bring her upstairs."

Forty-Three

Making it easy for Hank was not high on my to-do list. I struggled and thrashed as he dragged me up the stairs, wrapping me up in a half nelson and holding me aloft by my shorts.

"Let go of me," I said squirming and clawing at anything, mostly air, with my free arm. He just pushed harder against my head until I thought it would rip out of my neck. Down the hallway, he flung me into the sterile bedroom and I crumpled into a heap on the floor. Hank grabbed a black, straight-backed wooden chair from the dressing table and thumped it in the center of the room. Picking me up by the shirt collar he slammed me into the chair. I kicked him in the leg as hard as I could, possibly doing more damage to my toes than his leg. He smiled as he backhanded me across the face. The sting subsided and the taste of blood seeped into my mouth from my lip, now split. My eyes started watering but I just stared back at him.

"Feel like a big man now? Hitting someone half your size? You're just a fucking coward." More Lucas déjà vu.

"You know what? You're right," he said, grabbing me off the chair and plunging his knee into my stomach. All the air shot out of my lungs as I collapsed on the floor. I couldn't breathe. I was suffocating, gulping like a fish stranded on the sand. Mom, give me some air! Smirking, he opened a door to a long walk-in closet filled with neat racks of women's clothes from what I could see. He pulled a rumpled brown paper bag from behind one of the racks and moved the dresses back in place, making sure they were in their original perfectly ordered space.

Finally, I was able to gasp some air and my lungs stopped burning. I wasn't going to die although I definitely felt like hurling. Pulled back into the chair, my head spun and everything was a blur. My hands were yanked behind me and bound tightly with heavy plastic ties, cutting into my wrists. I recalled DaKota's funeral and seeing the ligature marks on her wrists. I heard a ripping sound and felt my leg become part of the chair. I looked down; my leg was duct taped to the chair leg leaving my stump free. The hit I had taken from the stake split about an inch of scar on my stump and I watched drops of blood hit the white carpet. I tried pulling my arms but only the straps wouldn't budge without slicing into my wrists.

Breathing was getting easier but I still felt nauseous. That's the last thing I wanted to do, get sick in front of Hank. I pushed the queasiness aside and replaced it with anger, determined not to give him the pleasure of watching me puke. It turns out he had a different plan in mind anyway.

Grabbing what he could of my short hair, he yanked my head up and slapped a strip of duct tape over my mouth. I tried moving my head but he just pulled harder. I was sucking in as much air through my nose as I could, trying not to suffocate.

Hank bent at the waist so his face was inches from mine. "I'm going to solve a mystery for you. I know you're just itching to find out exactly how your, what do you call yourselves, partners? What a load of shit that is. Partners. Anyway, how your little partner met her fate. Better still, I'm not going to tell you, I'm going to give you a demonstration."

Images of DaKota's bedroom the night I found her leapt into my brain. I tried to cry out but it all came out as a mumble.

"What's that? You don't want to know?"

I shook my head.

"Oh, that's too bad. I really thought you wanted to know. Well, that's okay. I'm going to show you anyway. Just because I'm a good guy."

He went to the bed and I heard the bag rustling. He came back holding a small white can with blue and black printing. The can had some sort of trigger mechanism on the top that held what looked like a long red cocktail straw.

"See this?" He held the can up to me and I saw the words "Dust Be Gone" on the front.

"Don't worry. There's nothing to be scared of. It's just air." He pumped the trigger quickly twice to prove his point. The can made two short loud hissing sounds, not unlike the air hose at a gas station.

"Here's the cool part," Hank said. He turned the can upside down and gave the trigger one long squeeze. A whitish-gray cloud shot out of the tube, about six inches in length, dispersing outward from one end to the other.

"Cool, isn't it? This stuff gives you such a great buzz. All I wanted to do was show poor DaKota how good it could make her feel. She was feeling so down and out, you know? I just wanted to lift her up some, but she put up a fuss and," he said shrugging, "I guess she got a little too much. It's a shame really. You want to try?" he said holding the can in front of my face. I shook my head. I could feel my eyes watering.

"No? Aw, come on. You don't know what you're missing."

I just kept shaking my head 'no' as best I could.

"No, huh," he said pretending to think for a minute. "Oh I know what's missing."

From his pocket he produced a small metal cylinder that made my heart stop. He unscrewed the top and poked the red straw down into the white powder and then carefully reattached it to the can of air.

"You don't mind do you?" He made fast work of two ragged lines of coke he'd cut on the dresser.

Almost three years since my last line of coke. Mom, please save me from this. This isn't going to happen, is it? Tears dropped on my cheeks and breathing was getting difficult with my nose starting to run.

He walked over to me, eyes wide and black, a maniacal grin on his face. "Come on, I know this is your favorite stuff. Don't you remember all those great feelings, the strength that you could do anything in the world? I know you miss it. Once a junkie, always a junkie."

I started screaming as best I could but all I tasted was the bitter adhesive from the tape. I thrashed back and forth in the chair, trying anything to keep him away. Hank pushed the chair down and sat on my lap facing me. I kept flailing my upper body, trying to tip the chair over, trying desperately to keep him away from me.

The next thing I knew Hank caught me with his forearm under my chin, pressing my head to the back of the chair. He held the can upside down, jammed the red tube up my nose and pulled the trigger.

Forty-Four

If there was a way to get instantly baked, this was it. Everything moved. I watched Hank get off of me but he appeared to go very slowly and leave a faint vapor trail. My head stayed back resting on the chair. I let it loll from one side to the other. Initially it was a peaceful, but intense buzz, but I could feel the coke swimming into my system. Memories sand-blasted through my brain. My nerve endings danced as if they were electric wires cut loose and flailing through the air. I tried to shake my head, shake the wooziness away and stop the high-speed buzzing in my brain, but it held on.

Hank leaned over and ripped the tape off my mouth. I didn't feel any-thing; I may have even smiled between the gulps of air I was trying to swallow.

"You bastard," I said as I tried to stop myself from giggling while tears streamed down my face.

Hank patted the top of my head. "You be a good little girl now. I have some other things to take care of. Then I'll be back to have some more fun."

He reached into the bag and pulled out a long rod that had a black molded plastic handle attached to a thin red rod that split into two prongs at the end. He held it in front of my face and clicked a button on the handle. Two electric sparks sizzled off the prongs.

"Ooooo," I said.

"Oh, don't worry," he said. "This isn't for you. Yet."

He left the room and I heard him thumping slowly down the basement steps. Even through the slowly fading haze I realized what was going to happen. Basement. Cattle prod. Pat. Shit.

I struggled against my bindings feeling strong enough to rip them apart, but somewhere knowing that it was all an illusion. All I accomplished was digging the straps deeper into my wrists. I thought about tipping the chair backwards to break it, but then realized my hands would be part of the breakage. I tried to jump up, tried to move the chair into the hallway. I had to stop that bastard.

"You really won't get very far like that," said a voice in front of me.

I looked up and there was a fuzzy figure leaning against the doorframe. I shook my head again and tried to focus.

"I know you, I think," I slurred. The fuzzy figure approached and pushed my chair back on all fours. I started humming. I think it was one of the band's songs but I don't really remember.

After about fifteen minutes, my vision started to clear, the merry-go-round was slowing and my sinuses were throbbing.

"Speechless? That's a first."

"So I was right. Jennifer Payne and Carolyn Hill are one and the same. Looks like your face cleared up okay, or was that a fake too?"

"What do you think?"

"Pat's downstairs," I said. "You've got to help him."

"Oh, he'll be fine. Hank won't touch him. Not unless you continue to cause problems. You are a tough one I'll give you that."

Jennifer walked over to the mirror and inspected her blond hair. She wore it loose unlike the first time I saw her in the restaurant. Opening a drawer and pulling out a brush, she carefully combed out each side until every strand was in place. Satisfied, she put the brush back in the drawer, closed it and turned back to me, smiling. Her eyes, however, were black; black with a fury buried somewhere deep inside, a fury that would surface if I pushed the wrong button.

"You just wouldn't leave it alone would you?" she said.

A light bulb went off in my head. "You're the one who called threatening me to stop. Are you the psycho that hacked off Pat's finger?"

She smiled thinly. "Naturally. At one time I was a nurse so there's no need to worry. If you had just gone about your business, running your little record store and playing with your stupid little band pretending to be a rock star, none of this would be happening. But, no, you wouldn't stop and now we have this…situation that needs to be dealt with."

"I still don't understand. Why did Hank cut my brake line? Why did you kidnap Pat? Why the entire charade about being in love with him? None of this makes any sense."

"I'm a bit disappointed. Pat always used to tell me how smart you were. Jesus, he barely talked about anything else but you." She stood and started pacing the room. "All that endless dribble about what a "cool" person you were and how proud he was of you. It was like he worshipped you, some royal princess to whom we were all supposed to bow before. Always on and on about family. What a great family you were. What a loving family you were. How close you all were." Her pace had increased and I saw she was wringing her hands in front of her. "Family this and family that. There were days that I wanted to scream. Seriously. Sometimes I thought if I had to endure one more second about his wonderful family I would..."

"Kill someone?" I offered.

Turning to look at me, her eyes on fire, her lips pursed she said, "Oh, yes. There was no question, but, I am not capable of that. Believe me. I don't have what it takes to kill anyone or anything. Unlike you."

"Me? What the hell are you talking about? I haven't killed anybody!"

She stood in front of me. "Oh, no?"

We stared at each other in silence. I just didn't know what to think or what she thought I had done.

"Stand up," she said.

"That's a bit tough with my leg taped to the chair."

"You can do it. You can do anything according to Patrick."

I leaned forward and lifted my butt in the air, trying to balance on one leg. I thought I had it until forward momentum kicked in and I started tipping, the floor rushing up to meet my face. The chair, however, suddenly stopped. Carolyn had grabbed the top of it and was helping me regain balance.

"Come on. Hop this way," she said with a soft giggle. She held on as I hopped into the hallway, stopping at the open door to the darkened basement steps.

"There's no way I can go down steps like this," I said.

"Oh, don't worry. You don't have to." She pushed the top of the chair forward. All four feet hit the floor but then started to tip backwards toward the staircase.

"Whoa," I screamed. Halfway down the chair stopped, Carolyn's foot on the rung between the legs. She pushed it down so all four legs were back on the floor.

"Thanks," I said. She just smiled.

"Now. I want you to say hello to your brother."

I looked at her, confused.

"Go ahead. Say 'hello.'"

"Pat?" I called over my shoulder.

"Chynna?" The voice was weak and garbled, as if he was losing his voice.

"You okay?"

"Of course he's okay," Carolyn snapped. "Now, let's play a little game." She went into the spare bedroom and came back with a similar chair mine. She placed it on my left side and sat, her back to the living room.

"I'm going to ask you some questions. You have to answer me as best you can. For every wrong answer, there's a penalty that Hank will administer." She said, her eyes moving to the door.

"Pat!" I screamed.

"Oh there's nothing he can do about it."

"What about right answers?"

She cocked her head to the side thoughtfully. "I never considered that."

Fear and panic took up permanent residence in my gut. "You're insane."

"Mmmmm, possibly, but that really doesn't matter now does it? So," she said sitting up straight and smoothing her pants, as if she were a teacher about to start a lesson, "Ready? First question. You killed DaKota Gibson didn't you?"

"No!"

She looked at me, almost sadly. "No. That's not correct. Hank?" she called. It was followed by a sizzle, then a scream from the basement. Hank was using the cattle prod on Pat. A vice grip of helpless panic seized my chest and sweat broke out on my forehead. "Pat!" I screamed.

"OK," Carolyn said, appearing nonplussed by anything that was happening. "Next question. Why did you kill DaKota Gibson?"

Through clenched teeth I said, "I did not kill DaKota. Hank did. He admitted it to me."

"Hank?"

Another scream from Pat. I thrashed in my chair rocking it side to side, screaming, trying to break the bonds. I was breathing hard and bathed in sweat. "What makes you think I killed her?"

"Oh no, that's not right. You're not allowed to ask any questions until you answer one correctly and so far, well, you are not doing very well. Maybe you'll get better. We have a lot more questions to go through. Like this one. Why did you steal DaKota away from me?"

"I didn't steal DaKota from anybody. I didn't even know about her relationship with you until two weeks ago. I swear that's the truth. I didn't find the pictures until after DaKota was dead. I didn't know. I swear I didn't know!"

Carolyn sighed, looked down and shook her head. "No. I don't think so," she said. "What do you think, Hank?"

"She's lying. She'd say anything now."

"Hmmm. I'm afraid I agree with Hank."

Then I heard Pat's voice. "No. No. NO!" Followed by another sizzling sound and a howling scream.

"I'll kill you," I screamed through my tears. "I will absolutely fucking kill you. You and Hank. You are the sickest people I know and if you had any guts you'd untie me and face me one on one. There's absolutely no excuse for you and that psycho freak downstairs continuing to walk on this earth."

Carolyn got up and slapped me hard, but I kept yelling as a distraction to keep her from turning around and seeing two uniforms and Douglas creeping through the house towards us, guns drawn.

"Fuck you. You think you can get me to stop, you twisted bitch? You and Freddie Krueger in the basement should be buried alive."

"That's a bit harsh, don't you think?" she said with a smirk.

No answer was necessary as one of the uniforms grabbed her from behind, put a hand over her mouth and dragged her back, kicking and thrashing into the living area. Douglas knelt down to undo the tape.

"Stop," I whispered. "Pat's downstairs." Douglas's eyes widened. "He's chained to a bed. Hank is torturing him with a cattle prod. You've got to get Hank up here and call 911. We need paramedics for Pat."

Douglas moved me away from the door opening, picked up the chair Carolyn was sitting in and hurled it down the hallway. It bounced off the wall, smashing a full length mirror and tumbled in pieces across the floor, leaving a gash in the woodwork. I could hear Carolyn struggle harder in the living area.

Douglas pressed his back against the wall next to the door, his gun pointing upwards and held in both hands.

From the basement Hank called, "What's going on up there?" Douglas put a finger to his lips.

Hank was ascending, one step at a time. Then there was silence. I looked at Douglas. He was trying to hear Hank's steps.

Then all hell broke loose.

"Ow, god damn. Holy shit!" It was one of the officers from the living room.

I turned and the uniform that was holding Carolyn grasped his hand as blood poured down it. Carolyn had blood around her mouth from where she'd bitten him.

"Hank! He's at the top of the stairs with a gun! Unhhhh," the other uniform stunned her with a taser and she collapsed on the floor in a heap.

Fast footsteps on the stairs, going back down. Douglas whipped around into a spread legged stance in the doorframe, pointing his gun down the steps.

"Shit," he said and started down, clumping with his cast-encrusted leg.

"Call 911!" I shouted at the uniforms.

"Already have."

"Pat! Are you okay? Pat!" I called over my shoulder. No answer. The two uniforms were still dealing with Carolyn. "One of you guys want to get me out of this chair?"

"Wait a second," one of them responded. I couldn't see them anymore. I heard a crash below, as if someone had knocked a shelf of junk onto the floor, and then the sound of glass being smashed.

"Come on!" I screamed. One of the guys came down the hall. "I was helping the other officer wrap his hand up. Crazy woman almost bit clean through him."

He ripped the tape off my legs. "Mother of..." If that's what waxing feels like I'll never do it.

"Miles? You have the cutters? Going to have to cut the cuff straps."

"Fine, fine, just do it. Hurry."

Just as he cut them a gunshot exploded and shouting voices erupted outside. The officers ran and I hopped into the living area. Through the darkness and the pouring rain I saw Hank standing on the dock, in one hand he held Jaycee's ponytail yanking her head back, in the other an eight inch gleaming blade poised at her neck. On the dock lay Jaycee's gun.

"One more step and she's dead," Hank shouted.

"I missed the little prick..." Jaycee started to say until Hank yanked her head back harder.

I knew the cruelty this psycho could dish out but I'd had enough. I was not going to live with the blood of one more person on my hands. I hopped onto the porch. One of the cops grabbed my arm but I shook him off.

"Where are you going to go?" I shouted, taking small measured jumps forward. "We have Carolyn inside and you're trapped on the dock. You've got nowhere to run."

"Stay back or I'll fucking kill her. I swear. You know I will."

"Yeah? And then what? Jump in the bay and swim to the mainland? Even you aren't that stupid."

"Get back!" he screamed. I stopped but I could see confusion flicker across his face. "I'm taking her in the boat. You'll never find me. I can put in to shore anywhere or just abandon it and swim. And as for her," he said pushing the edge of the blade against her throat, "she'll make good bait once I cut her up in small pieces."

The heavens opened and the rain suddenly came down in sheets. Visibility was almost nil in the thirty feet that separated us. I thought about running straight at him through the rain. I had a slim chance he couldn't see what I was doing if I could do it fast enough while the rain was in full force. With one leg, though, I knew I'd never be fast enough. He was inching back towards the edge of the dock and the speedboat.

Something on my right was suddenly blocking the rain. I squinted through the wash and saw Douglas, his eyes riveted in a cold stare at Hank.

"Bastard stunned me," was all he said and slowly walked toward him.

"Back off right now, man, or she's going down. I'm not fucking kidding."

Douglas didn't stop but veered off to the side giving Hank and Jaycee a wide berth. A step at a time he moved to the end of the dock and purposefully took out his gun.

Hank laughed, "Not a chance, man. Put that down now."

Douglas quickly raised his gun and emptied it, one shot at time, into the gas tank of the speedboat. The fuel drained in streams into the black bay waters. Hank stared in disbelief.

"Now what, asshole?" Douglas said, calmly, the rain streaming down his face.

"I still have her boat, shithead," Hank yelled, nodding toward Jaycee's boat, which was docked behind Hank's at the end of the dock.

"But you have to get through me first," Douglas said. "And if you hurt that woman, the officers here will blast you off this dock in pieces so small the fish won't even care. Give it up."

Hank was trapped and he knew it. I moved closer, hopping as quietly as I could. It is true about trapped animals being the most dangerous. Hanks face showed confusion, fear and anger, twisting his head from side to side, looking at me, then at Douglas. With nowhere to go he let loose a growling scream. I moved as fast as I could, and flung my body at him, but not before he pulled the knife back. Jaycee started to move but wasn't fast enough and Hank plunged the blade into her side. She let out a deep howl of pain and crumpled to the pier at the same time I hit Hank full force, sending us tumbling next to Jaycee.

Rage exploded as I scrambled to my knees above Hank, clasped both hands together and slammed them down on his face. His nose easily gave way again, blood and cartilage splashing across his cheeks. Even so he had not relinquished the knife and in his pain was thrashing his arm wildly. I felt hot stab in my arm as the knife slashed across me but I didn't care. I jabbed both thumbs hard into Hank's eyes. The agony was enough to make him drop the knife and convulse, holding his hands to his face, screaming.

I snatched the blade off the dock and gripped it with both hands. "This is from DaKota," I growled and raised the blade with both hands above my head.

"Chynna! Stop!" Douglas screamed through the rain. "Put the knife down. Slowly."

I glared at his face, hate, anger, rage pushing me on, wanting to complete what I had started.

"Don't do it," he said. "It won't bring her back."

I looked down at Hank, now unconscious, his face stained pink from the blood running from his eye sockets, diluted by the rain.

"It's over," Douglas said quietly and I felt him gently take the weapon from my hands.

The power was draining from me. The other cops were attending to Jaycee, cautiously moving her into the house.

The rain still beat against me and it was starting to turn cold.

"Come on inside," Douglas said offering his hand.

Forty-Five

Getting everyone to Manahawkin Hospital on the mainland proved to be a bigger chore than necessary. Initially, only one ambulance showed up, which took Jaycee, alive but unconscious, and Hank with an armed escort. Pat and I went in the second one when it arrived. Carolyn was transported in a cruiser.

Douglas presented me with my foot, cell phone and shoes. I was too exhausted to find out how he got them from Jaycee's boat.

In the ambulance I made a quick call, then sat and held Pat's hand while the paramedics checked him out. Pat's mouth and lips were covered with sores from repeated strips of duct tape being stuck on and ripped off. The two attendants snapped medical terms I didn't understand back and forth. Out of the back window I could see we were leaving the island, crossing over the causeway. I was still bothered. I was trying to fit everybody into a puzzle that just wouldn't take shape.

One of the attendants started treating the wound on my arm. The slash inflicted by Hank separated the Scorpio tattoo on my arm in two.

"Is he going to be okay?" I finally asked.

A female attendant who could have easily been an Olympic weight lifter smiled up at me. "Oh, I think so. He may not look it, but he'll be fine. What happened to his hand and foot, do you know?"

I shivered just thinking about it. "He had as finger and toe amputated."

"Well, whoever did it knew what they were doing. It's a clean wound, stitched up nicely. Not infected."

I stared out the back window. I couldn't talk about it anymore.

Later that night, after everyone had been stitched up and treated, Douglas and I were sitting in a small lounge area the hospital set up for visiting families.

"You all right?" he asked.

"Yeah. I guess so. How did you know where to find me?"

"Your friend Jaycee, who is a character and a half by the way. I kept calling and calling your cell phone trying to reach you. She finally picked it up and we exchanged information. Once she told me what you had done I knew there was going to be trouble."

"How did you know that?"

He said, "New information uncovered by the Philadelphia police."

"Such as?"

Just then the door to the lounge area opened and in walked Dr. Eileen Kane.

"Interrupting?" she said.

"Not at all," I said and got up to give her a big hug.

"Sergeant Douglas, I think you remember Dr. Kane." I said. "Doctor Kane made sure I didn't lose my mind after the accident."

"I'm glad you called me," she said looking me square in the eye. "So how are you?"

"Okay, I think. I still have a crap-load of unanswered questions."

"I think we all do," said a voice at the door. Gralewski walked in and sat down in an empty chair facing the sofa, flanking Douglas, who looked at me and rolled his eyes. I pressed my lips together to suppress a grin.

"Please," said the Detective, "don't stop on my account."

I started to speak but Dr. Kane squeezed my hand. "Detective, this woman is a patient of mine and we were in the middle of a confidential discussion. If you will excuse us?"

"And who might you be?" Gralewski snarled.

She told him. "Well, as this Detective was already in here I didn't think it was all that confidential."

"Detective Douglas was here at Ms. Lennox's request."

"Actually," said Douglas, "I think that Detective Gralewski might want to listen in to this." My eyes widened giving Douglas a "are you nuts?" stare. "Doctor, may I see you out in the hall for just one minute, please?"

Although I could tell she was suspicious, Dr. Kane and Douglas went in the hall and closed the door. I could see Douglas speaking and Dr. Kane nodding.

"So," Gralewski said.

"Don't bother," I retorted.

The two came in from the hallway and sat. "Chynna," said Dr. Kane, "Detective Douglas has convinced me that allowing Detective Gralewski to stay would be beneficial at this time, provided that all discussion in this room is confidential and may not be used in any way outside of this room."

"Look," Gralewski said, "Your client has been involved in a capital crime, she can't hide behind that rule. It's just not going to wash."

Dr. Kane looked at me. "How do you feel about that?"

I looked at Douglas. "How do *you* feel about that?"

"I have no issues," he said with a broad grin.

"Works for me," I said.

"I think maybe you better start by filling the Detective in on today's events."

I told them the story with Douglas inserting tidbits from time to time. When I was finished, Gralewski smugly said, "So you expect me to believe this guy confessed to the killing? That's convenient."

I shrugged. "Tough. He did."

"Well, let's take a step back," said Dr. Kane. "I've spoken with the mother this afternoon. I'm here because Ms. Lennox called me. I think she initially wanted me to be available for her brother, but the Police here learned of my credentials and asked me to talk with Mrs. Payne."

"Payne?" Gralewski asked. "Who's that?"

Dr. Kane continued. "The woman's name is Jennifer Payne, the young man, Hank, is her son. His name is..."

"Jackson Payne," I chimed in. Jaycee nailed that one.

"Correct," Dr. Kane gave me a smile. "There is no Carolyn Hill. Jennifer has no sister. She has a brother but no sister. Jackson, as I said, is her son. He's had quite a few run-ins with the law here, mostly drugs and assault issues."

"Is there a Mr. Payne?" I asked.

"If you mean does Jackson have a father? Yes, but there is no husband."

Douglas looked at me and said, "The information I told you I received today validated that our friend, Mr. Lucas Hill, has a dubious past. Before he became a millionaire real estate tycoon, no one had even heard about

Lucas Hill. He just sort of appeared. Further digging uncovered a document in a Nevada courthouse, a request for a legal name change some eighteen years ago. Mr. Lucas Hill was the new name. The original name was Daniel Payne."

"So," I said, "they were married at one time. Why did he change his name?"

"No," Douglas said, "they were never married. They're brother and sister."

The weight of that settled in the room. Dammit, the pictures I saw in Lucas Hill's office and in Jennifer's bedroom were the same man. I was trying to find a place for that in my head but it just wouldn't sit still.

"The picture..." I muttered.

"What picture?" asked Douglas. I explained the portrait of their father. Then I asked, "And Jack?"

Douglas looked at Dr. Kane, who barely nodded, and then at me. "Their son."

"Oh, God," I breathed.

"How good is this information?" asked Gralewski.

"I can corroborate it," Dr. Kane said. "I heard essentially the same story from Jennifer. She told me quite a lot today. You might have trouble using it because she was heavily sedated at the time. She said the activity didn't stop with his birth. Daniel and Jennifer never stopped being together. He went out and made the money but she kept her distance from everyone as much as possible. Their incestuous behavior went on for decades and when Jackson was in his teens, they both turned to him."

"Holy shit," I said.

"I know this doesn't make it easier, nor is it an excuse for his behavior, but when he was taunting and torturing you and Pat, I think, sub consciously he was going after Jennifer and Daniel. That's an assumption on my part," she said it directly to Gralewski.

"Damn," I said under my breath.

Dr. Kane explained, "It is a known pattern for incest victims to reenact their trauma in the exact way they were victimized. If Jennifer continues to get help, the past may come out but I am certain both she and Daniel were sodomized by their father. Incest frequently happens through generations. In this case Jackson seems to have found an alternative method to venting his anger."

I was digesting all this, or at least trying to. Trying to make it all fit together into something I could recognize. Something I could understand. I looked at Douglas. "So…" I said. He put his hand up to stop me and gestured to Dr. Kane. She took my hand. "There's more," she said. "Jackson was not the only child born to Daniel and Jennifer. They had another one prior to Jackson. A girl. Her name was…"

"Aw, shit, no!" I yelled.

"Yes. Her name was Jessica, who was adopted as Jessica Holt-Gibson, later known as DaKota. From the story Jennifer told me, it sounds like she hid the pregnancy from Daniel, who by this time had become Lucas Hill and was building up his empire. When DaKota was born, Jennifer gave her up for adoption. I don't know why. Maybe to protect her. Maybe some shred of sanity came through at just the right moment to spare DaKota a life of hell."

"But she was still sufficiently nuts to have an affair with her own daughter," I spat out.

"Her past trauma was stronger than anything else she felt."

I started crying. I couldn't stop. Dr. Kane just sat, holding my hand, waiting for me to stop. I wasn't wailing, just a ball of sadness draining down my face. It kept flooding out, and I didn't even know why. Douglas handed me a box of tissues he grabbed from the side table.

"So," I said through my sniffles and tears, "why did Hank kill her?"

"Let me ask you something first," Douglas said. "How was DaKota just before she died, say a week or two before? I know you told me things were fine but I am assuming that was a lie."

"Bite me," I said half smiling through my tears. "She was distant. She broke up with me. Didn't want to talk to me, didn't want to play with the band. Something was bothering her but she wouldn't say what."

"Uh-huh."

Then it hit me. "She found out, didn't she? She found out Jennifer was her mother. She had an affair with this woman then found out later she was her mother. I mean her birth mother. She had been searching for her birth mother and found her. I never knew she was adopted until after she was dead. She never told me. She found out, didn't she?"

Dr. Kane said, "I believe that's partially why she was killed. I think she discovered everything. More than just Jennifer being her Mom, I think she found out about Jennifer and Daniel and Jackson. How, I don't know. I think the realization of having had an affair with her birth mother probably disturbed her so much she threatened to blow the whistle, go to the Police with the whole story."

Douglas said, "That's what the rat in her dresser drawer was all about. Hank, um, Jackson was protecting the family secret. She was going to rat them out."

"So he trashed DaKota's?" I asked.

"More than likely," Douglas said.

I thought for a moment. "But what he was doing in my apartment?" I said out loud to no one in particular.

Douglas said and looked at me quizzically. "I didn't know he was at your apartment."

I told them about the night DaKota's was trashed and being bowled over by someone shooting out of my apartment. Douglas shrugged not having an answer.

We all sat in silence for a moment, just long enough for the explanation to sink in. "The poppers," I said. Everyone stared at me as if I was speaking Latin. I looked at Gralewski and said, "The nitrous oxide poppers you found in my apartment. Hank put them there to frame me, to make it look like I had provided DaKota with the junk found in her lungs."

"Again," Gralewski grumbled, "convenient."

Dr. Kane continued. "DaKota must have contacted Jennifer with her discovery and threatened to go to the police. Jackson found out and went to his Father, Lucas, and told him about DaKota's existence and what she was planning to do. Lucas had Jackson kill DaKota to keep the family secret hidden. It was soon after her death that Lucas came after you, yes?"

I nodded, in stunned disbelief. "What has Pat got to do with all this?" I said just staring into space.

Dr. Kane sighed, and said, "Jennifer had it in her mind that you were responsible for taking DaKota from her when their affair ended. I think your relationship with DaKota was the final hurt, the final rejection that sent her over the edge. She blamed you for that rather than DaKota. Her real and imaginary bonds to DaKota were too strong. So she went after you. You took something of hers that she held deep and unseen in her heart and soul. She was going to take something from you in return."

Gralewski spoke up. "Hold on a sec. The timing of this doesn't make sense."

"Sure it does," said Douglas. "DaKota ended the affair with Jennifer. We assume she still did not know she was her mother. At some point after that DaKota and Chynna became lovers. Jennifer finds out about it and makes a plan to get even."

Dr. Kane chimed in, "Whatever piece of Jennifer that gave DaKota up for adoption was enough to create a personality that longed for a normal life, a life where family members respected boundaries. My guess is that over time, this personality became 'Carolyn'. When it was time to lure Pat into an affair, Carolyn was called in, probably close to the same time DaKota learned of her mother's identity. How she found out is still unknown, but my guess is Hank or Lucas purposely let her know. DaKota is disturbed enough that she breaks up with Chynna and threatens to go to the Police with everything. Carolyn doesn't know this is going on and continues with her plans to nab Pat in revenge.

"Learning about DaKota's murder was too much for Carolyn once she realized who was behind it. Whatever fragile balance of rational behavior she possessed crumbled under the stress, and the lines between Carolyn and Jennifer became extremely blurred."

I leaned back into the sofa cushions and gave out a huge sigh. I had no more questions. I had no more of anything. Spent and numb, I wanted the lights to go out so I could sleep forever. All this pain, all this useless waste. How did I get in the middle of it all? I didn't want any more of it.

"I'm going to go see Jaycee and Pat," I said to Dr. Kane.

"Good idea," she said, with the warm smile I wished I could bottle and take with me. I started to leave the room but then stopped in front of Gralewski.

"Well?" I said.

"What?" he asked.

"You have nothing you want to say to me?"

He shook his head, "Not until I check all this out. Could be total crap for all I know."

"Asshat," I said walking out of the room.

I walked down a long corridor. It was late and quiet. Here and there a television filled dark rooms with a blue glow. In room 304 Jaycee lay quietly in the darkness, her chest rising and falling in sleep. I leaned over the bed and brushed a few strands of blonde hair from her face, which caused her to stir and peer out from heavy lids.

"Oh," she said in a groggy tone. I smiled.

"Thanks for coming back," I said.

"Mmmm. You're lucky I did or you'd be fish bait," she said, her eyes closed.

Under sedation, some of the hardness of her features gave way; she stopped being on-guard. It made me curious to know what about her life had pushed her to the extent it did, why she felt she needed to wear the tough exterior. In a hushed voice I asked, "Why did you come back?"

She groaned and pressed her head deeper into the pillow.

I quietly chuckled and said, "You're so obvious."

"And you're nuts," she said not opening her eyes. "Jumping in the bay. Surprised you didn't sink like a bloated mackerel."

I stayed long enough to watch her drift back into a deep peacefulness.

In room 312, Pat was propped up in bed, the top of which was raised. He looked cleaned up and content. I sat in the chair next to his bed, put my arms on the raised railing and rested my chin there. All the lights were out except the small fluorescent lamp over his bed. An IV was attached to his arm. I didn't know what it was for but I figured the hospital staff knew what they were doing. Besides, I didn't have to know. I already knew too much for one day.

Forty-Six

September. School was back in session. The ground under my feet became a bit more solid as each day passed. I returned to town, still somewhat dazed but not confused. Pat was home and itching to get back to the restaurant, but the doctors wanted him to take it easy for a week first.

"I'll go crazy if I sit around here for a week," he said to me on the phone.

"Go for a walk. Will do you good."

"For a week? I'll walk to Boston and back."

I thought about the last time I saw him at the restaurant before all this happened and asked myself, yet again, if there was anything I could have done to avoid everything he went through. Self-flagellation kept rearing its ugly head in my brain, even though Andi and Dr. Kane were doing their best to keep me from holding pity parties. Randomly changing the subject often seemed to help. "Think up some new recipes. When do you see Eileen again?"

Sometimes I'm too obvious for my own good. Using Dr. Kane's given name was tantamount to implying, or at least pushing, a relationship outside of the normal Doctor-patient realm. Pat hesitated, and then said, "Thursday. How did you know I was seeing her anyway?"

"Well, someone has to keep tabs on you as you, obviously, don't have the capacity for staying out of trouble on your own."

When I returned to The Slipped Disc, I found a recent copy of *The Trenton Chronicle* on my desk with a screaming full page headline, "So Long, Scumbags" written between a press release photo of Lucas Hill and a mug shot of DaKota's Dad. Snevley completed his digging while recuperating and unmasked Mr. Gibson as the silent money partner to the Family First project, which also implicated him in the murder of his adopted daughter and the fire-bomb deaths of all the people at South 26 Upstairs who were not lucky enough to escape. A sticky note was attached to the newspaper that read, "You owe me. Be by to collect after plastic surgery heals and I'm beautiful again.–S"

Lucas remained in a coma. Mr. Gibson was on his way to meet Bubba, his new cellmate. Strangely I felt no anger, just a deep sadness that the two Dads in DaKota's life both wanted her out of the way. She didn't have a chance.

After an hour of filing most of my desktop contents in the circular file, I headed out for a walk through town. Geoff was, once again, trolling for nubile young muffins and had the A.C. set on frostbite so I let the sun's rays work their warmth into me. For the first time in a while I felt relaxed. Happiness was something different. The wounds left by the whole incident, both mental and physical, were gradually fading into retirement and were slowly letting me get back to my life. Working into my first permanent prosthesis grew easier by the day. There were patches of time when I scarcely thought about its existence, which were sometimes followed by acts of sheer stupidity like forgetting to take it off when taking a bath. Duh.

Inside Grace's, I spotted Douglas on a coffee run dealing with one of those cardboard cup holders filled with steaming drinks. "Here I thought cops just ate doughnuts," I said walking behind him.

"Do you see any in the vicinity?" I sat on Grace's stool in the back. The store was packed so I knew my order would have to wait. Douglas and I had not had much contact since that day on Long Beach Island, outside of a few calls concerning lawyers, the trial and the usual police minutia. Whether I had to show up at any trial or hearings for Jennifer and Jack was still up in the air. For the time being, I turned all that worry over to Mom and Jason, in that order. I just didn't want to think about it anymore.

"Everything okay?" Douglas called back to me.

"Fine as frog's hair," I smiled back. Why an old Nana Lennox expression choose that moment to make an appearance is beyond me. He shook his head with a grin, "That's a new one on me. If nothing else talking to you improves my regional vocabulary skills. Sabina has been bugging me to invite you over for dinner. You must have made quite an impression apparently. She wants to celebrate, in her words, how thoroughly you humiliated my unpleasant partner."

"Name the date and time. I'd love to come over and support her ganging up on you."

A broad smile slowly creased his face.

"You can get that image out of your head right now, Perv."

Forty-Seven

That night I lay in bed just listening to the fans move the air around the apartment. The oppressive humidity had broken but the heat remained. My mind was wandering in a never-ending stream of consciousness. Something was gnawing at me. I reviewed all the pieces to the puzzle and everything appeared to fit but there was something deep inside demanding some attention. Around two in the morning I was tired of trying to fall asleep and climbed out of bed, chugged some cold water out the fridge and watched the full moon cast shadows across the kitchen floor. One of the reasons I tolerated the heat of the third floor was being able to sit on my front porch in my skin late at night and connect with life, allow myself to be enveloped by the pulse of the earth and the sounds of the night. More than anything else I wanted to talk to DaKota, knowing what I now know. Just to tell her it was okay, to tell her I still loved her no matter what happened in the past. Somehow, just to tell her to keep going. I closed my eyes letting the visions of her smile, her touch and her laughter dance in my head.

The next sound I was conscious of was the birds. Birds? The sun wasn't up yet but I cracked my eyes open just enough to confirm morning light had appeared and I was still curled up on my Adirondack chair on the porch without a stitch of clothing. I casually melted to the floor and crawled back into the apartment. Yeah, I was on the third floor, but being arrested for indecent exposure was not on my agenda.

Once the sun was up and I was decently attired, I breakfasted on the porch. The morning breeze surrounded me as the neighborhood showed signs of awakening. From somewhere below I heard wind chimes. Even though the second floor was empty and about to be reoccupied in a few days, the chimes on DaKota's porch were still hanging there. I smiled. It would always be DaKota's porch.

I fished out the key from Daffy Duck's head and descended. The locks had not been changed. A lack of furniture and a new coat of paint had transformed the apartment into an empty shell echoing ghosts of the past as I walked through the kitchen, the living room and onto her porch. I had no desire to visit the rest of the apartment. I gently took down the wind chimes, walked back into the kitchen and turned to look one last time. Of all the memories that my brain could have recalled, the one that stuck was shuffling through the debris after Hank worked his magic. It's not the one I wanted to take with me; there were so many other good ones. I needed to let this one go.

I tossed my key on the counter, and then closed the locked door behind me.

The chimes fit perfectly on my porch. I'd always have DaKota to talk to when no one else was around.

Which reminded me; I had one last piece of business to clean up.

Susan cracked her door open an inch following my fist pounding on it. "Oh. Come to say goodbye I assume?" she said. Her hair was wet and slicked back; it was tough to tell if it was greasy or recently washed.

"In your dreams, bitch," I said pushing on the door to let myself in.

"No," she grunted and pushed back hard trying to block access. I was not going to be denied and for a few seconds we were braced on either side of the door struggling to overpower each other. There was no way I was going to lose. I backed off slightly then did a full force rush with my body. We went flying, tumbling over each other into her kitchen.

The old-fashioned, speckled linoleum smelled like pine disinfectant but it couldn't mask the earthy, moldy smell in the air.

"Oh, you've got to be kidding me," I said, now standing and scanning her apartment. Susan was on her feet but remained silent. Plastered on the walls were no less than a dozen posters from life-size to camera snapshots of Xena, Warrior Princess. Well, Lucy Lawless as Xena. All the furniture was thick dark pine that was big in the seventies but was probably the closest thing Susan could get to the ornate hand carved structure of Xena's time. A complete set of Xena DVDs sat in a rack on top of the widescreen TV. On the right hand wall hung battle implements, an axe, sword and a mallet, the handles of which were tied together forming a criss-cross.

"And you think I'm nuts?" I said.

"Get out," she growled at me.

"You had the balls to give me shit about my relationship with DaKota and here you are living out the ultimate lesbian fantasy character. You're a total hypocrite." My amazement turned to anger. I wanted to take one of the weapons on the wall and beat her senseless.

Then I saw the evidence that made the last piece of the puzzle fit, the last unreachable answer that had been annoying me for weeks. The axe on the wall had a one-piece forged head; a large blade on one side and a rounded steel ball on the other side. I yanked it off the wall, letting the rest of the junk clatter to the floor. I looked at the ball end closely and smiled. Flecks of red paint were embedded into the pockmarked metal.

In the kitchen I held the evidence in Susan's face. "Looks like you've been battling vicious stop signs, huh?" Her face tightened but she didn't respond.

"You trashed DaKota's place, didn't you? You wailed on the stop sign using this," I said, holding the tool in the air. "I knew there was something I was missing and now it makes sense. No one else could have done it. No one else had access. That plus your little phone call to the cops complaining about the noise upstairs when no one was here. If Hank had trashed it when he killed DaKota I would have heard it."

"So?" Susan said, petulance rising in her tone.

"Why? Was this just some warped Xena fantasy?"

"You must think I'm stupid, but I'm not. You're the one who is an idiot. I saw you go back into her apartment that night. I knew you would; you're so easy to figure out. Leaving you there for a bit I came in and heard you scramble into the closet. See? You thought you were so clever but I knew you were in there. I was going to call the Police from here but then the idea occurred to me that I could do so much more. So, yes, I trashed the place. It was enjoyable, actually. Once the place was a wreck, then I'd call the Police, they'd find you there and have more reason to think you were unbalanced, and maybe take you away then."

I stepped back into the kitchen, still gripping the axe. "And the rat?" I said. A mild sadness crossed her face.

"Gabrielle," she said. "She was my companion. She understood the sacrifice." Her gaze hardened. "People would think it was just the type of thing you would do."

I was tempted to ask what DaKota or I had done to make her react this way, with this much energy and violence, but something told me the train was leaving the Crazy Town station and I wanted to be on it.

I stepped toward her, weighing the axe in my hand, judging its heft and balance, but my eyes never left hers. Uncertain, Susan took a step back and then flinched hard as a reared back and hurled the weapon into the living room with everything I had. The wall shook as the blade pounded solidly into it.

I smiled and said, "Bull's-eye." The axe handle protruded from the six foot poster of Xena, the weapon still vibrating right between the warrior's eyes.

Forty-Eight

At the Weekend Reminders meeting I shared about the urges to use that I'd been having since the Hank affair, including 'drunk dreams'–the dreams addicts sometimes get where we use in our dreams and wake up with the images gone but the urges remaining. I reset my sobriety date even though it wasn't technically necessary. I wanted everything to be part of a new start. I didn't want to use, but after the little taste Hank gave me, all the old addictive shit kept popping up in my brain. Without meetings I'd be back behind a Seven-Eleven dumpster in no time. Not because I wanted to, but because I was an addict and was powerless.

The first day of autumn brought the last of summertime breezes carrying the scent of turning leaves and the promise of fall. It was Saturday, Andi's day with the cognitive therapist.

As I dropped her off I said, "You promise to call me after you walk home?"

"Yes, Mum. Don't flip out if it's later today. I have plans this afternoon."

"Oh, really? And what might those be?"

"I think I fancy the young gent who has moved into the second floor flat at your place. I've been feeling a bit randy lately."

The young gent on the second floor was a greying, sixty-eight year old, part-time Philosophy professor at the University who was not much taller than me and weighed half as much.

"You do that," I yelled from the car. "Just don't call me when collapses on top of you from a heart attack." We both shivered a little at that thought.

The sky was too blue and the sun too warm not to head for the beach.

The sands were mostly empty; the tourists back to work and school. The lifeguards were all back on college campuses across the country. A few businesses stayed open all week, but most had gone to a weekend schedule, catering to those stragglers, like me, who refused to let summer go, or to the parents with pre-school kids that took advantage of off-season rental rates.

The good thing about September at the beach was a better than average chance that the sun would stay warm and the sound of crashing waves didn't have to fight with the din of the crowd. On the other hand, without the people, it was easy to feel sad that another season had come and gone, and that colder weather was just around the corner.

Today, however, the sky was cloudless, the sun was hot, the humidity low and the day glorious. I was in my usual beach attire; tank top and shorts, slathered in SPF ten thousand. Only today, instead of watching the waves from the sand, I was gliding over the bay, checking out my new aviator shades in the greenish water as I looked over the side of the boat. Jaycee stood at the wheel in her usual denim work shirt, this time with her pony tail stuck through the back of her baseball cap. She sported a pair of Blues Brothers cheap sunglasses, keeping an eye on the buoys in the bay as we chugged past them. I gulped the last of my Coke, got up and put the can in the plastic bag we used for trash hanging on a thumb tack pushed into the row of cubby holes.

"I have a question," I said, yelling over the whine of the motor.

"Uh-huh." She acknowledged without looking at me.

"What does Jaycee stand for?"

"Why does it have to stand for anything?" she asked.

"Because it does and I know it, so give."

"Only if you swear to never repeat it or use it. Because if you do, I will have to kill you."

"Cross my heart," I said, drawing an "X" on my chest.

She hesitated before confessing. "Jacaranda. My Mom had a thing for those flowers. Don't know why, she just did," she said. I let that sit without a response, just feeling the motion of the boat over the water. Jaycee broke the silence and said, "How can I trust you to not reveal my true identity?"

"I can create a tontine and we can sign it in blood," I suggested.

"Create a what?"

"Never mind. I have a better way to seal the deal," I said, with a smile.

I guided her face to me, removed her sunglasses and pulled my lips to hers; soft, moist, our tongues gently caressing. Jaycee released the throttle and the engine wound down to an idling purr, allowing the sound of the water lapping against the hull to accompany us. Her hands, rough but gentle touched either side of my face.

We released, both of us grinning. She was a good kisser; what a great place to start.

Jaycee throttled the boat back in motion and said, "Not bad."

"One more question, if I may."

She sighed and shook her head. "Do you always talk this much?"

"Who the hell is Pete?"

She threw her head back and laughed. I had never seen her laugh like that before. All was right, all was good. "It's a long, long story," she said, shaking her head and smirking.

"Good," I said, smiling. "I've got lots of time."

THE END

About the Author

Jim Cooper has managed a movie theater, been a disc jockey, film critic, photo studio manager, real estate developer, baker, IT developer, paperboy, men's clothing salesman and corporate mailroom drone. He thought he'd give writing a go. He lives in New Jersey with his wife and two rescue maniacs, um, dogs.

www.ingramcontent.com/pod-product-compliance
Lightning Source LLC
Chambersburg PA
CBHW070548130626
46556CB00001B/67